THE OPERATOR

AN IAN BRAGG THRILLER BOOK 1

CRAIG MARTELLE

CRAIG MARTELLE

Website & Newsletter:
https://craigmartelle.com

Facebook:
https://www.facebook.com/AuthorCraigMartelle/

Ian Bragg 1—The Operator
Ian Bragg 2—A Clean Kill
Ian Bragg 3—Replacement
Ian Bragg 4—A Fatal Bragg

I can't write without those who support me. From families and friends at home to the readers who buy my books, you've been there for me. It's not who I am that matters as much as the quality of the people who surround me.

The Ian Bragg Thrillers team Includes

BETA / EDITOR BOOK

Beta Readers and Proofreaders - with my deepest gratitude!

Micky Cocker
James Caplan
Kelly O'Donnell
John Ashmore
Sabrina Ford
JR Pomerantz
Michael Penmore
Rob Kerns

And a special thank you to Kate Pickford for her initial guidance to put the book on solid footing to deliver what you have just read. I hope you found it entertaining and a good read.

Version 1.0

Cover by Stuart Bache
Editing by Lynne Stiegler
Formatting by Drew A. Avera

CHAPTER ONE

"All the world's a stage, and all the men and women merely players: they have their exits and their entrances; and one man in his time plays many parts..." William Shakespeare

I am not until I have to be.

I kill bad people for money. Not a lot of people, but a lot of money. Maybe one day I'll retire, but I think I have not yet reached the top of my game. Make no mistake, it is a game. But a deadly one. I like the game. I get to do what they wouldn't let me do in the Marines. Rid the world of bad people.

Someday, I'll settle down with a wife who would love to see the world. Be a tourist. Be a nobody and not have to work anymore. Retirement. It's not on my radar. Not yet.

I'm still in the game.

I was on my way to my next job. The Peace Archive had accepted my bid and put a hard limit at two weeks. That gave me thirteen days to find my target's schedule, find the weaknesses, and one day to satisfy the contract.

Satisfy it by changing his status from living to dead. Confirmation would earn me the second half of a substantial fee.

The Peace Archive. A name that misled. A clearinghouse for hired killers.

My thoughts focused on today. Plan for tomorrow, but lived in the here and now.

I clicked my wipers to high. The car, a late model beater. A Ford, I think, but I didn't care. As long as it ran.

The car was a tool, like any other tool. Purchased when needed, used, and dumped once I was done with it. It was my way. I have no need for material wealth. I have no one to flaunt it to. Only a job to complete. Make the world a better place. And then move on to the next job.

The rain pummeled the windshield. I was tired of the deluge assaulting me on the approach to Seattle, although it had only started fifteen minutes ago. Well-lit restaurant signs shone at the end of the off-ramp. I looked over my shoulder, signaled, and exited. I selected the biggest restaurant of the bunch, the one with the most people. It was easier to disappear in a crowd.

I parked in the middle of the lot, not too close for anyone to notice. Not too far, either. Nondescript. I let the car run while I waited for Rush's *Limelight* to finish. Listening to the words. I touched reality in a different way, no dream to be in the limelight. I preferred living outside the camera's eye.

I pulled my floppy hat tightly over my head and buttoned my overcoat. I can't have people remembering me, or if they do, without a description. I want to be the nice guy next door. *Kept to himself. Always a kind word, quick smile, or helping hand.*

That's me. Somewhere.

The restaurant was only a third full. Camera globes

dotted the ceiling. They were hard to miss. Probably half of them didn't work, and no one had bothered to get them fixed. Too much cost. Too little gain. Resolution too low to be any good except in reducing insurance premiums.

A run-of-the-mill burger joint. Common. Predictable. A place where everyone goes but no one knows anyone else.

It had a touchscreen ordering system and automated delivery. The few employees working behind the counter bustled here and there. Machines did most of the real work.

I kept my head down while ordering, my hat pulled tightly around my face to help me avoid the camera at the top of the screen. All the dome video feeds stuffed into an overused digital storage space being overwritten every couple hours because the restaurant refused to pay for more. This one was different and the only one of sufficient clarity to get a good picture of me. No one needed to know I was here. I kept my head down and used my knuckle to tap the touchscreen.

I ordered, paid with a gift card, took my number, and waited.

I watched those around me. It was my way.

A girl with dimples and a boy in his best blue jeans and a clean t-shirt. They giggled and laughed but weren't holding hands. Maybe a first date. An elderly couple. She steadied herself on one arm while he worked his cane with the other. Going out for a treat. Workers in their high-viz vests. A family of five looking haggard, counting their money to see what they could get. And a bunch like me, dripping wet, trying to read a menu they knew by heart or waiting for their order.

Same old eat-and-go. A little bit of everything. The

door opened delivering new customers while the rain sounded like white noise, a background din.

In walked two young men who had the look—sunken but darting eyes, shifting stance as if torn between running or fighting. A fist in a pocket around an obvious shape.

They were casing the place, and they were bad at it. Druggies needing cash quick to fund their next fix. And they were about to mess with my lunch.

A robbery meant someone would call 911. I had no intention of being interviewed by the police. My food hadn't come yet, and I wasn't going to leave without it. At the count of three, they were going to ruin my day.

Walk away. Go to a different place, I told myself. I was the worst at taking damn good advice. I could smell the burgers and fries. I wasn't ready to head back into the rain.

I made the decision and strolled up to the two before they split up to gain a tactical advantage like they'd seen on TV. As I said, bad at it. I grabbed their wrists. "You are not going to rob this place. Not now. Not ever. Get the hell out of here." I used a low voice. I meant business. There could be no doubt.

A ding sounded behind me. My fries were ready.

When I stared them down, it wasn't the look of a normal person making a hollow threat. There was something different about people who had taken another's life. A part of my soul was missing, the part that said it gets easier the next time. And the next. Most could sense it. Some, like these crackheads, could not. They started to struggle. One tried to push away and pulled his hand from his pocket. An old-time police special, .38 caliber, well-worn. Probably passed from doper to crackhead for decades after one of them had stolen it from his old man, a cop.

The one with the .38 needed the most attention.

I had to remove the first junkie from the equation. A quick finger strike to the throat sent him staggering back, both hands reflexively snapped around his bruised windpipe while he gasped for air. This freed me to deal with Mister Aggressive. I still had him by the left wrist, but he was right-handed. The pistol was coming up. His head was completely unprotected.

Generating power from my waist, I hammered a heel strike to his temple, right behind his eye. His body went slack, and the .38 fell from numb fingers. He started to go down. I caught him, pushed him back into a bench seat intended for those waiting for their orders. The pistol clattered across the floor. I arranged him to look like he was napping.

In a way, he was. Everyone near the counter watched. Not what I wanted, but it was better than having the police show up. I smiled at the employees behind the counter and picked up the pistol by the diamond grip. I unloaded it and prepared to toss it in the trash. The second crackhead was already out the door, running as fast as he could while still holding his throat.

Two weren't as good as one who knew what he was doing. Crime wasn't their profession. I'd bought them another day free from the gray-bar motel.

The patrons had stopped to watch the exchange. The old man nodded to me while his wife looked on in horror. The family clutched their cash and stared at the ceiling, praying in thanks that they had not lost the last of their money. The kids had not noticed.

Good for them. It was nice to be young and innocent. I reached toward the trash can's opening.

A hand stopped me. It wasn't the hand of another druggie. An overweight man stood there. He fished in his pocket and pulled out a badge. He had been in line near me. I had missed that he was a cop. That kind of stuff could get me killed. He was a greater threat to me than the crackheads, but only if he wasn't managed. The more official, the easier to manage. Everyone had their leverage points.

I gave him the tight nod of brothers in arms.

"Don't want to leave that laying around for someone else to find." He gestured to hand it over.

I turned it butt first and gave it to him, making sure I didn't touch anything that would leave a print. Waiting with the six bullets from the old revolver, I rolled them in my hand to smudge any marks. The officer pocketed the pistol. He didn't seem to care about the ammunition.

"If we could keep this between us, I hate the paperwork," I offered. "I just wanna eat in peace."

"Me, too, pal. Nice work." The man was an old hand. He faced the other patrons. "Nothing to see here, enjoy your meals." He gestured for calm with an easy look and resumed his place in line, taking in the menu over the counter. He preferred to order in person rather than use the touchscreen. I scanned the delivery area for my order. It had not yet appeared. The employees stared at me.

I waved my ticket and smiled again. Robots shouldn't need encouragement.

"Coming right up, mister," one of the flesh-and-blood workers said. A young kid with a college degree. *Management.*

He snagged my order from the conveyor and threw in an extra burger, double super-sized fries, and a large chocolate shake. "Thanks," the young man said while pushing it toward me.

"Can you make that to-go, please?" I wanted to eat in a dry place that smelled less like a wet dog than my car, but some things were not meant to be. It was time to go.

The manager bagged it and set the bounty before me.

"Much obliged. Take care of your employees, and they'll take care of you," I advised before claiming my lunch. On the way out, I slipped a twenty into the hands of the praying family and kept walking. No need to look back. I knew everyone was watching.

It was still better than a formal police interview.

I stuffed the bag inside my jacket and let the rain fall on my shake. I wouldn't drink it, but I wouldn't toss it while they were watching me. I had to look appropriately appreciative of their appreciation. It was a way to keep them loyal. I needed strangers to be loyal to me.

How to be a leader while working alone.

CHAPTER TWO

"The most difficult thing is the decision to act, the rest is merely tenacity." Amelia Earhart

The lemons did little to cut the disinfectant smell that greeted me. A higher-end boutique hotel. Not a chain. Chains kept better records and tracked their guests no matter where they went. I preferred not to have that.

Textured cream and gold wallpaper brightened my room. On a clear day, I was supposed to see Mount Rainier through the oversized picture window.

Fourteen days in Seattle probably wouldn't be enough to get a clear day.

I wasn't going to stay at a dive in a seedy part of town. I had worked the higher costs into my bid, along with the price of the car. With success comes opportunity for more success at a higher rate of pay. This had been my biggest bid, and The Peace Archive didn't flinch when they accepted it. There was no negotiation. That told me I should have bid more.

I didn't get to see who else bid on a job, only the number of other bidders. I wished I knew the numbers the other two had thrown into the hat. I don't mind a little competition to help me sharpen my game, but it bugged me to think I was the lowest bidder.

I knew a couple of the other operators. I had not stumbled across this opportunity blindly.

A private invitation had shown up on the welcome mat of my condo in the suburbs of Boise. That led to two people I knew from the Marine Corps. They'd introduced me to the Peace Archive.

One of the men had been an officer. He had given me a hard time during my tour in the sand. A captain. They called him "Skipper." I called him "Asshole." Maybe he had been grooming me all along, to see how much I could take. I handled it all, following the stupid rules of engagement. I could have cleared a whole town if they would have just let me. We used the tools they gave us, but not the right ones.

In my opinion, the world is a tool chest if one knows what to look for. A little gasoline and laundry detergent for a Molotov cocktail. A little bleach and ammonia for chloramine gas. An irritant in low doses, it sent a strong message. Fertilizer and diesel fuel packed into a dumpster. A large crane tossing steel girders about. A bulldozer to clean up the rest.

So many missed opportunities, but only for offing bad guys. Too often, we couldn't tell who was who. Kill 'em all and let God sort 'em out wasn't a viable strategy. Not everyone needed to go. Only the bad ones. Back to working with our hands tied.

The skipper appeared different from when I'd last seen him in the desert eight years earlier. Maybe that was the benefit of civilian life. He looked harder, yet less like a Marine.

Same with my old platoon sergeant. He had seemed to get me. We got along just fine. Band of brothers and all that.

They had new names, too. They told me this in low voices in the privacy of my condo. Then we went for a walk in a nearby park, oddly vacant for midday. The test? My willingness to kill someone I didn't know. I had laughed. Better than killing someone I did know.

They were deadly serious. I was put into the bidding pool based on what they had seen from our time together in the Middle East. They trusted that when it came down to it, I would pull the trigger without hesitation. I didn't want to be restricted to using a rifle. They said they didn't care what I used as long as the contract was satisfied without bringing a great deal of attention to it.

Yes. I could be an operator.

Why not? For Corps and country were good reasons, but making a living killing bad guys?

A month later, my condo was sold for what I owed, and I disappeared.

A year and six contracts later, I was a multi-millionaire. Richer than I ever thought I would be, and I'm still in the game. Six targets removed without leaving a trace. Nothing pointing back to me or The Peace Archive. I was a rising star.

At least in my own mind.

I checked the room because that was something I always did. I pulled the blanket back and slapped the middle of the bed, watching for anything to pop up, dust, bed bugs, things that shouldn't be in clean sheets. In the shower, I checked the vent for dust and the caulking for mold. Bathroom vents always bore the burden of humid dust sucked into the fan. This was no different, but it wasn't completely blocked. I used a wet wad of tissues to knock off the biggest chunks, then tossed it all in the trash.

I looked for buttonhole cameras hidden in various nooks and crannies, from the overhead lights to the vents to spaces behind the toilet to hidden areas behind mirrors to equipment in the room: lights, the smoke detector, sprinklers, emergency intercom, clock radio, air conditioning unit, and television. Five minutes showed me what I needed to see.

Nothing hidden, but right there in the middle of my personal space, overlooking the bed, the hotel's smart TV sported an integrated camera. I took the room-service menu, creased it in half, and tented it over the top center, blocking the digital view of my room. Little of the screen was blocked, just in case I wanted to watch TV.

Usually I didn't. When I was in my room, I focused on the target, putting myself into his or her shoes, finding a weakness, and devising a way to exploit it.

I set my iPod in the clock radio and brought up my playlist. It was simple: every Rush album in one long stream. I selected random and hit play. I closed my eyes and listened. *Between the Wheels* from *Grace Under Pressure*. The volume had been turned down. I fixed that.

But not too loud. Can't have complaining neighbors. *Between the Wheels* was a hard song about a hard present that would lead to a tough future. I listened through the first refrain before getting down to it.

I pulled a new laptop and a phone with a hefty load of pre-purchased data out of my duffle bag. I had paid cash for both at a Walmart two states away. I needed my own data until I could get my virtual private network, the VPN, active before using the hotel's Wi-Fi. Too much potential to be dirty and leave a trail. I hooked the phone to the charger and brought it to life, activating its mobile hotspot.

There was only one thing I needed the computer for—the internet. I had websites, logins, and passwords memorized. No small feat since they were all different. Once the laptop booted up, and after using Edge to download Chrome and a VPN, I installed the new programs and rebooted.

The VPN created an encrypted tunnel between my computer and a remote server. From there, I could make it look like my computer was anywhere in the world.

I figured a search on a political figure in Seattle should come from neighboring Vancouver. I typed in the city name and waited as the VPN rerouted me. Once established, it was two-click easy to change over to the hotel's Wi-Fi.

The search started simple.

James "Jimmy" Tripplethorn, an up-and-comer on the Seattle city council, ostensibly on his way to the mayor's office. Someone was spending big to keep that from happening. "Jimmy." The word reminded me of a bad dick joke. "Kick me in the Jimmy!" From *Beavis and Butthead*. Not the highest-quality television, but it applied. He was a politician. "Dick" might be a great name, but "Kicker" was to be my nickname for him.

Important to dehumanize the target. Made pulling the trigger easier.

The timeline was tight, giving me less opportunity to make it look like an accident. I needed his medical records. I needed to see his schedule. I needed all available data on him. I'd consolidate it on a small-sized USB drive, wrapped within foil that I could hide inside an electrical outlet or a light switch.

I read as much as I could to paint a picture of my target. I never saw anything about professional politicians that I found appealing. I think meeting one in real life would only reinforce the poor impression I had of them.

Kicker was heavily in the public eye. That increased the challenge but made gathering information on him easier. It also increased the payout. I should have bid more and demanded more time. I'd read the conditions and was given a full week to bid, but I pitched it in two days. They had accepted the bid and confirmed the contract. That made it sacrosanct. I was under the gun, a three-quarter-of-a-million-dollar gun.

I assumed killing politicians had a way of riling up the masses. Bizarre, since I thought everyone hated the so-called public servants. Maybe it was just me. Or maybe I was more honest with myself than the average Joe.

I searched the media websites for articles. I watched short news clips where Councilmember Tripplethorn spoke. I re-watched the clips, looking for people who were always with him. His wife was there more often than not, standing in the background. They put a good face on the team. There he was driving away from a rally in a red Ford Escape hybrid. He wore suits but never a tie. He liked speaking extemporaneously on location about whatever issue plagued the day.

Never let a good crisis go to waste.

Tripplethorn was there but didn't take facetime from the people in charge: the fire chief, the police detective, the corporate CEO. He waited his turn to speak instead of seeking the limelight.

The picture of him as a politician was emerging. A reserved opportunist. Well-spoken. Said the right things. More fans than enemies. Lived a reserved lifestyle despite his wife coming from money. She stayed in the picture at the edge of Kicker's spotlight, whispering to him before he went live. The power behind the throne?

I descended into the dark web to confirm more intimate details, like his credit history and his medical record.

A modest home in the high-rent district that was paid off. The posted dirt was speculation and innuendo. I figured I would find the real stuff when I dug deep enough. All politicians had secrets. Kicker seemed better at hiding his. Probably the same with most successful politicians.

After three hours of searching and digging through the refuse piles of the dark web, Jimmy Tripplethorn remained a mystery. Someone had decided he deserved to die, and in an odd way, I had agreed. I had to find out why for my personal edification before I pulled the euphemistic trigger.

I had his home address. I'd take a casual drive past tonight, and again tomorrow in the daylight. See it better, but they could see me. Cameras could record me. The two trips through by a nondescript vehicle now wouldn't register in two weeks if I had to make the hit in the neighborhood. I could not go back to Jimmy's house after tomorrow, except on foot under cover of darkness if that was where it would take place. So many questions needing answers.

I closed the laptop and locked it in the safe before using my credit card-sized multi-tool to undo the screws to the switch plate in the bathroom. With the thumb drive at the bottom of the light switch's junction box, I replaced the plate.

It was hard not to look at myself while performing this quick operation. The mirror in the bathroom didn't paint a pretty picture. I looked tired when I should have had the boundless energy of youth. Well, almost youth, not quite middle-aged. A drink of cold water was refreshing but didn't quite do the trick.

I needed to kill some time and clear my mind. The hotel had a fancy lounge to provide such a distraction.

Time for a drink.

The hallway smelled pleasant, a touch of lavender wafting from periwinkle walls. It was much better than the disinfectant in my room. I took the stairs to the ground floor and followed the signs to the lounge. Touchless doors swished open as I approached.

A long bar occupied the area to the right. To the left, a small dance floor and a stage where a live band could play. Tables filled the free space.

Three couples sat at the small square tables, nursing their drinks. Two older businessmen sat at the bar, engrossed in their conversation. Two younger guys were at a table for four, trying to impress three women about my age. The lounge's window shades were down, making it hard to see more detail. I chose a seat at the bar near the television. A college basketball game played.

I ordered my favorite drink, orange juice with grenadine. I know they call it a Shirley Temple. It was embarrassing to order, but they were what I liked. As always, there was the slight hesitation and the lip twitch where the bartender wanted to say something. I dropped a twenty on the bar and smiled. "For your silence, my good man."

He laughed. Nothing like the truth to keep people honest. "You got it, buddy. A *Thunderbolt Special* coming right up."

Silence *and* loyalty.

Because I'm a nice guy. I keep telling myself that. It's easy to believe, except for the day job. Aren't we told our job shouldn't define us?

I'd go with that.

The basketball game played on. A three-point shooting

contest ensued, where each team dropped bombs from afar. The score started to run up quickly.

One of the women from the table showed up to order drinks. I looked over my shoulder. The two young men had paired off with the two thin women.

"The music stopped?" I asked her. She looked at the speakers overhead where the jukebox played Kenny G. The reference dawned on her. She shrugged. "Join me?" I waved to the bartender and dropped another twenty in front of my drink. "I'll get Ms…"

"Jenny Lawless," she filled in.

"Ms. Lawless' drink." I stabbed a thumb over my shoulder. "Those four are on their own."

"Coming right up." The bartender looked at her, and she stared back. He finally had to ask. "Your drink?"

"Whisky sour." She reddened and looked away from checking me out in the mirror. She turned her attention to my glass. "A Shirley Temple?"

"Thunderbolt Special," I corrected

She creased her brow and shook her head. She figured me for a liar. The potential companionship was dead on arrival if I couldn't turn things around. I pointed at the bartender. He looked up from adding Gentleman Jack over ice cubes. "It *is* a Thunderbolt Special," he confirmed.

"What's in it?" She opened to the new possibility.

"Orange juice." He held up the jug of Simply Orange and tossed the right amount into her tumbler with the Gromme and a dash of egg white. "And grenadine."

"A rose by any other name," she said.

I knew how she saw herself, keeping an arm in front, sub-consciously putting the chair between her and me to hide her shape, averting her eyes to avoid seeing any judgment. She was what some considered a curvy girl, a little heavier than her two friends, but far more beautiful than she gave herself credit for.

She'd parried my thrust expertly once she knew the rules. I was intrigued. "Sparkling eyes and sharp wit will make for wonderful conversation."

"Are you for real?" She twirled her hair around a finger before tucking it behind an ear.

The bartender glanced at the group behind her. She looked at the money in her hand. "I was going to buy them drinks for my entertainment." She turned to me. "Looks like I'm covered." She shoved the bills into her purse.

"I'm a business consultant, and I'm here on a two-week gig. What about you, Miss Jenny?"

"Three-day conference, but I don't live too far away. An hour's drive." She smiled. Genuine, with her eyes. Green with flecks of brown. Expressive.

"If you would be so kind, Miss Jenny, tell me a story with a happy ending." I sat back and took a drink. A little heavy on the grenadine. I'd ask him to dial it back for the second one. The clock behind the bar suggested I had an hour to kill. As the lady had said, "Looks like it's covered."

"And you're going to sit and listen?" she asked with a slight head turn. Feigned or real skepticism? My redemption was in sight.

"I see you have been the subject of too many poorly trained suitors who tried to impress you with their knowledge. If I interrupt while you're talking, it will only be to ask clarifying questions. And for the record, I am not married, and I do not have a girlfriend." I took another sip and rolled my finger for her to begin.

"A suitor, huh? Sounds ominous." Her cheeks flushed. I shook my head and gestured for her to start as if waving her to me.

A schoolteacher who'd moved into her parents' house

after they both passed away. It still choked her up. No debts. She had hobbies like crochet that she did for nieces and nephews thanks to her prolific sister and brother, who lived on the other side of the country.

She called them often. Jenny described a life that was ideal for some and hell for others. I wasn't one to stay home and enjoy my white picket fence. Then again, I didn't need a lot of friends, just a few to have a drink with every now and then. After an hour passed too quickly, Jenny intrigued me even more.

She talked about today's educational foundations, her use of online training methods to bolster her classroom instruction, the writings of Thich Nhat Hanh, the founders of the nation and their personal desires for a greater nation, and so much more. She flowed through her narrative as if delivering a well-practiced soliloquy on issues that mattered to me. I was an audience of one, tailor-made for every subject she wanted to talk about.

Mesmerized. She made me think things I'd not thought before. She made me want to spend more time with her. I found the revelation intriguing.

I ordered a third Thunderbolt for me and one for Jenny. Two whiskey sours were her limit. She was starting to giggle.

"You don't want to get me drunk?" she said, biting her lip and looking up at me, her long eyelashes tickling her brow.

"I do not. I have a meeting tonight, and I need to be lucid. There's no sense in only one of us getting lit."

I checked my watch. A second hour had gone by. I stood up and put a gentle hand on her shoulder. It hurt me to have to go. She saw it on my face.

"If you don't want to go, then don't."

My soul cried out in pain. There were no options to call

in sick in my line of work. The Peace Archive implied that bad things would happen to operators who missed their mark. *Very* bad things.

"I am left with a horrible choice. I must attend my appointment. They pay me a great deal to do the work I do. I don't have the option to skip it, but I would if there was any way possible. I'm not quite ready for this night to end."

"I was thinking...maybe a nightcap?" A shy smile. Demure. Picking up guys in bars wasn't her thing. I liked that. She didn't want her evening to end, either. I liked that, too.

"Give me your number, and I'll call you tonight after my meeting. We can talk about what tomorrow might bring, besides takeout Chinese or something better. I'm not sure I can think of anything else at present."

"I love Chinese takeout."

I wasn't surprised.

I unlocked my phone and handed it over. She dialed her own number while I traced a finger along the skin of her bare arm. When the phone in her purse vibrated, she stroked it gently before shutting it down. She slowly looked up at me before handing my phone back. I took her hand and kissed her fingers.

"Until next time, Miss Jenny Lawless." I hesitated for a long moment before forcing myself to walk away. I looked over my shoulder when I reached the end of the bar. She smiled and raised her hand in a subdued wave, then shook her head and dropped her arm. I checked. No one was looking, so I blew her a kiss.

Her friends and the young men were long gone. Few people were in the bar, even though it was still relatively early. The small crowd had gone for real food instead of microwaved bar appetizers. A line cook would have made the hotel good money. Maybe they did better with live music.

I wouldn't be there if a band was playing. Not my thing. I prefer the quiet and the one on one of a soft voice with sharp wit behind it.

I'd have to find a place for tomorrow's dinner, or I could just ask Jenny. She would know. Until then, I had a lot of work to do. Mister Jimmy Tripplethorn and I needed to get better acquainted. I wanted to see the place Kicker called home. Google's satellite view had given me a good idea of what it looked like from above, and the street view wasn't bad either, but there was nothing like seeing it in real life.

CHAPTER THREE

"Glory follows virtue as if it were its shadow." Marcus Tullius
Cicero

The rain had stopped. I didn't know when. The ground
was wet. I suspected it would always be wet. No respite for
my water-resistant loafers. If it started raining again by the
time I reached Kicker's house, my view wouldn't be great,
but I wanted to scout approaches and exits. Better done
driving slower, reasonable on a rainy evening. I'd view the
house tomorrow at normal speed if it was clear.

The drive was easy. I had known where my target lived
and picked a hotel that was fairly close but still two towns
away. It took me twenty minutes to get to the
neighborhood. I was surprised it was not gated. Good for
me, bad for Kicker.

I made the turn into the neighborhood, a
homeowners'-association-controlled area. The telltale
signs of bushes trimmed to exacting standards. Mailboxes
spaced evenly. Home colors consistently pastel, yet earthy.

I didn't see anything that looked like community security besides the ubiquitous signs in windows that declared the resident to be members of the neighborhood watch.

While they kept their curtains drawn and shades down.

No one was watching anything on a dark and drizzly evening.

Maybe no one wanted to see anything. I was willing to oblige them by not being seen.

I drove casually, not the twenty-five miles-per-hour allowed, but closer to fifteen because it was evening and children could be in the street. I didn't ever want to hit someone's kid.

Saw too much of that in the desert. Unintentional, but tragic all the same. There was no need for it. I had happily ventilated a couple terrorists who'd run a bunch of kids into a convoy. We'd hit two before we could stop and were able to get them to the hospital in time, but nothing had saved those who had used them as weapons. We didn't even try.

Maybe Kicker was the type to let his kids play in the street, tempting fate or making a statement. I could do him for that alone.

Perfect front yards suggested the neighborhood kids played elsewhere. Backyards or the community-approved and aesthetically pleasing playground.

The parents chose to live in this community and signed draconian HOA rules. A good school district. Rubbing elbows with the upper crust. It wasn't my concern how they managed their life choices. I only needed to understand enough to operate within the neighborhood's constraints. Do what I needed to do. Be unobtrusive, and no one cared. No loitering. A single drive-through at a reasonable speed and no one noticed.

Jimmy's home was up ahead on the right with the rest of the even-numbered addresses. The porch light glowed, the mist creating a rainbow ring around it. Welcoming and warm.

A man in the yard holding an umbrella over a giant poodle. It was Jimmy, looking unlike what I expected of a politician. In an instant, I had a picture of a man focused on holding an umbrella over his dog. The look on his face suggested something more than his turn in taking the dog outside. Average height, athletic build, a sweatshirt that was getting wet. An old ball cap to keep the rain off his face. He got wet while his dog stayed relatively dry. He seemed unconcerned with his own discomfort. He said something to the dog, making the white tail wag.

I wondered why they weren't in the backyard. It was raining just as hard up here. Maybe his backyard was under construction or flooded. He didn't look around to see if anyone was watching. Didn't even glance at the car driving by.

The front door opened. I was almost past, struggling to look without turning my head. An angry woman yelled and shook a finger. Tricia Tripplethorn. I couldn't hear what she said. He hurried the big dog back inside.

I was too far away to see what happened after that. I continued around the block and drove straight to the front gate. I stopped at the first stop sign, dialed up *Subdivisions,* and let it jam.

The exchange with his wife was an unexpected treat, but it threw variables into the equation. I didn't like undefined variables. I compartmentalized the information for later, when I would review it with additional refined searches online. I needed to start looking into the wife, Tricia Tripplethorn. I wondered how often she'd sounded that out before deciding to take Jimmy's name.

I closed that door on the evening. Being able to think in one channel without being distracted by what was going on elsewhere was unique, or so I'd been told. Block out the stuff that didn't matter when thinking about that which did. I didn't know any other way.

I wasn't big on distractions when it came to thought processes. I changed thought compartments.

I tapped the screen to call the previous number dialed on my phone. She answered on the first ring.

"A gentleman who keeps his word?"

"Honorable is what I go for."

She laughed with an angel's voice. "I thought about it and realized I spent two hours telling you my life's story, but I don't know anything about you, Mister Ian Bragg. It's your turn to tell me a story."

Ian Bragg. My operator cover, the name on my identification. It had not yet been compromised. I'd get a new one if it became public with the wrong people. Contrary to popular opinion, getting a new identity was neither easy nor cheap, and was fraught with as much risk as riding an old name.

"I only have fifteen minutes before I'm back at the hotel, and I need to get some sleep since I have an early day tomorrow. My job is a bit demanding, so I'll be quick. Let me tell you about my time in the Marines..."

When I pulled into the hotel's parking lot, I said goodbye and that I would talk to her tomorrow. I closed that door within my mind and returned my focus to the job, building a portfolio of Jimmy Tripplethorn. I walked through the lot to the front entrance, taking my time to breathe deeply of the heavy, humid air. It smelled clean as if all the sins of a big city had been washed away.

Unlike Kicker's sins, for which his wife allowed no forgiveness. *Tell me your secrets, Tricia.*

I strolled in, took a hard right to the stairway, and climbed the single flight to my floor. I left the stairwell and headed for my room.

Jenny was strolling down the hallway wearing the hotel's bathrobe and carrying a bucket of ice. She stood in front of my door, swiped the card, and stepped inside.

I hurried after her, pushing through the door to find that it wasn't my room. It was the one next to mine.

Time stood still. She looked at me. I held the door halfway open, torn about leaving. I was in between compartments within my mind.

"You can stay," she offered, setting the ice bucket down and turning toward me, loosening the robe's tie and letting it fall open as she walked. Creamy smooth skin. Vibrant. Inviting.

I caught her halfway and pinned her tightly against the wall to kiss her fiercely. She responded with energy, electricity, a fire deep within. Promised passion.

Kissing her cheek on the way to her ear, I whispered, "I have a long day tomorrow that starts early. If I stay here, there will be no sleep whatsoever, will there?"

I traced a finger around her face. Her chest rose and fell with quick breaths.

No. Her lips parted, and I heard the word but couldn't be sure that she had spoken aloud.

My hand seemed to find its own way inside her robe, gently touching, then down to follow the curve of her bare hip.

She shrugged off the robe and started unbuttoning my shirt. I backed away until she had me pinned to the other side of the room's narrow entry. One piece after the other, my clothes fell to the floor.

"I need sleep," I reiterated. She smiled and snuggled close to me, naked body pressed hard against mine. I closed the door to Kicker's world and strolled into Jenny's, wide-eyed and willing.

I surrendered to the inevitability. There would be little sleep that night.

I managed to make it back to my room before I had to leave for Seattle. I thought of Jenny's smile one last time before pulling the credit-card-sized multi-tool from my wallet to remove the screws from the light switch panel in the bathroom. I needed the thumb drive to annotate my thoughts regarding the Tripplethorn home. I had to solidify my plan.

An operator worked alone, starting with almost no information, building a profile, and executing the contract. There were no links to The Peace Archive. Ever. The high pay came with high personal risk. There had been no training. Besides my recruiters, I had never met my contractors.

I liked working alone, even though it had its limitations.

I felt like I needed to meet the people who hired me. Could we work our way up? What was their cut of the fee for far less risk? Was that by invite only? There was no employee handbook and no one to ask. That made certain things difficult. So many questions and so little time.

Morning brought clear skies, but the forecast threatened rain. At the crack of dawn, I threw open the curtains. There she was in the distance, crowning the tops of nearby trees—Mount Rainier. The hotel's brochure had not lied. It was a nice view.

I needed to go into the city. Downtown Seattle. Collect information. After a quick shower, I put on my clothes from yesterday. A stop to buy a new wardrobe was in order. Salvation Army definitely and then maybe Kohl's.

I was not a slave to the fast-paced world of high fashion. Comfortable clothes that didn't stand out. What more could a working man want?

Chuckling to myself at my humor, I locked my computer in the room's safe and hid the thumb drive. I needed the cleaning crew in my room. Do Not Disturb brought questions and unwanted attention. I could put the sign out in a few days, after establishing that I had nothing to hide.

I opened my door quietly so as not to wake the neighbors, one in particular. I shut it carefully and hurried to the steps and down.

Through the well-groomed lobby, where a lone older woman wearing an oversized apron loaded the free breakfast buffet. I checked my watch. Still ten minutes before it was supposed to open. I pulled out a ten-dollar bill and strolled into the small restaurant.

"We're not open yet," the heavy-set woman replied.

I offered the cash. "A muffin and coffee? I have to hit the road to downtown, beat the traffic. What is it with Seattle commuters?"

She smiled easily and waved off the cash while gesturing with her head to help myself.

"Take it." I kept it in front of her. "We're all working for a living. You're doing me a solid, and I appreciate it."

She slipped the money into her apron. "Do you want something else, something hot?"

"Do you have sausage biscuits?" We all have our weaknesses.

"I'll bring one out." She trundled into the kitchen. I fixed my coffee with flavored creamers and snapped the lid tightly onto the recyclable cup. She reappeared with two steaming packages. She showed them to me before dropping them into a bag and handing it over. "You look like you could use some meat on your bones."

"I'll get it if I eat too much of the good stuff." I bowed my head to her. "See you tomorrow."

I strolled to the car, feeling refreshed and sharp despite having only catnaps through the night. That door threatened to open. I pushed it closed, smiling at my last vision of a woman I had just met. Sleeping soundly. Hair messed, but radiant.

I fired up the tunes and drove away, looking forward to joining a million friends driving into the city.

Hurry up and wait. I'd eat while stuck in traffic. Wednesday. Only a few workdays left to see the bustle of the daily grind, and most importantly, Tripplethorn's role in it.

Six contracts under my belt and they had all been wildly different. Still, I'd agreed the targets needed to die. I wondered if the other operators had my same sense of justice and honor. Marine veterans. I hoped so. It was The Peace Archive's job to deliver good targets. People who were despicable human beings. For me, Jimmy Tripplethorn would be lucky number seven. I would find the dirt that had so far eluded me. I had no doubt it was there.

The drivers in the traffic slowdowns looked like they were doing something else, able to drive while applying makeup, singing, gazing at the scenery. Anything and everything. Most were alone. It was the way of the modern world. Very few used the mass transportation many demanded. It wasn't convenient enough. We like our conveniences.

I listened to Rush's *Marathon*, ate my breakfast, and focused on my next steps.

Collect info until I could test a premise and a backup.

Simple if it didn't need to happen in a busy city in front of a perpetual crowd. If it did, I needed to start building that attack plan soon. The hits were easy. Escape was hard. Getting away required all the forethought and planning that could be put into it. "What could go wrong?" was the single most important question in walking through every step of an exit strategy.

I selected a parking garage five blocks from City Hall. As early as I was, the place was already ninety-percent full. I dutifully followed the others filling space after space. The daily commuters driving mindlessly.

I swung wide to pull into my spot. Maybe I should have bought a Prius for this gig. It would have looked less out of place than my bigger car that barely fit. I waited for the next slot to fill before squeezing out. I took care not to door-ding my tiny commuter neighbor.

The other drivers headed toward the many offices in the area, most carrying the specialty brew they'd bought on their way in. I left my cup in the car. I had no desire to advertise the hotel where I was staying. Nothing to connect there with here or here with me.

I had two hours before the city council's first meeting of the day. I had that long to learn how the council members got into the building if they weren't already there.

I would watch for the red Ford Escape hybrid, but that was a long shot. I knew what to look for, but that didn't mean I'd see it. The paparazzi didn't follow him around, so I wouldn't get instant updates on every single movement like one could with a celebrity target where hashtags followed them through their lives. Politicians didn't have fans like that. The media had a different agenda when following politicians.

Media and politicians. They deserved each other, but they weren't doing their job when it came to Tripplethorn. No one was that clean. *Come on, people! Pick up your game,* I chided in the safety and comfort of my mind.

I would never have a press release in my job.

Exactly how I liked it.

The misty cool weighed heavily on each commuter as they rushed from the garage toward their day jobs in fantastic office buildings, a sea of shining metal and glass. I pulled my floppy hat tightly over my head before stepping from the shelter of the garage onto the exposed sidewalk.

Despite being downtown, the air carried the unmistakable scent of the Pacific Northwest. Salt of the ocean splashed across a pine forest. A coffee shop with a healthy clientele. A place to hear the gossip. I joined the line and waited, playing with my phone while paying attention to the conversations around me. Most were inane. A waste of good air.

But one talked about the council. I moved out of line and browsed the pastry counter to get closer.

To listen.

I hemmed and hawed at the choices.

"Today's agenda is garbage. They won't be talking about anything that matters. Tomorrow afternoon! That's when you'll see the fireworks."

"I think you'll see plenty of smoke and fire today as they posture for a better position."

I already had the city council's agenda for the next two weeks. What I didn't have was why there would be fireworks or posturing. The two people moved to a table. I jumped back in line, and the person I had been in front of let me into my previous spot.

"Mighty nice of you. Much obliged." I tipped my hat in

appreciation while keeping my head ducked to hear the former conversation.

"I'm in no rush to get chained to my desk," the older woman behind me offered.

"Don't I know that! I think I'll stay here for a while. The Man can loom a little less today."

She nodded with a look that said she'd been there before, as recently as yesterday.

With my turn, I ordered whatever I would get the quickest. A fresh house special, pre-brewed and filling a hot pot sitting on the counter. Black, straight up. Medium. I threw a five on the counter and walked away to snag the table next to the two who had been talking about the council, but their conversation had moved on to youth soccer. They left before saying anything else that interested me.

I twiddled my phone absentmindedly while sitting at a table for two. I sipped my coffee sparingly, frequently looking outside. People filling the area until it threatened to burst, no one leaving. The big city at the beginning of a regular workday. The viability of a hit during the transit was shaky. Too many people.

Right amount for surveillance. Easier to hide in a crowd.

I listened and watched while taking care to look unobtrusive. The coffee shop cleared out quickly as the hands on the clock crawled toward the official start of paid time. I filed out after them and followed a mob of desk jockeys up the street, walking toward City Hall. All of them peeled off before getting to the big building near the top of the hill. I stopped when my final unknowing compatriot disappeared before getting me there.

I found a dry spot under an overhang and leaned against the wall, looking for anyone going my way. It took a half-hour before the clouds separated and blue sky peeked through. A small group of men in suits walked by, their expensive shoes click-clacking on the pavement of Capitol Hill. I fell in behind them.

My business casual wasn't out of place. I wondered if they were on their way to the courthouse to one side of City Hall, the municipal court behind it, or a big law firm in the tower looming over it all. I didn't care as long as it got me to City Hall without me walking alone. Make any facial recognition work that much harder if it was in place, despite the privacy regulations forbidding its general use.

See the lawyers in their natural habitat, armed with the latest legal theory, looking for prey, I thought. They turned toward the courthouse, leaving me by myself. I continued straight past City Hall and looped around the far side to the main entrance where police and other armed security maintained a presence.

The closest parking garage sat on the uphill side of James Street, less than half a block from Seattle City Hall's main entrance. I took a closer look. A man in a suit walked out of the garage and almost into me. No surprise since I blocked his way.

"Excuse me, can anyone park here? I parked way over there and hiked all this way to get to City Hall." I pointed generally down the hill but not toward where I parked.

"It's open for anyone, but you pay for the pleasure of parking close. I had to wait for someone to leave before I could park, and now I fear I'm late, so if you'll excuse me." He looked to be in a hurry. I stepped out of his way and uttered an apology.

I waited for him to round the corner before strolling downhill. The first city council meeting was supposed to start in less than an hour. I decided to watch the building from a coffee shop across the street.

Within thirty minutes, I had the answer to one of my questions. Five of the nine council members, including Mr. James Tripplethorn, hopped off a bus that stopped in front of City Hall. Maybe they parked somewhere else. Or an offsite meeting? Or alternate offices?

It begged more questions, which I would find answers to easily through better-tailored searches. Tomorrow I'd be right there, watching to identify routines. I searched quickly to see if the council proceedings were livestreamed. They were. They made no secret of it and encouraged people to watch. But I had no headphones.

Plenty of small shops around for the locals' convenience. I strolled casually to one and bought a cheap pair of wired headphones. I didn't trust having the Bluetooth active on my device, so a physical connection was called for. Next to the checkout counter stood a display with Seattle Seahawks 12th Man baseball caps. I grabbed one of those and a Washington Huskies cap and dropped them on the counter with the headphones.

I looked for a quiet cafe to listen to the two-hour council meeting. An hour and fifty minutes remained.

A sidewalk seating area suggested the morning rush had already passed and the lunch crowd had not yet arrived. A couple sat at a table. They didn't look happy.

Not everyone can be a shining bundle of perpetual joy like me.

I ordered a fruit platter and another coffee, availing myself of the bathroom inside before it arrived.

The couple had ratcheted up the volume. They were intruding on my peace. I covered my earbuds with my hands to try to tune them out. The server came by and gave the two a big hairy what for before chasing them away.

She stopped by my table to apologize.

I pulled out the earphones. "No need to apologize. I'm sorry you had to do that." I wanted to ask if I could get her something or wipe a table if she needed to take a break, but that would have made me too memorable.

She laughed. "That's okay. Let me know if you need anything."

"I do, but on a completely different note. Maybe you know. How can I get an item on the city council's agenda?"

"Through their staffs," she replied, looking around to make sure no new customers had arrived. "You can request a meeting with the councilmember, but unless you're a donor or a high-powered special interest, they won't pay attention. All except Jimmy! He is open to the people. He'll walk down the street and ask us what we think."

"He has time for that?" I pressed, looking for insight into his personal engagements and how far beyond personal security lines he would cross.

"He makes the time. He's either with the council or in his campaign headquarters. I think he's going to be the next mayor. That'll be good for Seattle."

Someone has paid a lot of money for a different outcome, I thought. *Much cheaper than donating to a political action committee.*

"I think so, too." I glanced at the livestream. They were still in session and going strong. It was time for both of us to move on.

"If you'll excuse me." She bowed gracefully before turning to clear the table of the couple she had kicked out.

I still hadn't heard any posturing or fireworks. It all seemed like inane garbage. I continued to listen while using my phone's browser to find the address of the campaign headquarters. Kicker had an office right here and in a second one located in his district to the northeast.

The Seattle office sat only a few blocks away. An easy

walk. I waited another twenty minutes until the session was ready to wrap. The last for an early council day. I finished my coffee, stuffed a twenty under the cup, and walked out.

Next stop, Jimmy Tripplethorn's campaign headquarters. I strolled through the humidity. It added a cool bite to the air, but I was happy it wasn't raining.

CHAPTER FOUR

"When sorrows come, they come not single spies, but in battalions." William Shakespeare

I thought about the arguing couple. The server had handled it like a champ. I could have tossed them on their heads, but getting involved wasn't good for me as an operator. If the couple had become violent toward her, I would have been in the middle of it in a hurry. Can't abide those attacking someone for doing their job. Then again, maybe she could handle herself in that arena, too. Sometimes I assumed too much.

I wanted to be likable. Strangers loyal to me. But then other strangers would know how dangerous I could be.

In the pros and cons of my line of work, that wasn't a pro.

To shake off any observers, I headed down the hill and walked parallel to the street where the headquarters was located, taking off my jacket and hat and bundling them under my arm. I came up on the far side of the campaign headquarters and turned back toward City Hall.

A cascade of signs was plastered out front. "Vote Jimmy!" "Tripplethorn. Triple win—you, your community, AND Seattle." I strolled into the lobby of the twelve-story office building, where more signs directed me to the third floor.

The office building was not a great place for a hit. No access to the street. A staff who buzzed with activity but not a lot of people. It was too high-profile, funneled through a single entrance, unless there was something hidden in the back, opening to a service corridor. That would swing the needle in my favor.

This would be my only visit.

The workers were motivated to help. I strolled in, trying not to gawk at the riot of red, white, and blue.

"Are you here to volunteer?" a perky college kid asked while trying to affix a button to my shirt pocket. I let him have his way with my clothing while I peered past him. The arrival and main area looked to be a cross between a warehouse and a call center. In the back, a number of office doors were closed, all with their lights on.

"No, but how can I help Jimmy without volunteering?" I smiled from under my 12th Man hat, trying to appear to be a believer.

"Spread the word! Put a sign in your yard, signs in your windows, a bumper sticker on your car, wear your pin, and share, share, share!"

"I should have figured. I don't have a yard, but I do have a car. Can I get all the stuff here?"

He led me to a side wall that looked like the bargain section in a dollar shop. I took a variety of display materials, just one of each.

"How about something for less well-represented communities?" He led me toward the back without waiting for a reply.

More bins held more materials. Pink and rainbow prevailed. I took one of each to cover all my bases.

"You're the best, wild man. Thank you." Likable. He probably saw me as an old man. I should have punctuated my exuberance with "Groovy."

"Jimmy is the best! That's why we're all here, to support our future mayor by doing our part!"

I smiled at him and started to walk out, but hesitated when I reached the front door. "Do you mind if I watch how you guys work with the public? I don't want to be clumsy with my message. I'm sure you are old hands at this."

"We are motivated to win!" my escort blurted with the greatest enthusiasm. "You can sit over here and listen to our message volunteers as they carry the word to future fans and followers."

"All the way to the White House?" I asked in a low voice. My escort beamed but put a finger over his lips.

"Wouldn't that be magnificent?" he whispered, shielding his mouth to conceal his glee. I nodded, sealing our conspiracy.

He gestured to an open table, where I grabbed a chair and dragged some of Tripplethorn's literature over to me. On the table were haphazardly tossed copies of the councilman's schedule for the week. I swept one into my stack of reading material.

I turned my focus to the operators making their calls.

"Join us…"

"Be on the right side of history…"

"Show how much you care about Seattle…"

"Be a winner..."

Emotional engagement charging the atmosphere. Rarely did the volunteer get asked a policy question, but when it happened, they had lists of prepared answers for everything from healthcare to stop signs. The volunteer would thumb through and read the wording to deliver it exactly as intended.

I wondered who shaped the words, Kicker, or a psychologist to elicit the most positive response from the listener? How about one of the civil affairs types, the kind I had met in the Corps running around the desert and creating chaos? I understood what they were trying to do, but they missed the target too often to unleash them on a hostile population. The officers, "zeros" as we called them, kept civil affairs behind the lines.

The fault was strategic, not tactical. We employed them too late. They sucked at damage control. The few places where they went in first worked much better. In those villages, we didn't have to drop the hammer. Civil affairs got people to go along with authority. If done right, the locals bought into it. If done wrong, they fought back.

Most likely folks from PsyOps. Psychological Operations. No doubt they were well-suited for political campaigns, although no politician would admit to using PsyOps. Poli-Sci. *Should be Poli-Psy...*

When detached from the warfighters, they were little more than a propaganda machine. Just like a campaign office.

Welcome to the binary world of today, where people are forced to be with us or against us. Be a winner, vote for Jimmy. The enthusiasm and joy the callers showed while delivering the message were persuasive in their own right.

It made my skin crawl. I hadn't bothered to look at the

candidate's platform because it didn't mean anything to me. Just words. Actions mattered more.

A commotion near the front. The volunteers reacted by jumping to their feet and cheering. I stood to see what was going on. In the flesh, Jimmy Tripplethorn. All smiles and waves.

The volunteers started clapping. I joined them with a sedate golf clap, trying not to stand out. Kicker wove through the crowd, pressing the flesh with the volunteers, greeting them by name. He rolled down the phone lines before noticing me.

"A new volunteer?" He thrust his hand out. "Call me Jimmy."

I was older than most everyone else in the office except for two octogenarians handling the elderly calls. "Not a volunteer." I took his hand and gripped it firmly, enough to let him know he wouldn't establish handshake dominance. He smiled as he let go. "But here to see how I can do my part for Mayor Jimmy Tripplethorn."

I saw someone lift a personal phone. I moved sideways to turn my back to the camera.

"From your mouth to God's ears. But I'm here to serve the people. It's not about me, but Seattle and the good folk living in this district. What's your name, friend?"

"Randy Bagger." I'd never used the name before, and I wouldn't again. Jimmy moved on. Two of the office doors opened, and executives stepped into the open area. One man. One woman. The campaign managers.

Kicker entered an office in the back, with the two executives following. They closed the door behind themselves. I picked up my bumper stickers, signs, schedule, and buttons and stuffed them into a Tripplethorn bag—fully biodegradable, of course—and headed for the front door. I looked straight ahead, avoiding making eye contact with any of the staff.

I needed no pictures of me with Jimmy Tripplethorn. If there had been training on being an operator, it would have had a strict rule against being seen with the target as part of the main directive of never making contact with the target. *Am I comfortable killing someone I don't know?* I had laughed off the question, but not anymore. Killing a person took a certain sense of distance that I had never crossed before. I had never killed someone I knew. This would be a first.

I had shaken the man's hand.

It was time to change my perspective.

The campaign headquarters was a far softer target than City Hall. I couldn't make the hit at City Hall. It was too well guarded, too hard to get in and get out without more time to look for weaknesses. But Tripplethorn wasn't important enough to rate private security, not yet, but any day now. That made him vulnerable almost everywhere else for the time being.

Time to get a little deeper into Candidate Tripplethorn.

I looked for the door to the service corridor. It was located next to the stairs, and I pulled the handle. I was pleasantly surprised that it wasn't locked. Shrugging in confusion in case a camera captured me, I continued through the door and down a narrow corridor to the back of the building. I took a left where the corridor accessed a back door for each of the offices.

A cleaning man was there. He barely looked my way. Two doors were labeled for the campaign headquarters. When I reached the old man, I stopped.

"I was looking for the stairs. They seemed much easier to find before." I held out my hands. He looked at the bag dangling from my fingers.

With raised eyebrows, he studied my features.

"You're not a fan of Jimmy Tripplethorn. Can you tell me why? I haven't decided yet."

"Bah!" He threw his hand as if telling me to go away, but his ire wasn't directed at me. "Any kind of cult like his tells me all I need to know. Squeaky clean. Bah! I've lived here a long time, worked right here for all of it. Politicians come and go, but I have never met a clean one."

I leaned close and covered my mouth with a hand. "What do you think he's up to?"

"No good!" the man declared, smiling with pride at his answer. He turned back to the trash he'd collected, preparing to haul it away on a small cart.

"Too true," I agreed ambiguously. "Do you clean these offices?"

He nodded while continuing tying up the bags.

"After hours sexcapades?"

"Don't I know it! I start early, and you should see the stuff left in those offices."

"Jimmy's, too?"

He shook his head. "He's too smart to be caught with that." The old man tapped his nose with a finger. "Up to no good, I tell you."

I tapped my nose in reply and waved before turning and walking away.

He hadn't told me anything but had confirmed what I was seeing. Could kick me in the Jimmy Tripplethorn be clean?

Then who wanted him dead? Was there a crime element that feared for their existence? More questions.

In the stairway, I checked for cameras and how the doors secured. Alternate access points, possible escape routes. On the ground floor, the stairs continued to a lower level, but I headed out, looking away from the lobby camera by scratching my face and yawning. I left the building because my work there was done.

Across the street and one building closer to City Hall, a café sported a second-floor terrace. I went in, intending to spend time there, waiting and watching, learning the comings and goings of those who worked in the building where the campaign headquarters was located.

It was barely one in the afternoon. I had missed most of the lunch stampede.

A delivery driver pulled into a loading/unloading only spot in front of the office building across the street. He tapped on his phone. Two minutes later, my ebullient guide from the campaign office appeared with two of the telespammers. They loaded up with bags and boxes, staggering under the load on their way back into the building.

An alternate approach for getting something inside or creating a diversion. So many options for an opportunist like myself.

A plan was starting to form.

I had clothes to buy and one more pass to make through Jimmy's neighborhood.

I had already eaten too many times that day but ordered anyway to secure my seat on the terrace overlooking the building with the campaign headquarters inside. I pulled the schedule out of the bag. He was a busy man, and thanks to the campaign, they had every hour for the next week planned out. I wondered when they would have the schedule for the following week ready.

Did I risk going back in, or did I move my schedule up? Nothing said I had to take the full two weeks to execute the contract. I decided going back into the campaign headquarters carried too much risk.

Flashing at me like neon lights was today's schedule.

Starting at six tonight, Tripplethorn had an evening of meetings at the district campaign headquarters. I needed to be there to scope out his arrival and departure. He had another identical set of meetings on Monday.

Opportunity knocked. Would I answer?

CHAPTER FIVE

"I would rather walk with a friend in the dark than alone in the light." Helen Keller

Nothing happened across the street while I watched and waited for my side salad and sparkling water. I felt like I'd seen what I needed, and anything more was wasting time. I ate quickly once my food arrived and left as soon as I paid, hurrying toward the parking garage with my car. I walked with a sense of purpose. It wasn't how normal people walked. It was how Marines walked when they had something to do. I forced myself to slow down, slouch a little, and look somewhere other than where I was going.

I remained aware of my surroundings while focusing on the way ahead, making eye contact with those near my path to confirm they were not a threat.

Down the hill and into the parking garage. I had to pay at the entrance but hadn't brought my ticket. I went to the car to get the receipt. The garage was completely full. I returned and paid in cash, earning a few coins in change. I returned to my car with my freshly validated pass.

Getting out of the garage was easy. My phone guided me to a Goodwill less than five minutes away. A spot opened up on the street, and I pulled right in. I looked around suspiciously, never trusting the luck of the world. Karma had a way of causing grief. But lightning did not strike.

I went inside.

Finding my size was easy. Thirty-two was commonly available and dominated a portion of the rack under the sign showing the waist sizes. I thumbed through to pick up the rattiest pair of stained pants I could find, along with a nice pair of skinny jeans because that's what the majority of the staff in Kicker's office had been wearing. A pair of long-toe shoes, three button-downs, a sports coat, a pair of workout shorts, and a couple of t-shirts later, I was ready to go. I dropped my bundle on the counter.

The checkout woman went about her business with a clinical detachment that said she didn't want to be there. The total on all the items came to seventy-five dollars. I counted out four twenties and laid them on the counter. "The rest is a donation for the good work you do." I scooped up my new wardrobe and left before she could answer.

I chucked everything into the backseat. That was it for clothes shopping. I had my outfits for the next twelve days.

Before pulling out, I spun up Rush's *The Analog Kid* and rocked to the opening riff, encouraging me to get into motion. Sing it, Geddy.

I had enough time to get back to the hotel, dump my trash, and get in a workout. It looked like dinner would be much later than I had originally thought. I better give Jenny a call.

"Yes, lover," she answered in a sultry voice. I had to pull over to look at my phone to make sure I'd called the right number. "Ian, are you there?" Sultry had been quickly replaced by panic.

"I am. You gave me heart palpitations, and I had to pull over."

"Is that a good or a bad thing?"

"Makes me wish I didn't have a late meeting that just got called. I have the afternoon off and am on my way to the hotel to squeeze in a workout before I have to get back."

"You won't be able to see me tonight?" She sounded sad. The extremes of a potential relationship. So many stories she was telling herself. "I was too fast, wasn't I?"

I smiled. "Are you kidding me? I can't wait to see you. I only wanted to tell you that I can bring dinner but expect it might be closer to ten. Can you wait that long, or do you need me to send something earlier?"

I thought I heard a sob. I had no idea what was going on.

"I've been waiting my whole life for you," she managed to say. I had to look at my phone again. I don't know why that surprised me. I knew how the game was played, how to be kind by listening and asking questions. That the self-conscious were the most emotionally vulnerable.

But this wasn't a game. I didn't make love to a woman I didn't care about. I needed that more than the physical act and the intellectual engagement to trigger the emotions. I needed the whole package. I'd found it hiding behind the sparkle in Jenny's magnificent eyes. I lived the dichotomy of an operator's life. I wasn't supposed to care about people, but I did. That gave me solace in doing what I had to do.

"The sun came out today to shine on your beauty." It

sounded much cooler in my head. "Corny, I know. Sorry. I'll call when I'm on my way tonight. Get some rest. You're going to need it."

"I can meet you at the hotel. I'm only fifteen minutes away."

"For a workout in the *workout* room!" I clarified. I had a couple hours, but I needed to continue my research into Kicker and his wife, despite a growing desire to make my life worth living.

I could take my computer with me for my impromptu stakeout, but that was a tradeoff, and I couldn't make tradeoffs. No. It had to be an early night. Sleep and then research. I could go with four hours. That would work.

It begged the question, how much energy did she have?

I had work to do. The sort that ended in death, either my target's or mine.

The compartment in my mind Jenny Lawless had wandered into remained open. I tried to contemplate what the next twelve days would bring, but it was a fog in which much remained hidden.

One day at a time with an eye toward Monday, based on what I saw today. Eyes on arrivals and departures at the district campaign headquarters, with a list of people who were critical. They would be first in and the last to leave. They were the ones I had to outwit.

They all had their weaknesses. I only needed to find them.

But first, exercise the body to keep the mind sharp.

A nearly empty parking lot. I had no idea what Jenny drove, so I didn't know if she was already there.

An empty lobby, not even an attendant at registration. I continued upstairs and straight into my room to dump my new-to-me clothes on top of the low dresser. I dropped my clothes from yesterday and put on the shorts and one of the t-shirts. I bent down to lace up my all-terrain shoes, good enough for running, working out, or everyday wear.

A soft knock on my door signaled the arrival of my guest. I shoved my keycard into my pocket along with my phone and answered the door. A brief shoving match ensued. I blocked Jenny from coming in, and she blocked me from leaving. I wrapped my arms around her and kissed her until both of us had to take a breath. "Put on your workout clothes and join me."

Her face dropped.

I waved her off before she could say anything. "You remind me of Ashley Graham. I've know your clothes size, and I like you just as you are. But *I* need to stay fit, and I want you to join me. Being healthy isn't about weight or size, it's about what's in here working like it's supposed to." I tapped the center of her chest before taking her face in both hands and kissing her again. "I'll be waiting for you. Workout room is on the other side of the lounge."

I slapped her on the butt a little too hard because she jumped. I instantly started to apologize, but she laughed. "I'm going, I'm going. Ashley, the plus-size model? And how did you know my sizes?" She tossed her hair as she pulled out her keycard.

"Ashley the supermodel. No other qualifiers." *How did I know her sizes?* I had folded her clothes for her because she had left them in a pile not far from mine. It was hard not to smile at what happened after that.

Down the stairs and left to the sparsely apportioned workout space. A bench to do ab exercises. A treadmill. A stair-stepper. A machine with a stack of weights for upper body exercises. Typical hotel stuff, even at a higher-end place like this. The only difference? This equipment was new instead of half of it sporting out-of-order signs.

I started with the upper body machine on a low weight setting so I could run up a high number of reps.

Jenny walked in and glanced at the two plates on the stack. "There's a method to my madness," I said, even though she hadn't been judging. I wanted to impress her.

She hopped on the treadmill and started walking. I increased the weight through the chest press, standing with my back to the stack and pushing out, then turning toward it for curls. Not optimal, but my options were limited. I couldn't break up the workout by my usual push day and pull day. In the run-up to this gig, I had missed too many days of working out. I needed to be in shape as part of my exit strategy. People might try to stop me. I might have to run for my life, maybe fight my way through. Even being jacked up on adrenaline, I needed to be in top shape.

Never skip leg day.

After a half-hour of weights, I hit the stair machine. Jenny was sweating like a goat and breathing hard, but she didn't give up. I increased resistance and jammed hard on the stair-stepper, powering through a hundred flights. I slowed my pace as a warm-down. After an hour of total time in the workout center, I was finished. Jenny stopped the second I did.

She held on to the treadmill rail to balance her wobbly legs. "You could have quit earlier," I told her.

"That's not a word I'm going to let you see me employ."

My hand sought hers. That would have been my answer, too. Set realistic goals and meet them, then go another mile.

She leaned toward me, and I kissed her gently. I tasted salt from the sweat running down her face. The door opened, and others from her group entered. The two from last night. They stared. She recoiled as if we'd been caught smoking in the bathroom. I ignored them and urged her close for another tender kiss.

"You missed the last session," one of her friends interrupted. Jenny casually leaned back, smiling at me, eyes sparkling. I was happily lost in the moment. The friends had her back. "We will give you the down-low, so your principal doesn't think you were screwing off."

Jenny sighed and turned back to me. "I had high hopes of getting you into the shower," she whispered. "But duty calls."

I checked the clock on the wall, pursing my lips with the calculations. "There is nowhere near enough time to do you right before my meeting. I'll take a raincheck, and since this is Seattle, I'll be able to cash it that much sooner. Dinner's on me." I took a step toward the door, and the women moved aside. I looked over my shoulder. "I'll see you tonight."

Women my age giggling like schoolgirls. I didn't know if they were happy for their friend or just wanted juicy gossip. I didn't let it bother me.

When the workout room door closed, that compartment in my mind closed with it. I breathed deeply and felt good but tired from the lack of sleep. That didn't matter. I could sleep later.

Councilmember James Tripplethorn, I'm coming for you.

The Tripplethorn district campaign headquarters nestled between a dry cleaner and a convenience store. Cameras covered the building, and roof-mounted units looked out over the parking lot. Across the street, a well-lit gas station stayed busy with a constant stream of traffic. Telltale surveillance globes lingered in the roof over the pumps.

I parked around the corner in a dead zone between active businesses. I waited until traffic picked up, then got out of the car. A series of trucks raced by, interfering with the view of a lone pedestrian trying to get off the street. The well-worn and stained pants sagged because I had not tightened the belt all the way. I wore my trench coat over a t-shirt but left it open to better deliver the effect I wanted.

Down and out. Homeless. The type most people chose to ignore. I found a spot in the shade at the edge of the parking lot and took out a bottle of clear Gatorade. It was the real thing because I needed to rehydrate after working out.

The casual observer would not believe it was anything other than disguised booze.

Hiding in plain sight. Showing people what they expected to see.

Improvising. A Gatorade bottle of booze could be an incendiary device when shoved through a car window that would incinerate anyone inside. And no one would see it coming.

All I needed was confirmation of how Kicker came and went, along with an exit strategy. I casually drank my Gatorade while sitting between a bush and a light post. The campaign offices were well lit, with few people inside. Over the next hour, volunteers and staff arrived, parking in the middle area since the strip mall businesses were still open and the front row was filled.

I watched for the Escape hybrid, but my target didn't drive himself.

Kicker arrived with his two campaign managers from the Seattle office. I'd seen their names on the roster. He rode up front, with Antoinette Bickness. Ken Renton reclined in the back seat.

They pulled into the reserved spot right up front. Kicker and Ken climbed out, shutting the doors and waving. Antoinette backed out and maneuvered around the lot to park farther away from the front door. She chose a spot annoyingly close to me. A woman by herself. Shouldn't she be afraid of a vagrant?

She got out and stared at me while I let my head loll as if I were in the confused state between drunk and sleep. Antoinette strolled toward the office without looking back. She had not seen me in the downtown office, and I had taken great pains to look different now. I was safe, but not as safe if she had parked away from me like she was supposed to.

Confidence. No fear. I expected she could defend herself, an important point to log into the system. If Kicker was surrounded by fighters, an exit strategy required more distance or total isolation for the hit, limiting my options.

A handicap-plate van pulled up and parked in the spot reserved for Councilmember Tripplethorn. The side door popped, and a wheelchair emerged. The van closed itself up after the volunteer joined the team. Two other handicapped slots were already filled.

The candidate maintained a robust group of volunteers representing all walks of life. Of course he wouldn't park up front if others needed the space.

My lip curled of its own accord. *Who wants Jimmy Tripplethorn dead?* The more I learned about him, the more I liked him. The janitor saw behind the scenes and hadn't found any dirt. He had minor allusions regarding the others. It made me wonder. Was Tripplethorn the right target, or should it have been someone else?

My contract had been explicit—Jimmy Tripplethorn had been marked for death.

The Peace Archive couldn't afford to make mistakes like getting the target wrong. They commanded the utmost in trust.

Honor among thieves. Or killers.

I sat in the mud dressed like a hobo, thinking about honor.

Go-time arrived. Six in the evening, when the meetings were supposed to start. Kicker sat on a table while the others faced him from a semi-circle of plastic chairs. From those handling the phone campaign to the sign personnel to mid-level and upper-level political execs, the meeting was a who's who of a political campaign. All shapes and sizes represented.

From what I could see, the meeting was lively, with laughter and engagement. A fun campaign with fun people. Who was running for mayor against him?

The incumbent. Others who had declared their candidacy had quickly withdrawn. Who wanted the status quo?

Nobody.

Was that why Candidate Tripplethorn was having fun? Was he a shoo-in? Was the incumbent that tied to his position that he had to kill Kicker to keep his job?

Dirt! It remained elusive. I needed to expand my search. Friday was going to be an online day. I would dig into all the nooks and crannies because he had to be hiding something.

I moved to sit on the curb, leaning back against the light pole. I pulled up the collar on my overcoat to keep the perpetual mist off my neck. The Washington Huskies ball cap kept it out of my eyes. I sat still and waited for the target to make a mistake.

It was like working as a sniper in the Corps. I had not gone through sniper school, but I had shown that I could shoot, running up mid to high shooting scores on the rifle range. We needed the capacity to reach out and touch people, even if we had not been given the assets. They put me into the role.

In Iraq, I had tagged three terrorists from a thousand yards. They had been planting improvised explosive devices, IEDs, along the side of a main road. There was no doubt they were bad guys. I applauded their diligence as each picked up after the other fell until there was no one left. The bomb squad guys found a series of shaped charges that could be triggered remotely, but they had not yet been inserted into the holes to the side of the pavement.

They wrote up an award for that, but then took it away when I got into a fistfight in camp. They figured it was better than putting me up on charges. I did, too. I didn't want to go to the brig. The assholes guarding combat-zone prisoners had no sense of humor. They transferred the other guy out of the unit and behind the lines. He had been harassing Muslim women, ripping their veils down and laughing. It was easy enough to tell a man trying to hide beneath an abaya without doing what he was doing.

He did it for kicks. Established his dominance. Doing that garbage around me had been a bad choice. The skipper agreed, but the scumbag and I had to be punished in our own ways.

Medals didn't pay the bills, but then again, neither did getting busted down a rank. I got to play sniper a second time, but no bad guys raised their ugly heads.

I imagined the crosshairs on Jimmy Tripplethorn's

chest. In my daydream, I never pulled the trigger. In real life, I was going to have to.

Find the dirt!

The second hour of the meeting involved a lot of notetaking, with Antoinette and Ken doing most of the talking.

A pizza delivery driver showed up around eight in the evening. Kicker himself stepped outside to help the driver carry the boxes. They spread them out on tables along the side wall. Jimmy shook hands with the driver before he left. The young man seemed pleased when he hopped into his car.

Jimmy Tripplethorn handed out the plates with a smile as the crew lined up to grab a bite to eat.

Reminded me of a church picnic. I thought back to the janitor's words. *Cult like his…*

Eight-thirty rolled around, and a red Porsche Panamera Turbo growled into the parking lot. It rolled slowly to the front row and took a spot reserved for the now-closed dry cleaner.

Tricia Tripplethorn stepped out and softly shut the door. She fixed her hair and adjusted her hat before facing the campaign headquarters. Mrs. Tripplethorn took a deep breath before throwing her head back and striding toward the door. I stood to get a better look. Even in high heels, she moved quickly.

Someone inside noticed her and pointed. Heads bowed, and the mood instantly darkened. Antoinette made herself scarce by disappearing through a rear office door. Tricia walked inside to little fanfare except from her husband, who rushed to greet her. The remainder of the meeting was a one-way presentation from Jimmy to his volunteers. It only lasted another ten minutes before he called it a night. The team straightened the office quickly, piled the empty boxes near the trash, and excused themselves one by one.

Ken tried to make small talk, but all the while, he inched toward the door. I wondered where he thought he was going. He had ridden with Antoinette. When Tricia turned away, he was out the door like a shot. He headed my way, so I started to stagger toward the street. I made it to the bushes, where I was able to turn back to the campaign office.

Antoinette was already out the door and on her way to the car. Nearly all the volunteers and staff had left. Small groups were gelling in the parking lot. I stumbled closer so I could listen, but that backfired when the volunteers hurried into their cars and locked the doors.

I moved away, giving them space so they could feel safe once more. I sat on the curb, which limited my view but made me less threatening. Cars backed out and drove away. Antoinette and Ken rolled toward the parking lot entrance. I bowed my head so they wouldn't get a good look at my face. The office manager and the Tripplethorns were the last ones out. I staggered to the light pole and leaned against it.

Jimmy waited until the office manager locked up. They shook hands before the young woman headed for her car. Jimmy waited until she got in and drove away before joining his wife.

She stood with her arms crossed. He got into the car while she looked around. I crossed my arms, too. She stared at me, and I thought I saw a smile crease her face before she climbed in, backed out, and revved the engine to bark the tires while sending the car darting toward the entrance.

I waited until everyone was long gone before dumping my empty Gatorade bottle in the trash and finding a crosswalk to get back to the side of the street where my car was parked.

The picture was getting clearer. I needed a lot more information, but I knew what to search for. I knew that Tricia Tripplethorn had paid a small fortune to have her husband killed.

CHAPTER SIX

"What really matters is what you do with what you have." H.G. Wells

Once I reached the car, I took off my muddy pants and chucked them into the trunk. I'd been wearing my sweaty gym shorts underneath. I smelled like Goodwill. I needed another shower. Jenny was going to get her wish.

It had been a while since I had eaten. My overcoat was muddy, too. I folded it and placed it on the passenger floor. I dialed up Rush, *2112.* The first half of the album was long enough to get me back to the hotel. Space sounds and laser beams. I called the last number dialed from my phone.

"You're early," she answered promptly.

"Chase the other men out of there, lover, because I'm only bringing enough for the two of us."

"That's funny. What are you getting?"

"Tried and true. General Tso's and stir-fried green beans with fried rice."

"Stalwart. What are you getting for me?"

I waited for a moment. "A test." Talking out loud helped me work through it. "We have not eaten together, so I have no insight into what you might pick at versus what you go for first, besides six-footers with brown hair and brown eyes."

"Still waiting for an answer."

"I am being forced into a bald-faced guess. Stir-fried udon with chicken."

"I give you an A-minus. Egg foo young would be my first choice."

I pursed my lips and grunted. "Just when I was getting to like you, you drop this nuclear depth bomb on me. What other dark secrets are you hiding from me?"

"I have a pentagram tattooed on my backside."

"I am positive that you do not, which leads me to believe that you could be trying to lead me astray on the egg foo young. I'll get it, but I'm going to be watching closely."

"Fair enough."

"I'll be there as soon as humanly possible." I hung up and concentrated on driving.

Rush extolled the virtues of a guitar on the second track of the album.

Traffic was light and the drive was quick. The Chinese place was a mere block from the hotel. I ordered our meals. The egg foo young came with a second container for the gravy. I wasn't sure about it, but that's what she had ordered. I wiped a drip of General Tso's sticky sauce off the side of the foam container and tasted it. Sweet with the right amount of bite.

At the hotel, I bundled the overcoat over an arm and hurried into the hotel, wearing my gym shorts and a worn t-shirt. I waved my keycard at registration on my way past. I took the steps two at a time on the way up.

Miss Jenny was leaning against my door, waiting. I rushed to her and slammed into her, almost dropping our dinner in my desire for a hug and more.

Her nose wrinkled.

"I know. I smell. I fell in the mud, and this was the best I could manage." I swiped us into my room. "I'm not a fan of cold Chinese, so if you can bear with me, let's eat, and then I'll take a shower."

"I'm not sure I got fully clean before. I could probably use another one," she taunted.

"Deal." We spread the food out on the desk. I held the chair out for her. I sat on the short dresser next to her, dumping half the rice into the General Tso's. She poured some of the gravy sparingly over the fried egg pancakes. She took one bite with her mouth closed and stopped chewing almost immediately. I knew that look. "Try mine."

I secured a cube of chicken with my chopsticks and held it out for her. She took it carefully, smiling as she chewed.

"Gimme," I said without fanfare, putting my former dinner in front of her and taking hers for myself. I snagged a pile of my green beans before they, too, became communal property.

"You would do that?"

"I don't see you as a person I have to take care of, that I have to protect, but if you prefer what I have, then I give it to you willingly. Also, keep in mind that I'm a Marine. I'd eat the asshole of a goat if I was hungry enough."

She rocked back and made a face before leaning toward me. "I didn't know such things *were* done."

"Welcome to your new world. And please, don't order egg foo young again."

61

"You know I will," she replied.

"I know. I just wanted to go on the record as having stated my position."

"I'll make it worth your while." Her smile and the sparkle in her eyes promised more.

"It already has been." I had to put the egg foo young down to keep from spilling it as she came for me. The warmth of her body and eagerness absorbed me. I remained hungry but would be satisfied in a different way.

Dinner ended before we'd eaten. First, a shower for two, and then an adult, calorie-free dessert.

Exhausted and spent, I was out cold by midnight. Four hours later I woke, refreshed. Jenny was still asleep, covers pulled up to her chin. Her naked skin, warm under the sheets. Smooth and tender. The curve of her hip. She purred at my touch but didn't wake. I got up because I had a great deal of work to do.

I glanced in the mirror as I got my thumb drive out from behind the switch plate. I looked far better than I deserved, the result of emotional engagement, physical fitness, and intellectual stimulation. Yet, a dark cloud hung over my head. I filled the one-cup coffee maker and let it deliver a cup of the hotel's "custom" blend.

The challenge of the day was a contract to kill Jimmy Tripplethorn that wasn't going to work for me unless I ran across something buried so deeply that no one else could find it. I could pay the money back to The Peace Archive, but I doubted that would save me. If I didn't pull the trigger, another operator would, and then they'd come after me, too.

Unless I could get the contract canceled, which meant leveraging Tricia the Wonderbeast. I decided that name fit her—wondrous in her own mind and a beast to everyone else.

I removed my computer from the safe. The desk remained cluttered from dinner last night. Dinner had only been sitting out for six hours. The egg foo young wasn't good for anything except the trash, but the General Tso's was palatable, as were the cold green beans. I wolfed the food down without remorse, trusting that Jenny would sleep until the small restaurant was open and I could treat her to a free breakfast.

She had the last day of the conference, and I had to get my head straight about my contract. That meant information.

The VPN obscured me while the dark web opened up the world of those who stayed out of view while shining light into the darkness. My first task was to find the Wonderbeast's email before trying to gain access to her private bank records. What passwords had she used? What were the patterns for creating new ones? Humans were predictable.

I quickly compiled a list of seven different email addresses that had been used by Tricia Tripplethorn. Her publicly available commitments appeared to be random.

She did not have a nine-to-five job. She occupied her time as a board member of two different major corporations. Seattle Pacific operated with ten billion in assets, and Husky Express Airline looked like a potential merger candidate with Alaska Air. Lucrative positions.

Yet, they lived in middle-class suburbia.

There was far more to her than being Mrs. Jimmy Tripplethorn. Her maiden name was Barrows. A daughter of *the* family. Daddy was a billionaire.

He lived on his yacht year-round. With a crew of twenty, it was almost as long as the biggest Coast Guard cutter. It sported its own helicopter and submarine.

If that was what people wanted to do with their money, more power to them.

So, why had Tricia Barrows married a no-name with a master's degree in public administration?

And where had their relationship gone sour? Tricia was no longer a fan of Jimmy Tripplethorn's. I'd seen two different interactions, and neither convinced me that their home life was a happy one. The rich spouse generally had no problem retaining wealth when divorcing the poor partner. So why kill him? There had to be another reason.

Had it always been the plan to become the mayor herself without having to do any of the politicking? Ride the sympathy wave into the big house.

Another rabbit hole, but it was important to understand her motivations to help me leverage her away from continuing the contract. I needed to know what made her tick. I started digging, peeling away layers of noise that hid the private life of Mrs. Tripplethorn.

She was far more active than her public persona showed. Her social media pages had been carefully cultivated. Happy-go-lucky with the obligatory two children, now eight and ten. The giant poodle in the family pictures. Endless fun. A picturesque life.

On pages that were grossly open for all to see. It was a presentation purely for public consumption. What was the real story? What happened behind the scenes? I looked into her personal email for that.

Passwords she had used in the past that had been compromised.

Hu5kyMacGreg0r
Hu5kyTunn1c!1ffe
Hu5kyKje!!berg

I smiled to myself. A clear pattern. After a quick search, I accessed the Wonderbeast's email and typed in,

Hu5kyMacGreg0r. The screen flashed and the webmail's inbox appeared. She had over five hundred unread emails. I skipped those and went to the sent folder. What did she tell others?

Day to day tasks. Childcare. Friends get together. An invite to Daddy's boat for a meet and greet with money brokers.

I tried the other accounts. One password to bind them and in the darkness show the way.

I built a list of who she sent notes to, copying the email addresses into a spreadsheet. I looked away to let my eyes focus on something besides the screen. I'd been staring for almost two hours.

The sun was up and casting light around the window shades. Jenny was still asleep. I'd have to get her up soon.

A simple Hotmail account made up of letters and numbers caught my eye. I accessed that account and tried Wonderbeast's current password. It opened.

Only twelve emails total, and eight of them, she had sent to herself. I read through them one by one, then re-read them. I clicked on the sent folder. Nothing at all. I leaned back and crossed my arm as I battled with the secret email account. A yawn broke my reverie. Jenny was sitting up. She let the sheets fall from her. I closed my laptop and tried to switch compartments, but I was still in Tricia Tripplethorn's world. I had been pulled in, and it wouldn't let go. I looked blankly at the beautiful woman in my bed.

"What's wrong?" She stood in all her Venusian glory, stretching while she stepped toward me. She kneeled next to me, running her hand through my chest hair. The Wonderbeast disappeared into the recesses of my mind as the blood rushed through me.

"I was still thinking about today's schedule. You have to check out today, don't you?"

"I do not. You won't be getting rid of me today."

I pulled her to her feet. On the dresser, my two access cards lay beneath my cheap wallet. I removed one and gave it to her. "I'm here for another eight days. You don't have to leave me."

She looked at herself. "Where am I supposed to put this?"

I let my eyes wander casually over her naked form. "I hadn't thought that far ahead. I was making a statement."

"And then what, Ian? What happens to us when you have to go?"

I chewed on my lip before taking her face in my hands. "I don't want to leave you behind. I'm thinking of leaving my job."

She frowned, her eyes wrinkling with internal anguish. "I don't want to be the cause of anyone leaving their job. I don't know if I can support us both. My life is boring," she stated in a rush.

I looked at the floor. "I have plenty of money. I don't have to work for years if I don't want to. I was thinking of a world cruise."

She raised her eyebrows and contemplated me. "This is a side of Ian Bragg I didn't know existed."

"When this job is over, you'll learn all there is to know about Ian Bragg." I led her back to the bed, stripping bare before lying beside her. The world could wait for us after a proper welcome to the new day.

The revelations of the past twelve hours had changed my perspective in entirety. I had a lot to do to get myself out of the crosshairs.

And it started with removing Jimmy Tripplethorn's head from the guillotine. A politician. What if he was the last honest one? I refused to be the instrument of his demise, solidifying corruption's hold on power. The Wonderbeast was the key to making this right. What to do about her?

But first, what to do with my new bedmate…

CHAPTER SEVEN

"Keep it simple and focus on what matters." Confucius

The free breakfast was hopping. Jenny and I took two empty seats at a table for four, where she knew the other two occupants. I wanted to run for my life but smiled and suffered through it.

I sat uncomfortably with a perpetually full mouth, trying to avoid answering the shotgun blast of questions. I looked at Jenny for help, pleading. She touched my arm and came to my rescue.

"Such a busy day ahead! Ian doesn't have any time. We're running late because of so much sex! The clock just kinda loses meaning." I tried not to choke on my Lucky Charms, refusing to look up. The silence at the table went on for too long. I had to see. I lifted my head to find three women staring at me.

I cleared my throat. "Jenny meant to say, a late dinner followed by an engrossing movie and stimulating conversation," I countered, trying to sound confident.

They started to laugh. It was the best move I could think of.

"With a comeback like that, he's a keeper," one of the two stated. Jenny squeezed my hand.

I felt like I was thinking more clearly than ever. I got lost in her eyes. I had had other girlfriends, but they'd never lasted long. I had stuff to do, and they didn't want to be a part of it. Timing. Focus. The Tripplethorn job made me question what I was doing. It had always been easy. My mind tumbled through a cavalcade of thoughts.

Because I was a player. The deadly game continued, and the more Jenny became embroiled with me, the more she risked. And she didn't know it. The revelation would come soon. That would tell me if we had a relationship or a fling. Her eyes drew me in.

I knew what I wanted. I watched my hand caress her cheek.

A voice in the distance spoke. "The music stopped, but everyone watched as they kept dancing."

One of our table mates. I didn't know what she was talking about and had to ask. "I'm sorry, what?"

She waved a hand to take in the entirety of the dining area, filled mostly with women attending the conference. They started to clap. I glanced at Jenny. Her cheeks flushed, and she tried to look down. I tipped her chin toward me and kissed her.

Her lips tasted of maple syrup. I tucked her hair behind her ear and kissed her again, then quickly stood. "It's a full day. I *will* see you for dinner."

I tried to walk casually from the restaurant, but it was difficult with all eyes on me. I never liked being the center of attention, and now was a particularly bad time, not that there was ever a good time for someone in my line of work.

I headed for my room to build a full target profile on Tricia Tripplethorn. I had no idea how to confront her but would find a way. I *had* to if I was to have a future.

A future with the exquisite woman with green eyes and a musical laugh.

———

Jimmy Tripplethorn was on the morning news. A five-alarm fire burned in the manufacturing area of the northeast district. The local mayor and fire chief stood center stage, describing the efforts to contain the blaze. Jimmy stood in the back, looking appropriately concerned. It didn't appear to be an act since he could barely be seen. A reporter asked him for his opinion, but he waved them off, pointing at the fire chief and telling her that he was the one with all the information and in charge of the scene until the fire was out.

She didn't like that answer and came back at him. "So, you're just going to do nothing?"

The fire chief and the local mayor looked at Councilmember Tripplethorn as he instantly became the focus of the press conference.

Jimmy rose to the occasion. "Political processes happen best when carefully discussed and evaluated toward a well-defined goal. Working with incomplete information and being in a hurry accounts for why we have so many misbegotten laws on the books. If this is arson, that calls for one response. If this was from an HVAC system not up to code, that's a different reply. We will do what we need when the time is right. For now, we will give Fire Chief Hanson the support he needs through funding authorizations for the extra police for traffic control, impact assessment on the power grid, firefighting supplies, and the cost of a thorough investigation. Please don't confuse a politician's role in emergency management with those who are physically engaged with managing the emergency. *Our* job is to make sure they can do *their* job."

The reporter glared at Jimmy but didn't have a comeback. The press conference closed, and the view cut to what the helicopter could see as it circled the still-raging fire. The firefighters poured water on the neighboring buildings to keep them from burning. They'd already written off the first structure. The press had the decency not to say it out loud.

Jimmy left the briefing and peeked around the vehicles as if looking for someone. He worked his way around the outside of a fire engine. One of the news crews followed him at a distance, filming him from behind. Jimmy found a fireman sitting on the truck's step, his head hanging. Jimmy kneeled beside him, talked to him before giving the man a hug and moving on.

The video cut back to the fire to show a section of wall caving in. The fire flared into the void but quickly died down. The combined efforts of numerous crews brought the breach under control. The news feed returned to the studio, where they showed a map of the fire's location and the blocked streets surrounding it, advising viewers to avoid the area.

They finally cut to a commercial because the station had bills to pay, no matter the level of emergency.

I had seen enough. I trusted that Jimmy's good-guy image was not feigned or choreographed. Jimmy led by example.

My fingers flew across the keyboard as I searched for anything related to Tricia Barrows. She'd kept most of her pre-marital assets in her name. Who knew the modest-living Tripplethorns maintained vacation properties in Italy and the Cayman Islands?

Would the media put Jimmy under the spotlight and reveal this hidden wealth? Was that motive enough to have your husband killed? If Wonderbeast wanted to be the mayor, would they find this information and publish it to smear a grieving widow? Or she was tired of the scrutiny while being condemned to middle-class suburbia and wanted to rejoin the upper crust of society.

There were too many potential reasons. I needed to find something to point in one direction over another, a crack to widen.

I accessed the Wonderbeast's hidden Hotmail account. Four emails from a single account, sent every two days, with the last a week ago. Each one contained no more than a few sentences.

The first one read: *The view is spectacular this time of year. You should see for yourself. Drive like you are the only one on the road.*

She never replied to any of the emails, but the subsequent notes suggested a reply had been sent.

Not the view you thought. It gets better. Climb the highest peak and keep climbing.

A call to action? I could see this as a possible negotiation with The Peace Archive, but it was like they were speaking in a different language. Inconclusive and not compelling.

The third email was even more cryptic. *A chair. The deck. A cloud. Margarita.*

And the fourth email epitomized brevity. *End.*

If there was a transfer of money following receipt of that last email, I'd have a potential link. I tried to get into her bank accounts, but her primary password did not work. I expected she would have been alerted about an attempted login, so I left it at one try. She probably used a recommended strong password, unguessable, unlike those related to her affinity for her alma mater and women's sailing. I looked at the financial institutions that pulled up under her name in the recesses of the dark web, three different ones that appeared to be in just her name.

But the important information remained hidden from me.

The elder Barrows, grandfather to the Tripplethorn children, maintained a public presence only through whatever his media relations team and corporate entities provided. I could find no private email accounts for him or that anything of his had ever been hacked and made available on the dark web.

He would have to remain a mystery. Going after him was out of my league, but his daughter didn't play by the same privacy rules. She needed to take a lesson or two from her old man if she wanted to play the game.

She was in my territory.

I needed to have a private chat with the Tripplethorns, but it needed to be in a place that I picked, that gave me an advantage. Never let the enemy choose the battlefield. That was one of our problems in the Middle East. We were always in a hurry. We could have simply blockaded towns and made them come to us, but no. We had to go in and root out the bad guys.

It changed the dynamic. Increased the danger.

I laced my fingers behind my head as I leaned back in the uncomfortable hotel chair.

I was just a grunt, savvy with the net and possessing common sense that helped me get answers to hard questions, but this job called for more.

The Peace Archive. There was no one to call for help. The beauty of their system was in the independence and disconnection. No one was linked to anyone else as far as I knew. I had two private bank accounts in the Cayman Islands. They transferred money into one, I moved it to the second. I let it build up.

I used Western Union to send myself cash, or rather, send cash to Ian Bragg.

So how was I to make this happen? I shut the laptop and reclined on the bed, propped up on pillows while I stared at a spot on the wall, working through scenario after scenario where I talked to Jimmy about his wife. Why would he come clean with me? What would it take to have a candid conversation with the Wonderbeast?

Put her on her heels. Force her to remedy the error of her ways. What authority did she respect?

I needed to peruse her other emails and see what she let slip. I closed my eyes as I tried to think.

Next thing I know, someone kissed my neck. I nearly jumped through the wall.

"Whoa!" Jenny thrust her hands in front of her to hold me back.

I worked to catch my breath and slow my heart. I had lived alone for too long to be comfortable with pleasant surprises like that.

"You looked so adorable sound asleep, I couldn't help myself. Note to me. Don't wake Ian out of a sound sleep."

I shook my head. "I don't remember falling asleep." I took her hands in mine and held them. "I was thinking about my client. I'll need to meet with them tomorrow, but I have Sunday off. What do you say we do something nice together? A hike if the weather cooperates, or a movie in a theater? Anything where I can be with you?"

"You can count me in." Jenny climbed under my arm to lounge on the bed next to me. "I was thinking about this morning…"

I waited until I realized this was the part where I was supposed to say something. "Why did we meet?" I dodged with a question.

"Because you came to the bar for a Shirley Temple, and I was with people who could not have cared less if I was there or not."

"That's pretty harsh. I have a different take. We were meant to meet. We are meant to be together. I know your parents are gone, but I am asking your father in heaven for permission to court you."

"He would have liked you. He respected the military but never served. And he loved my mother to the moon and back."

"Is that what you're looking for, Miss Jenny? Someone to love you like that?"

"Is it too much to ask?"

"Ask? No. *Demand*? Yes. That's why your new favorite drink is grenadine and orange juice."

"I don't think that's my new favorite drink, but I'm okay with it being yours."

I thrust out my hand. "It's a deal."

She laughed and contorted her body to shake hands with me. "Does this make us partners?"

"I think it does. What's for dinner, dear?"

She rocked back.

"You are not pulling that on me!" she declared. "You bought dinner last night, so it's my turn to treat. I know a place that's not too far. I'll drive. Are you good with steak?"

"I'm good with a good steak, but the best burgers are usually in steak houses that are only okay with steak."

"What I hear you saying is that if I don't like my steak, I can have your burger." Another test. I was ready.

"Of course, as long as you don't mind waiting while I order another burger."

"I remember something about a goat's asshole." Jenny put a hand on her hip and gave me the side-eye.

"Just because I'll eat it, it doesn't mean I like it. I prefer the finer things in life." I wrapped my hands through the crooks of her arms and hugged her to me, holding her tightly.

Jenny nibbled on my earlobe before whispering, "I love you, Ian Bragg."

I knew it was coming, but that didn't change the surprise or my mumbled reply. "Me, too."

The saga of Kicker and the Wonderbeast melted away for the moment. Tomorrow they'd be back with a vengeance. Tomorrow, Jimmy's schedule said family time with Grandpa. That meant I would go to the private berth of the Barrows' yacht to see how the Tripplethorn family interacted. Learn what I could.

Insight would give me the edge I needed.

CHAPTER EIGHT

"One cannot separate the spider web's form from the way in which it originated." Neri Oxman

After an evening of excellent steak, ice cream, a stroll under the stars, and intense one-on-one entertainment, I slept for a solid six hours. Jenny remained asleep, as content as I had been. I took the opportunity in the early dawn to watch her sleep for a few moments and appreciate what life was offering me.

Karma? A reward for doing the right things or enticement to save me from going too far down the wrong path? Either one was good. No matter the reason, we would live for today to make life worth living.

I had work to do before heading out.

I accessed the web on both the public-facing side and from the dark side. I checked the Wonderbeast's emails and found the alert for my attempted login of her bank account. I deleted it and then went into the deletions directory to remove it from there, too. She wasn't as savvy as she might have thought. Having seen her arrogance, I suspected she didn't listen to people, if she bothered to ask for help in the first place.

What I found was most enlightening. I opened a new window with her private email. In the deleted directory were her replies that I had missed the first time through.

The view is spectacular this time of year. You should see for yourself. Drive like you are the only one on the road. Her reply to the first email was abrupt. *For this, I prefer someone else drive.*

Not the view you thought. It gets better. Climb the highest peak and keep climbing. Her reply was *A million steps to the top.*

Had the Wonderbeast paid a million dollars to do her husband in? I was getting three-quarters of that and never expected that I was getting more than half. The Peace Archive had more risk than me. They had to find the clients, which put them far more into the open than me.

The cryptic reply from the unidentified email address. *A chair. The deck. A cloud. Margarita.*

She responded in kind. *Ocean. Heat. Yellow. Napkin.*

She never answered the last email. *End.*

It came across as a substitution code—a word meant something specific. There was no repetition, nothing to analyze. A physical codebook would be required to link this series of emails to a negotiation for a murder for hire. A cipher, encryption at the letter level, could be decrypted through cryptanalysis. Too bad it wasn't a cipher, like a cheesy letter replacement. But I had more faith in The Peace Archive. They never came across as cheesy.

I went to her other emails and searched for three things: any mentions of "Margarita," the alpha-numeric email, and all attachments. That was no small task since she had a mountain of emails with attachments, but most were from so-called friends sharing recipes and memes.

I wondered if she cooked. I had to fight my immediate judgment that she didn't. Collect the data and see where it led. How much of her life was a façade? That was what I needed to unmask. Where was the real Tricia Tripplethorn hiding?

She had a friend named Margarita. There were no attachments with that word contained inside or any of the other codewords. Nothing to indicate that she had received a code sheet by email. How did one start a conversation about hiring a hitman?

And the other email address was not referenced in her regular emails. A lot of research right into a dead end. I checked the time. According to Jimmy's schedule, he was to be at the yacht by nine in the morning. Allowing for traffic. I needed to leave in the thirty minutes to be in place well ahead of the Tripplethorn arrival at Grandpa's place.

I took a quick shower and dressed in my skinny jeans, a button-down, and my suit jacket. I figured being dressed well would stand out less in that area.

Jenny's eyes were open and she was sitting up when I reappeared from the bathroom. I sat down on the bed next to her.

"Dress for success, Mister Bragg?" she said softly.

"Something like that. What are you going to do today?"

"Check out, take my stuff home, and bring a few things back just in case. Maybe you can come home with me for the rest of the weekend after you get back from your day."

"A road trip. Do you have Yahtzee?"

"Of course. And chess."

"Chess. A game that's more than a game. I also like Snakes and Ladders."

"I would have guessed Twister," Jenny countered.

"We don't need Twister to get excited."

She laughed. "You got that right. We can talk about the future of mankind, maybe fix all the world's problems with enough time and enough whiskey."

"Are you suggesting that you want to get me drunk?"

"No sense in just one of us getting lit."

Touché.

"If I must, for King and country, of course." My hand wandered freely across her bare chest. She leaned back and closed her eyes. I leaned over her for a kiss. "I have to go, but I'll be back, and then we have until Monday morning, when I have a ridiculous day. But let's focus on what we have now, starting when I get home to you tonight."

"Home," she repeated softly.

"If I'm not careful, this job will be the death of me, just when things are looking perfect."

Jenny had no idea how much truth there was in that statement.

"I'll do my best to balance you. We are partners, after all. What can I do to relieve some of your burden?"

"When I don't have to think about the job, you can keep me distracted. That is all I can ask for."

"I'm here for you. You need only ask." She let me go, watching me as if studying.

"I'll be back as soon as I can. Your place, dinner, relax with a movie, stimulating conversation, and whatever else strikes us."

"Until tonight." She didn't wave or smile. Just looked at me, respecting that I had to go to work while committing to wait for me.

I returned to her, sitting on the side of the bed where I could whisper into her ear, "I love you, too, Jenny Lawless." I willingly took the step from which there was no turning back.

I stood and hurried from the room. Once in the hall, I walked slowly, trying to close the Jenny compartment and focus on the job I had to do.

Anger flooded my mind. Why did The Peace Archive take a contract on someone who wasn't a scumbag? And why did Tricia Tripplethorn want her husband dead?

If she hadn't taken out the contract, I would have never been here, never met Jenny. The good came with the bad. I had ten days total to fix it.

I stopped by the hotel's restaurant, which was already open. I didn't need to work the serving lady for a meal, but it was Saturday. Someone else was working. I helped myself to a sausage biscuit and hash browns, both being kept warm under a heat lamp. Not the best, but better than nothing. I took a seat in the restaurant and ate quickly before doctoring a coffee with too much foofy creamer.

In the car, I set up my 1980s Rush Playlist. It started with *Permanent Waves'* *The Spirit of Radio* and would roll through the next three albums, *Moving Pictures*, *Signals*, and *Grace Under Pressure*. I should be near the marina well before the music ended. I'd listen to whatever was left, along with *Power Windows* and *Hold Your Fire* for the trip back.

I needed to catch the Seattle ferry to Bainbridge. It would drop me off in Eagle Harbor, where Barrows' *Euripides' Ion* was docked.

Traffic was heavier than I expected, almost like a workday. Good that I had given myself plenty of time. I sat in traffic and jammed, trying to think through scenarios where this contract ended without me being on the receiving end of a Peace Archive bullet.

What if I ended the Wonderbeast?

It wouldn't cancel the contract, but there would be no one to complain. I chalked that up as my last resort.

I turned up the music to clear my head. The soothing slow-roll intro of *Natural Science* wafted through the car before the pace picked up, almost frenetic as it called to me. Triumphant. Tragic. Such power.

Next up on the list was *Tom Sawyer*, followed by *Red Barchetta*. I wondered what she called her Porsche. I decided to refer to it as Barchetta. I suspected it would come into play at some point during this operation.

Once into the downtown area, north of the football stadium, the signs led me to where I wanted to go. A tollbooth funneled paid vehicles onto the *Wenatchee*, a two-hundred car ferry at the Colman dock. A special ferry left early on Saturday morning. During workdays, all the departures were after noon until nearly eight in the evening. A different way to commute.

They were already loading vehicles. I drove in and squeezed up front with the other eight early arrivals. I hopped out and locked the doors. I familiarized myself with the big boat. One never knew when that kind of knowledge would come in handy. It was easier early because very few people were on board. It was less obvious.

I strolled around the deck, watching people going about their daily lives. A young couple going for a picnic. A couple with children riding the big boat for cheap entertainment. The children wanted hot dogs, but the machine wasn't running this early. A bagged Otis Spunkmeyer muffin wasn't satisfying their craving. They both started to cry. I moved away because I could. The parents did an admirable job of ignoring the bawlers, much to everyone else's dismay.

At the aft rail, I could see other cars in the staging area. I should not have been surprised to see a red Escape

Hybrid waiting there. I shook my head slowly at my misfortune.

I had shaken hands with Jimmy. He would recognize me. I hurried back to the car and pulled my floppy hat out of the trunk. I wedged it onto my head before taking it off. I was dressed in business casual, and any of my hats made me stand out.

I tossed them back into the trunk. What to do to avoid being seen?

Disappear. It was a tight squeeze in the lower of the two vehicle bays. I headed topside to see where the Tripplethorns were going to park.

The red Escape was one of the first on the upper parking deck. I dodged toward the aft end of the ship and stayed in the shadows. The family did not climb topside but headed straight for the galley. I meandered that way, staying behind a tall man in case Jimmy appeared, but he was inside with the others, waiting patiently in line for whatever they were serving for breakfast.

People stopped to shake his hand before begging his pardon for interrupting Jimmy's family time. The Wonderbeast maintained a plastic smile. Her eyes told the full story.

Not amused.

Limelight came to mind. Mrs. Tripplethorn didn't like the limelight. *Why not a divorce like normal people? But you're not a normal person, are you?*

Jimmy gave his full attention to the kids as they sat at a table for four. The children ate, while the adults settled for coffee. Like a normal family. Jimmy ended up eating what his daughter left behind of her muffin. The older boy devoured his microwaved egg and meat surprise on a croissant. The children had foil-topped plastic orange juices. Jimmy opened one, and Tricia opened the other.

The family started chatting, laughing at the occasional jibe from one of the kids. Just like normal people. The Wonderbeast occasionally glanced around the galley. I could only guess she was looking for me.

I ducked away twice before the risk became too great. I worked my way to the aft end of the ship in time to see it cast off. We maneuvered away from the dock, the start of a journey across Puget Sound. I descended into the bowels of the ship, the lower vehicle deck to find four young men of various colors strolling through, checking vehicle windows before moving on. They didn't care when I walked past them to get to my car. They continued with what they were doing. I leaned against the trunk and waited. Two came up on me from my left side, while the other two were three cars back on my right.

"Got anything good you can share?" one of the men asked.

"Nothing. Take a look." I didn't unlock the car. The second tried the door handle, scowling at me when he found it didn't open for him. The first kept me company.

The other looked through the window. "Looks like a sweet music player. What you got on it?"

"Rush, man. All the albums."

"Never heard of them, but I'm sure they can be erased. We can put some good stuff on there. Unlock the door."

My *close* friend leaned toward me to reinforce the command. "He said, unlock the door."

I took half a step back to see if he would continue his looming routine. He followed. I lunged forward with a knee to the mid-section. As he started to double over, I guided his face into the corner of my trunk. I jumped over him and continued toward the second man. He fumbled getting a knife out of his pocket, pulling it up as I arrived, too late to stop my fist from catching him across the nose. I followed with a second punch to the temple to take him out.

Their two other friends rushed to their aid, but they had been too far back to do anything about it.

I crossed my arms and waited.

"I'm going to cut you bad," the bigger of the two claimed.

"Come on over here so I can pile you with this one. My money says lucky number four runs like a scared girl when it's just him while his three tough buddies are crying in their Cheerios. Come on, Big and Dumb, I don't have all day to teach you the meaning of life." Nothing like taunting a bully to unhinge them.

He hesitated as he passed the one whose face had had an untimely meeting with my trunk. Maybe not so stupid.

"We are only making sure the vehicles are secure. We work for the ferry service."

"Is that the best you could come up with? Now, get over here and take your lesson like a man." I picked up the unconscious man and held him in front of me. Would his buddy still be willing to use the knife?

All six foot three and two hundred pounds' worth rounded the corner of my car, with the fourth man, probably no more than eighteen years old and a hundred and thirty pounds, right behind him.

Both were right-handed. I lifted and shoved the body toward the big man's right side, blocking his vision for a moment. He did not let his knife go as the unconscious "friend" fell into him. The big man shoved his so-called friend away with his left hand.

I was already well into a roundhouse kick headed straight for the scumbag's 'nads. As my thug shield fell to the side, my heel, with all the power of a full-body turn, impacted the big man square in the choice bits, sending him staggering back until he fell over.

The slight man's hand shook as he brandished his knife at me.

"Put it away and help your friends. Get them away from me while you think about your life decisions. You can never win in this business. You will always find someone bigger, tougher, faster. If all you want to do is bully the weak, this is what happens, or worse, you get yourselves killed. People who have been picked on their whole lives have a tendency to get fed up."

"You got bullied?" he asked as he put his knife away, keeping his distance.

"No. I went in the Marine Corps before toads like these could give me any crap. The difference this morning? They were fighting to be pricks. I was fighting to win. Help these mouth-breathers out of here before Security comes. The last thing you want is to get your asses kicked *and* thrown in jail."

"What's your name, mister?"

"You haven't earned the right to know my name. Now get out."

He picked the first man down to help. Groggy, with a face that was a bloody mess, the two staggered to the elevator. The slight man hurried back to help the second one down. He was still out cold. The smaller man struggled to get him to the elevator.

I bent down and picked up the big man's knife. "If I see you again, I'll bury this thing in your throat." I waved the knife in front of his face. He groaned instead of talking. I couldn't tell if it was an apology or a threat. I gave him the benefit of the doubt and cut the belt on his saggy jeans. If he wanted to fight anyone else, he'd have to do it with one hand holding his pants up.

The youngest member of their gang returned to help the big man up. He remained mostly doubled over. Together they worked their way to the elevator.

I called after them, "You might want to put some ice on that." Big and Dumb groaned again. The bigger they are, the harder they fall. It seemed appropriate. I'd be long gone by the time those knuckleheads had their wits about them. The young man looked at me while he waited for the slow elevator. "You want to be tough, join the Corps. Don't beat up the weak. That's for candy asses like those three."

The elevator arrived and he bundled the others inside, jamming the button and watching me until the doors closed. If the message had gotten through, that was one less thug on the street. Three or four if I had made an impact on their lives.

I chuckled at my own joke before unlocking my car and getting in. I adjusted the mirrors to watch the elevators and stairs in case they recovered enough and got a wild hair. None of them had firearms, and they only had two knives left. I had the other two, a nice four-inch lockback Schrade, a Hunter. The other looked like a butterfly knife purchased in an Asian souvenir market. I wedged it against the floorboard and stomped on it to break the blade.

I folded the Schrade and pocketed it. It was a nice piece of gear, a prize won in battle. I'd wipe it down and ditch it when this op was over, just like everything else. It was all expendable. The value of things was greatest when they did not link me to Seattle.

Cameras had probably recorded the scuffle, but it was dark in the lower car deck. The images would be grainy and indistinct. My license plate would be irrelevant because there was nothing connecting me to the car. It was still in the previous owner's name.

It wasn't long before the *Wenatchee* slid into the

receiving pier. The ramp dropped, and we drove off in reverse order. The Tripplethorns were the first ones ashore and long gone by the time my turn rolled around.

I didn't see the four *amigos* again. Good for them. Better for me.

Bullies. Put in their place, forcing them to believe a life of crime would take them nowhere except to Painsville.

The bottom ramp opened, and I drove off the ship at the front of a parade of weekenders visiting the island.

I turned left once onshore to find Wyatt Way, which turned into Eagle Harbor Drive. It looped around the western end of Eagle Harbor to return to the Puget Sound side for the best view of *Euripedes' Ion*. Private property kept me from a position at the end of the dock. I drove past and parked in Pritchard Park, then strolled past the Japanese Internment Memorial and onto the beach.

Driftwood cluttered the area. The weather was pleasant, with a modest breeze. Cool, but it wasn't raining.

I sat on a stump that had washed ashore and looked over the harbor. I couldn't see the red Escape but knew it had to be close because the family of four neared the end of the dock. An older man waved from the boat, and the kids started to run.

CHAPTER NINE

"'Tis best to weigh the enemy more mighty than he seems."
William Shakespeare

Euripedes' Ion towered over the dock, making the other boats berthed in Eagle Harbor look small and insignificant. Jimmy and Tricia watched the children run to their grandfather. They launched up the gangplank leading to the aft deck, where he greeted them warmly, as a grandfather should.

A much younger woman waved from behind the elder Barrows. The second wife. The first lived in Cyprus, thanks to a generous payout from the divorce. I wondered how much of each parent the Wonderbeast had inherited and which one she embraced more. Was Jimmy a payback for her father replacing her mother with a younger woman?

I suspected if Jimmy left her, he'd get nothing. A prenuptial agreement. So why the hit? A divorce would make her look like a toad while his star continued to rise.

If he was gone, she could probably ride the wave to being mayor but would be stopped there.

None of it made sense. It made me question whether she was the one who had paid for the hit. I might have been hasty. Still, there was something going on with her. A secret.

Dirt.

I used my phone to zoom in on the *Ion*. From my seat, I had to look through the random boats tied up at the Bainbridge Marina. A couple walked out on the dock and looked into the water before strolling back to land.

I took the opportunity to go where they had gone, taking advantage of public access. Once on the dock, surrounded by a ragtag fleet of private vessels, both powered and sailing, I looked into the water at regular intervals as if watching for sea life.

At the end of the dock, I was a hundred feet from the Barrows and Tripplethorn families. The rear deck was open toward me, with the family lounging. Smoke belched from the funnel before settling down.

The Barrows' yacht was heading out to sea.

I sat down on the end of the dock, removed my dress shoes and socks, and rolled up my pants legs. I dangled my feet in the water, acting as if I didn't have a care in the world. I pulled my 12th Man ballcap down to shade my eyes and prevent Jimmy from recognizing me. I wore my sports coat and a button-down shirt. A businessman taking a break from the rigors of the daily grind.

Even though it was Saturday morning. I could have gone with more casual. An old seadog walked down the dock toward me, carrying two fishing poles and a bait box. He tossed his stuff into an aging cabin cruiser before heading my way.

"You lost, sonny?"

"Wondering what it would be like to leave office life behind to spend more time on the ocean."

"A fool's life, that's what!" He raspily laughed himself into a coughing fit. I had no idea what his point was. "I used to be like you, working in an office. Retired early and bought this luxury yacht."

I glanced at the old nag. He had to be pulling my leg.

"She was something once, but everything gets more expensive, and the money doesn't go as far as you'd like. I'm getting by. I'll eat what I catch. I could use a spare pair of hands if you want to see what it's like. I'm not going out very far. This ol' tug doesn't make the long trips anymore."

I was torn, but I wanted to see what the *Ion* was going to do. Jimmy's schedule said it was a day outing. The Tripplethorns had not brought extra clothes or backpacks to suggest an overnight.

"I have to be somewhere this afternoon, but I could spend the morning with you. I'd love to give Puget Sound fishing a try."

"Yeehaw! We'll catch us some chinook and maybe a lingcod or three. We'll be back a little after noon if you can sling bait."

"Let me run to my car and get different clothes."

"Don't take all day, Sonny. You got some deck-scrubbing to attend to while I get her ready to catch fish."

I laughed as I picked up my stuff and hurried back to shore, tiptoeing barefoot through the parking lot, through the rough undergrowth, and to my car. I swapped my jacket and dress shoes for my stinking hobo pants. At least the mud had dried. some of it cracked off on my way to *Bessie Mae.*

There was a distinct difference between someone walking with a purpose and someone just walking. I could ask the spry oldster about the big boat and her owner. One never just fishes. I expected the man would talk constantly while we were at sea. I'd give him a good day's work for everything he knew.

Because he wasn't getting any information from me.

After dropping off my clothes belowdecks, I returned wearing nothing but my dirty pants and a ball cap. No shoes. No shirt.

He looked me over skeptically. "What the hell happened to you?" He pointed at my side.

"Shrapnel. A gift from those who didn't like Americans stomping on their sand."

"I was Navy. Between wars, but I do love the sea. Now, stop goofing off, ground-pounder, and get to scrubbing."

"Yes, sir. Scrubbing now, aye, aye, sir." I took the proffered bucket and brush and started aft as far as I could go so I could keep an eye on *Ion*. Two crew stood on the dock, preparing to cast off the lines. "What do you know about that big boat? Who owns that kind of thing?"

"That's Clive Barrows. Baron of Ball Street. That's what we call him, anyway." I hit the deck hard, scrubbing at a year of grime. The old man hadn't cleaned his boat in a while, as if he'd fallen out of love with her. "Kinda like Wall street, but front lines. He owns a dozen convenience chains. Touch the front-line workers every day by selling them microwaved food and supersized Cokes. Those with their balls on the line, average people, not like you or me. I don't eat or drink that swill. Poison!"

Bessie Mae's skipper became easily agitated. The veins in his face throbbed, and blood vessels in his nose threatened to explode. He looked like he needed a drink. I was happy he didn't reach for one.

"No need to get spun up. He doesn't live in our world. I'm curious about his, though. Looks like a young family is on board. Who are they?"

"That's the next mayor of Seattle, Jimmy Tripplethorn. He married the daughter and right into all that money. She's the only heir, and old Clive is getting on in years."

"A second wife?"

"It's the in-thing for old rich guys. Trade for a newer model, if you know what I mean. I'm sure the newest Mrs. Barrows got herself a nice nest egg out of banging the old man in his later years, but the daughter gets the bulk."

"He's not that old, is he?"

"Older than me!" The skipper changed out the lure on one of his two poles, choosing a massive spoon over the hook and sinker of the other setup. "No matter. None of my business what he spends his money on. I'm just bitter that my pie gets smaller and his gets bigger."

He caressed the wood frame beside the driver's compartment above the cabin.

"Me and *Bessie Mae*'s been through some things, ain't we, old girl?"

"Your wife?" I kept my eyes on *Euripedes' Ion* as it turned about within the big harbor. I couldn't see who was driving it, but I knew who wasn't. Old man Barrows remained on the back deck, pointing out highlights of Bainbridge Island as if the children hadn't seen them before.

"Left. Turns out, she didn't like fish or me being retired."

"Left you high and dry." I tried to sympathize. Wonderbeast and the second wife were no longer on deck, only Jimmy, Clive, and the kids. They were too occupied with pointing and looking to bother with *Bessie Mae* or me. I watched them closely.

A good dynamic between Jimmy and his father-in-law. One of the crew brought out a pitcher and glasses. Looked like iced tea. It was still early, barely ten in the morning.

"Don't be watching the paint dry, skipper." I hopped off

the boat and threatened to untie the bowline. "Are we going fishing, or are you going to make love to your pilot's chair?"

"Hold your horses, dogface. I gotta do things in order."

"Eat me, squid lips!" With the *Ion* passing out of the harbor and accelerating, I returned to scrubbing the deck.

"Damn mouthy ground-pounders."

"Lazy-ass seadogs." My interservice rivalry game was strong. I had worked long and hard to perfect it. "Bell-bottom-wearing Mister Fancy Pants."

"Hey! Those were comfortable. I wish I had a pair that fit," the skipper countered, but he stomped around the boat, checking fittings and fluid levels. He finished back in the pilothouse, where he flipped a series of switches before turning over the engine. It groaned and cycled with a squeal.

I jumped to my feet. The sound had been uncomfortably close, the noise of an engine getting ready to blow.

It coughed and rumbled to life. A diesel. It didn't purr, but it ran. An overhaul would give it new life, but those cost money, and *Bessie Mae's* captain seemed to be a few dollars short.

"If I have to swim ashore because this tug breaks down, I'm going to be very put out. Very," I shouted over the engine's roar.

"Cast off the lines, pudknocker!" He waved indiscriminately. I jumped onto the dock, untied the bowline, and tossed it on board. I unhitched the stern line and carried it with me when I leapt into the boat. The captain laughed as he spun the wheel and eased *Bessie Mae* away from the dock.

A speed limit of five knots left us woefully behind *Ion*. It turned left once in the Sound and accelerated away. I kept scrubbing while looking up to keep an eye on the megayacht. The day's surveillance was coming to an end.

Bessie Mae turned right, cruised down the coast for a mile, and then slowed while the captain watched the fish finder. I realized he hadn't told me his name. He hadn't asked for mine, either. I would make do. Anonymity was my friend.

I quit scrubbing, leaving a night and day difference between the clean and the dirty.

"Come on, taxi driver, let's catch some fish."

"Hold your horses, dirt nap. Grab that rod with the spoon and get ready to let it out. When I tell you, toe rag, and not before." Laser-focused on his equipment, he held his hand out as if getting ready to call for wrestlers to start their match.

I unhooked the spoon, checked the bail, and prepared to send it overboard.

The captain idled the boat, letting it drift back the way we'd come. He kept his eyes on the fish finder. "You got a woman you have to get back to?"

"Have I ever! As much as I can handle and then some."

"A real spitfire, huh? We all need one of those. NOW!"

I tossed the spoon behind the boat and let it sink, leaving the bail open to feed the lure deep into the water.

"That's good. Tighten it up and be ready. I think we got some nice pinks beneath us. Don't set the hook on these. You yank the lure, you lose the fish. After you get a bite, reel him in."

It wasn't more than ten seconds before I had one hooked. I leaned back, letting the pole absorb much of the fight as I reeled. The fish started to run. I let him go. The drag was set light, and the fish swam away without much resistance. I dialed it up a little and reeled to keep the tension on the hook. Pull, run, pull. The captain cracked a beer and sipped it while I fought the fish.

Once the chinook hit the surface, he put his can down and grabbed the net. The fish headed toward open water. I pulled harder, letting the rod bend to work as a shock absorber. Reeling. Always reeling.

The captain jumped back into the cabin and added a little gas to get *Bessie Mae* moving forward, then returned to the aft deck. "Bring it down this side." He held the net where the fish couldn't see it. The chinook started to run, but it was getting tired. I horsed it the last few feet.

Quick as a rattlesnake, the captain dipped the net, scooped the fish, and dragged it aboard.

"Nice!" A quick measure showed we had a forty-incher, weighing in at twenty-five pounds. The captain slipped it into the cooler that doubled as a bench seat. I untangled the lure from the net. "Going for round two."

We doubled back and followed the same routine five times to put three more chinook in the tank.

After the fourth catch of the day, I had to rub my arms. They were getting stiff, and I had developed a bruise below my belly button where I'd jammed the butt end of the pole while fighting the fish.

"You caught 'em. You can take half."

"I'm staying in a hotel. No place for them, but you've shown me a great day. Let's head on in. No sense wasting gas with a good catch already on board. My compliments to you, Master Seaman."

"Four hooked, four in the boat. Not bad for a buckethead."

"It's almost like someone dipped them out for me. Squids know their own, don't they?"

"You better scrub the other half of that deck. Can't

leave it like that." He pointed at the unfinished work. "I'm taking us in. You go spend time with that lady of yours."

I pulled out the bucket and the brush, got back on my knees, and used my body weight to help put more pressure on the deck. I wanted to finish before we docked. It was a sense of pride.

The *Ion* was nowhere to be seen. Noon. I was going to get back early as long as traffic cooperated. I turned my attention to the deck and renewed my efforts.

I had a little bit to go when we docked. The captain told me to leave it. I couldn't. I tied us off and returned to finish the last of it. The old man carried two fish to the cleaning station. I cleared the deck before he returned, so I took the other two and carried them down the dock to where the old man carved away.

I flopped them on the table and headed back to the boat to get my clothes. I cleaned up as much as I could with a dirty rag. I needed a shower. When I made it back down the dock, I pulled two one-hundred-dollar bills from my wallet, rolled them up, and stuffed them into the old man's shirt pocket.

"You showed me a great time today. I don't take that for granted."

"I have all these fish and a clean deck. I should be paying you." The old man pulled out the bills and looked sideways at me. I held a finger to my lips.

"If anyone asks, I was never here. I wouldn't be able to live it down if anyone found out I spent the day with a squid."

He held out a fish-snotty-and-bloody hand. I took it, and we shook. cleaning table had a sink where I could rinse off, but it wasn't good enough.

"Anywhere around here to get a shower?"

"Inside. I'll let 'em know." He left his fish at the cleaning station and opened the door to the main building. "My friend here is going to catch a shower. Caught some decent chinook off Rockaway Point." He gave someone inside the thumbs-up and I walked in, barefoot and without a shirt. An older woman pointed in the direction of the restroom.

The shower was ratty and aged like the rest of the building, but it did the trick. I smelled like a new man, still barefoot, but I had on my nice pants and shirt. I bundled my nasty pants, holding them away from my body as I walked out the front door, through the lot, and into the neighboring park to my car. I tossed my pants in the trunk while I sat on the bumper to wipe off my feet and put my shoes on.

Besides fishing, what I had learned?

I had time to think on the drive.

If not the Wonderbeast, then who? I felt like I was back to square one.

Help would come to me through Rush. I scrolled to *Grace Under Pressure* and tapped *The Enemy Within*. I was taking the long way back to the hotel, avoiding the ferry by driving overland south and then east.

What to do about Tricia Tripplethorn? I needed to know where she went and who she met. I wanted to know where Barchetta went. I had to stop by an electronics store for a commercial GPS tracker. It carried the appropriate legal warning about tracking people without their consent.

Perfect.

I bought two. Thirty dollars each. Should have been illegal.

Would the Wonderbeast show up at the campaign headquarters on Monday night? I counted on it. I would browse her emails daily to find what else was going on in her life. It nagged at me. What was her role?

She had to get something out of it, but what? I needed

to continue looking for dirt on Jimmy, too. I had to dig into his emails if I could get in. A lot of work to do. I would take care of it in the morning while Jenny slept.

Traffic ground to a halt. I used the opportunity to give her a call.

She answered without preamble. It kept me on my toes. "Does this mean what I hope it means?"

"Your hopes are my desires. I am on my way to the hotel."

"I'm at my house, but I'll head back. Be there in less than an hour."

"I can't wait to see you, Miss Jenny." I waited for a moment before adding, "Don't get a speeding ticket."

"I'm grabbing my purse and keys on my way out the door. Soon, Ian." She hung up to focus on getting back to the hotel.

I turned up the car stereo. *Hold Your Fire* had just started. The album was over fifty minutes long. It should take me all the way to the hotel if traffic resumed at a decent pace. Saturday midday.

Where was everyone going? With the flow. Just like me.

But my destination was different.

Ride the tide. Turn when I had to. Only had to decide which direction.

CHAPTER TEN

"Exercise of body and exercise of mind are supplementary, and both may be made recreative and educative." John Lancaster Spalding

I pulled into the lot before Jenny. I hurried to my room to change, brush my teeth, and throw a few things into a bag for the rest of the weekend.

A gentle knock signaled Jenny's arrival. I waited without replying. She used her keycard and entered. "Oh! You're here. Why didn't you say anything?"

She strolled casually up to me, wearing a smile that broadened with each step.

"I gave you the key to my room. You need nothing more from me to come in."

She leaned back. "Housekeeping also has a key to your room." She rubbed her nose against mine.

"The difference is that I didn't give it to them."

"Point to Ian," Jenny conceded. "I smell fish."

"Funny thing," I started, looking down and shuffling my

feet. "Working with the client resulted in going fishing in Puget Sound. We caught a number of chinook."

"Ooh! I love fresh grilled salmon." Jenny's smile radiated brilliantly.

"Oh, no. I didn't have a cooler. Didn't think… I gave mine to the client. Dammit." The string of disjointed thoughts tumbled from me. "Can we buy some?"

"Of course. This is Seattle. The question is, can we buy good stuff?"

"Let's go shopping," I offered, trying to redeem myself.

"We want to cook it right after we get it. It's a little early, don't you think?" Jenny dropped her purse on the low dresser. She returned to the door and put the do-not-disturb sign out, then locked us in.

She stood by the door and casually unbuttoned her blouse.

I mirrored her movements. There was nothing else to say.

Jenny drove north to get past Lake Sammamish and then east and south. We held hands. Hers was warm and soft like the rest of her body.

"Grocery store?" I wondered what was for dinner. Jenny drove by a large chain store that touted fresh-caught salmon for sale.

"You didn't get your burger, so I'm taking you to a burger and barbeque joint. My treat."

"What's not to like about that? I'm sorry. I like good burgers but prefer great ones."

"I think they'll take good care of you. You can order whatever you want."

"Is this your neck of the woods?"

"About ten minutes from my house. I grew up here, but I don't know too many people now. Turnover as people move away and new commuters move in."

I understood that. "Still affordable for many who work downtown, but it's a long haul from here to the big city. A sacrifice the young are willing to make to get more for their money at the cost of their precious time."

"It's what my dad did," Jenny replied. "But he also loved to hunt."

"Do you shoot?" I expected his guns had passed to her.

"I can, but I don't. I'm not comfortable with just me going to the range."

"That's what we can do tomorrow. We'll send some rounds into paper and then clean the weapons, as it's probably been a while, hasn't it?"

"It's not something I think to do."

I wanted to see what she had in case we needed to defend ourselves. If The Peace Archive came after us.

"We'll fire them and forget about them. Then go for a hike or swimming or who knows what."

"Swimming! Like you want to be seen with a beached whale."

I gripped her hand tightly. "You can stop that talk right now. Purge those thoughts from your mind because that is the only place they exist. Definitely not in mine. I think about how beautiful you are and what you are doing falling for someone like me. I consider myself lucky to be with you. Maybe the luckiest man ever."

"But it's okay if we don't go swimming?"

"Of course, but not because you're afraid of what people will think. *We* are none of anyone else's damn business."

Jenny smiled, and her eyes sparkled as she pulled into the restaurant's lot. "Only our business, Mr. Bragg."

"Indeed, Miss Lawless. Let me get the door for you. It's the least I can do since you're buying. I shall embrace my role as a kept man."

"I've never kept a man before." She nodded at me. I got out and circled the car.

I opened the door for her and bowed slightly. "Neither have I."

She nuzzled close before taking my arm for the walk into the restaurant.

"Would you look at the time?" I showed Jenny my watch.

"We're acting like old people, eating dinner early."

"I haven't eaten since breakfast, and I'm hungry. Thank you for accommodating me. Jenny and Ian, being adults, ignoring all social norms as they venture through life."

"Philosophy. You don't strike me as someone who adheres to social norms. I've seen the clothes you brought."

I laughed and shook my head. My effort to blend in had been less than spectacular. "I don't care about a lot of things, but what I care about, I care about a lot."

"Like me?"

"A whole lot, and then some." I wanted to be clear. I opened the door, and she walked through and straight up to the hostess.

"Miss Lawless. Welcome to the Pighouse." She reached back for me. I wrapped an arm around her waist and nodded to the teenager behind the check-in stand. She raised both eyebrows while she gave me a quick once-over. She turned back to Jenny. "We have the anniversary table available if you'd like that. Are you celebrating anything special?"

"Thanks, Dara, we would. We are celebrating the love of life." Jenny turned to me. "Dara was in my class a few years back. A quick study and a most excellent student."

She led us through the half-full restaurant to deposit menus on an isolated table in the back. We took our seats across from each other. "The love of life, huh? I'm not sure I've ever seen you glow like this, Miss Lawless. Life must love you back." The teenager glanced at me before putting her hand on Jenny's shoulder for a moment before walking away.

I held her hands, not bothering to look at the menu, and once again surrendered to getting lost in her eyes.

Someone cleared their throat. I blinked before being able to look up. "Ah, there you are!"

He smiled without humor. "Can I get you something to drink?"

"Iced tea, sweet, please," Jenny ordered.

"Make that two."

"Are you ready to order?" he pressed.

"I admit that I have not yet looked at the menu. What do you recommend?" Jenny scanned the menu while I talked.

"The pulled pork sandwich is our specialty, complete with our homemade barbeque sauce."

"I'm torn. We came here for a burger, but when a restaurant has something they do best, it's hard to turn it down. I'm good with the pulled pork sandwich. I suspect there's a platter option with coleslaw and fries?" The server nodded as he wrote. "Miss Jenny?"

"Make that two. It's to die for."

"I hope not. Do I get to eat it first?" The server remained joyless as he collected the menus and left us to ourselves.

"What do you do, Ian?" Jenny braced her elbows on the table and rested her chin on her hands.

I liked that pose. I didn't like the question, but it had been inevitable. "I'll tell you at your house. My clients are rather private people, and this is a public place." We were isolated, but that didn't matter. I couldn't risk it.

"Interesting. I wondered how long you would go without telling me. No secrets between us. And no lies. Promise?"

"Those things are foundational to a strong relationship. I agree wholeheartedly. Please don't leave me."

"What kind of secret are you keeping, Ian, where you think I'm going to leave you?" The corners of her eyes wrinkled slightly as she held my gaze.

"Tonight, I will tell you everything. For now, I will explain that I don't love easily or freely. I'm amazed at how quickly I've fallen for you. This isn't a ploy to get some trim while I'm on a gig. I'm not sure I could be more surprised by how things are going. Makes me want to change my life goals and everything related to them. The start of relationships is usually powerful, where little things are easily overlooked. But I love everything about you, Miss Jenny. I wish to change nothing. I only want to be part of what's right in front of me. And that means I want you to be part of me, too."

Jenny leaned back and smiled without answering me. The server put our drinks on the table and disappeared without trying to make small talk.

When she finally spoke, it was with a shrug. "There's nothing you could say that would chase me away. I fear you are stuck with me."

I held out my hand with my little finger in the air. "Pinkie swear?"

"What, are we in high school?"

I held it there. She finally conceded, wrapping her warm finger around mine. "Be honest with me. Is the pulled pork any good?"

"I like it." Not the full commitment I was looking for,

but if that was the best she was going to give, I could ask for no more.

"Then we shall see how our tastes align." I got out of my seat and squeezed in next to her. She moved aside for me. I took her face in my hands and kissed her.

The flash startled me. A picture!

Dara was in my seat and smiling. "This looks like an engagement picture. I want to be the first to congratulate you."

I couldn't have a picture of me with Jenny. "Can I see it?" Dara pulled up the picture and held out her phone. Mostly the back of my head and my hands blocking most of Jenny's face. No one could tell anything from that, and most importantly, neither could web crawlers using facial recognition.

Dara leaned back and aimed her phone at us. "Let me get a nice one of you two. Congratulations, Miss Lawless! Who is the lucky man?"

I moved out of the seat and stood by the table. Dara looked dejected. "Shh. We'll make a formal announcement when the time is right. Keep the picture because that shows the face of true love, but please, no more. My employer would be put out if he caught me goofing off."

Dara looked confused. "Since when is eating dinner goofing off?"

"When your employer is as demanding as mine. They pay me a lot not to goof off." I held my finger in front of my lips. "Keep it on the down-low."

"Uh-huh," she mumbled.

"Down-low, Dara," Jenny requested in her teacher's voice.

She recovered quickly, straightening her shoulders. "You two make a great couple. If everyone had a relationship like yours, the world would be a better place."

A relationship like ours. What if the Wonderbeast had a boyfriend, a rich boyfriend who wanted to be richer?

The worlds in my mind were merging inconveniently. I was still in the game and needed to stay sharp.

A voice, both gentle and urgent. "Ian?" Jenny. I was standing, staring at the wall.

The two compartments were open, flooding into each other. Tricia Tripplethorn. Jenny Lawless. Worlds apart. Commitment. Betrayal.

The Wonderbeast was still in the middle of it. I hadn't been wrong. The Porsche. I had to know where she was going. Jimmy's days were long, and the kids were in school. What did she do with herself?

"Ian? You're scaring me."

"No. I'm so sorry, no! My day job. Dara's words offered a revelation. I see some things more clearly and others not so much, but I have a way ahead. Tonight when we're at your house. I'll tell you everything."

I sat down across from Jenny. She nodded, close-lipped, while she contemplated me.

"A man of mystery. I think you will keep me on my toes, Ian Bragg."

"It will be a good thing, too. We never want to grow complacent." I lowered my voice. "I hope you don't mind a world cruise when this is over. It might be six months long, but it will be epic."

"I don't have that kind of money," she replied, shaking her head firmly. "A partnership means we have equal parts to play."

"We shall discuss this later, and there will be no decisions without mutual agreement. Deal?"

"I'll hold you to that." She kept her face even, but the corners of her mouth ticked upward. I couldn't help but stare. Bachelor me of six days prior would be appalled. I embraced my evolution.

The server arrived before I had to come up with anything else because the truth of my life was the elephant consuming all the oxygen in the room. I needed to get it out so we could move forward.

Instead, we ate in silence. I peeked at her and she glanced at me while we chewed, barbeque sauce getting on everything. We were going to run out of napkins.

"I think we're supposed to lick our fingers," I suggested. My one napkin was mostly destroyed and no longer useful. "Or finish it without putting it down, eating two-year-old style."

I held it in front of my face and peered over the top of my sandwich. Sauce ran down her chin. She put her pulled pork down and wiped her face with the last vestiges of her napkin. She stood gracefully and strolled to the servers' station, where she snagged a stack of napkins, and returned to the table, waving them like someone who had received their lottery payout.

She dropped them on the table. "Men."

"I'm one of those. I would rather drive around lost than stop for directions. Just so you know. My secret is out, but it wasn't so secret. You already knew I was a man."

She took a deep breath. "I've dated both men *and* women."

I didn't know if she said that to shock me or it was a true revelation. I had taken a big bite of my sandwich and couldn't delay answering. She'd get the wrong idea. I replied with a full mouth, "So?"

"Some men have a weird reaction to that. Want a threesome or something."

I chewed fast, even though I wanted to enjoy the pulled pork. The barbecue sauce made for a perfect tang with the tenderness of a well-smoked shoulder. "I'm not some men. I have zero interest in spending intimate time with anyone other than you. I will spend the rest of my life proving it to you."

"From the L-word to a lifelong commitment. You move fast."

I used two napkins to clear the sticky mess from my hands so I could eat the coleslaw. "I spent half my life looking for you and don't intend to waste the other half. Let's get dessert to go."

"Make it so." A simple reply, appropriately geeky for me. I loved it. I hunted down the server to get a box and ordered lava cake for two with vanilla ice cream to go. When he came with the box and dessert, I reached for my wallet, but Jenny stopped me and handed over her credit card. Once our debt was satisfied, we headed out of the restaurant, hurrying to keep life from getting away from us.

Into the car and off, down the road, through a turn and then another, onto a side road. Jenny pulled into an older home. Yard a little unkempt. No picket fence.

She parked under a carport and not in the garage beyond. I guessed it was filled with junk.

Inside was a tidy house that smelled of fresh flowers, but there were none in vases. I would have to order some. Three bedrooms with a living room and dining room sharing space. The kitchen had worn corners on the counters, a shine on the appliances, and racks to hold the utensils of a master chef.

"Your mom was a good cook."

"She was magnificent. We never longed for a good meal."

Jenny put the lava cake on the dining room table, pulled open a drawer in the kitchen, and dug out forks and a serving spatula. Went to a cabinet for dessert plates. She sat down and I took the spot next to her, leaving the corner of the table with our dessert between us.

"What is your secret, Ian Bragg?" she asked as she cut the cake in half. When she finished, she fixed me with her undivided attention.

I didn't even have to take a breath. I had been holding it and waiting for the moment to say out loud the words I had never spoken before. "I was sent here to kill Jimmy Tripplethorn. You see, I kill people for a living."

Jenny's hand trembled but she carried on, nodding slightly before serving us both. She left her fork on her plate and watched me closely. I continued.

"Six total over the course of a little more than a year. I have nine days left to make the hit, but I can't do it. The others were bad people. It was easy to pull the trigger on them because their loss made the world a better place.

"But not this time. I've dug hard and can find no reason why Jimmy needs to die. The bad news is, the organization I work for, The Peace Archive, won't allow me to renege on the contract. I need whoever paid for the contract to cancel it. Even paying the money back won't stop the hit."

I pinched my eyes closed. My heart raced. Some tough guy. I felt like I was going to cry. I heard her sigh and then breathe rapidly. The silence dragged on. When I opened my eyes, she was looking at me, undecided. I looked into my lap and waited. The ball was in her court.

Jenny finally moved from her chair to kneel by my side, taking both my hands in hers and kissing them. "I can live with that. If that's all you have, then you are stuck with me."

CHAPTER ELEVEN

"Two heads are better than one, not because either is infallible, but because they are unlikely to go wrong in the same direction."
C.S. Lewis

"This job isn't that hard. Find the exit route, wait until the target enters the kill zone, make the hit, and leave. The hardest part is not having anyone to talk with, hammer out an idea or plan, make it better. You can help me think, save me from myself. Jimmy is the first politician I've gotten. The others were crime figures of one sort or another."

"Is The Peace Archive a government organization? Maybe a black program?"

I contemplated her question. I had missed the obvious. "That is a good question. Who in the government would want to kill a politician, an honest one? I think the answer to that is all of them. But who could afford it? It's at least a million dollars, maybe more. No government employees could afford this hit. Rich elected officials, maybe, but that's a hard theory to embrace because rich politicians destroy people with lies in the media. Destroying people's lives is a game to them. No. I think Tricia Tripplethorn is involved. Either her or an illicit boyfriend."

"No one likes her, but no one talks about it. I can see her having a boyfriend."

"Do you know her?"

"Of course not. I watch the news, and the future mayor and his family get a lot of airtime around here."

"Everyone assumes he's going to win. I haven't met anyone who doesn't. Why do you think that is?"

"Because the current mayor does stupid things and doesn't seem to care. In walks squeaky clean Jimmy Tripplethorn. No one is running against them. It's a two-horse race, and one is hobbled and crawling toward his deathbed."

"From my point of view, both of them are on their deathbeds."

"I'm sorry. I'm not used to thinking like that." Jenny continued to look up at me. Our ice cream was melting. The house seemed warmer than it should have been.

"I'm the one who's sorry. Why couldn't Jimmy be a bad guy no one would miss?" I scooped up a forkful of lava cake and ice cream and offered it to Jenny.

"A hitman who is tender and loving. Who would have thought?" She opened her mouth and accepted the bite of dessert. I took one and then offered her a second spoonful. She remained on the floor as I worked my way through my half of our dessert. It went quickly. I slid her plate to my edge of the table. "Did you go fishing today with a client?"

"I went to Bainbridge Island, where Clive Barrows berths his boat *Euripedes' Ion*. The Tripplethorn family went to see Grandpa. I was there to watch them, but they undocked and headed out to sea. A crotchety fisherman saw me on the dock and asked me to join him. He also provided some firsthand information on Old Man Barrows. So yes, it was one hundred percent a business trip until *Ion* buried us in her wake. Then we went fishing. Caught about seventy-five pounds of chinook. I think he wanted lingcod too, but we only had to cast five times to catch four fish. Then we returned to port, and I drove straight to the hotel. Oops, I stopped at the electronics mart and picked up a couple of magnetic GPS trackers. I intend to put one on the Wonderbeast's Porsche."

"Wonderbeast?" She looked at me with her lips parted and her tongue resting between her teeth.

"I call my targets by names to dehumanize them. Jimmy used to be Kicker before he turned out to be a decent guy. Kicker, as in 'kick me in the Jimmy.' And Wonderbeast is because she thinks she's wonderful and everyone else thinks she's a beast. Trust me when I say it sounds a lot better in my head. I don't usually say the names out loud."

"I'll take your word for that. I want to know it all. How does one get into the business of being an assassin? How do you contact The Peace Archive and accept a contract? I can't see how any of it works."

I cried out in brief panic, "Do not search online for The Peace Archive or my name or anything like that. They'll pick it up, and your ISP will lead them right here."

She got up, but only far enough to arrange herself in my lap and wrap her arms around my neck. "Are we in danger?"

"I told you I wouldn't lie to you." I looked down. "The answer is yes. I am always in danger, and now you've been seen with me. That was a poor decision on my part, but I wanted you to know how beautiful you are and that it was my privilege to be seen in public with you. But that selfishness has put you at risk."

Jenny kissed my forehead, then slowly caressed my face

with her lips. She rested her nose on mine and looked into my eyes.

"I feel incredible exhilaration knowing that. My life is different now, isn't it?"

"I'm sorry."

"I'm not." She dipped her finger into the chocolate atop the lava cake and drew a line from her jaw down her neck. She tilted her head back. "What am I going to do about this mess?"

"Whatever you do, don't get any on your clothes. It'll stain." Tacky, but it was the best I could manage with the blood rushing from my brain. I licked the chocolate off her neck.

I wouldn't have any problems with The Peace Archive until I was late with the contract, or whoever paid for the contract complained about getting pressured to cancel it. For the moment, Jenny was safe, but there would come a time too soon when we'd be on the run.

We made love with reckless abandon, like two people with everything to lose living the last of their lives to the fullest.

"Ian isn't your real name, is it?"

"It is for now. The name from before doesn't mean anything. That person is gone. I *am* Ian Bragg."

She nodded. I propped an elbow on the bed and supported my head in my hand.

"A world cruise doesn't sound too bad, does it?" I asked.

"It sounds like a great idea. I'll have to take a leave of absence from my job, but that means a substitute teacher will get her shot at a full-time job. It begs the question, can we honeymoon for the rest of our lives?"

"That is the question, now isn't it? Assuming they let me out of the game."

"Killing people is a game?" She wanted to know. She wasn't judging.

"No, but that's what I call it. A deadly game with only winners and losers. There is no second place."

Jenny nodded while I ran my fingers absentmindedly along her curves.

"Do you have Wi-Fi?"

"How backward do you think I am?" she shot back.

"I don't think you're backward, Jenny. My real question is, can I have the password so I can work."

"Don't you want to sleep with me?" Not a taunt.

I swallowed. "I will always want to sleep with you. It's for when I get up in the morning and you're still sleeping. I can only watch you for so long before I feel creepy."

She laughed, a light and musical sound. "I love Ian Bragg, no spaces. The Is are ones and Os are zeros."

I pulled the pillow under my head. "I think I can remember that, Miss Jenny." I closed my eyes, not realizing how tired I was, and fell asleep quickly. I don't know how long Jenny stroked my hair and watched me before she fell asleep too, pressed tightly against me.

I didn't bother getting dressed. I sat naked at the dining room table with my computer, using Jenny's Wi-Fi. My VPN hid any trace of my efforts. First order of business: dig into the Wonderbeast's emails and try to find evidence of a daytime liaison.

I accessed her unlabeled email first. A thirteenth email had popped up, and she had already read it.

Soap. Tree. Car. Water.

I dove into the deleted folder to find her response. *Noon Monday.*

Sent at six the previous evening. They would have either been still at sea with dear old dad or on their way back home. No codebook available. She couldn't wait to send her answer. It was important to her, despite the risk of sending it in the clear, not even cryptically worded.

If I could get the tracker on her vehicle before then, I could follow her from a distance. If not, I'd have to do it the old-fashioned way.

Her normal emails were a disaster, but I wanted to be thorough.

I turned off her email's system of marking emails as read when viewed in the preview pane. I browsed the previously read emails, looking for someone who shouldn't have been there. She didn't delete many emails.

I confined my search to the previous two months, then I moved to the unread. Tedious and time-consuming. I took notes on possible email addresses. Two hours and four cups of coffee later, I finished perusing the inane public life of Tricia Tripplethorn.

She confined her secret life to the cryptic private email.

Who was the mysterious sender hiding behind DN74XTW1?

I adjusted my VPN to make it look like I was searching from China. I typed in the letter-number combination. The return comprised subsets of the individual letters, but nothing exact.

A dead end.

I'd been sitting too long. I stood and stretched before strolling around Jenny's house. Family photos on the walls, the artwork Jenny had chosen to keep, and new items she'd put on display.

Art done by teenagers. Up-and-comers. Maybe.

She supported her students. They liked her, as Dara had shown.

Jenny was an innocent, living a sheltered life. Society, as it bubbled below the surface, was a hard place. I had not done her any favors by dragging her into my world. She said she was willing to come, but she didn't know the danger. An innocent.

She gave me something I hadn't realized I was missing —a partner.

In business. In life.

Jimmy Tripplethorn loved his kids. His dog, too. Did he love his partner?

I returned to the kitchen for another cup of coffee. I waited for the Keurig to deliver a Seattle's Best for me.

A soft footfall signaled that Jenny was awake. She hugged me from behind, sending a tingle all the way to my toes. She hadn't bothered dressing either.

"Did you find anything?" she asked.

I turned to face her and pulled her close. "You live a sheltered life," I said.

She frowned. "I meant on the internet."

"I'm sorry. I just finished strolling around your house, but I didn't open any drawers or anything. I wanted to know more about you. Everything about you."

"Sheltered?" Jenny leaned close, her nose touching mine. We spent a great deal of time talking that way. It was strangely soothing, yet fiercely intimate.

"Pictures, art, everything is from here. Local to this world."

"It's how I grew up. It's..." She struggled for the word. "Comfortable."

"And then I show up and flip everything on its head."

"I'm only going to say this one more time because I am the champion of self-induced anxiety. There's no reason for you to worry, Ian Bragg. I will go wherever you go willingly, no matter what that does to my life. I want to see the bigger world while sharing your world. I like comfortable, but I find that in you and not a place. How does someone like me get a 007 life? It's crazy, but it means cutting ties with my past. This is all new to me, but I am running headlong into it with my eyes wide open."

"Guns," I said out of the blue. "You'll need to be able to protect yourself, which means you'll need to be confident with a handgun."

"I'll show you my dad's arsenal." She backed away half a step, smiling at my response to her body pressing against mine.

I grabbed my cup off the Keurig and followed her. In the master bedroom, which still belonged to her parents, she opened the closet, exposing a handmade rack built to hold Mr. Lawless' collection. There were two pistols. First was a Browning M1911A1, the preferred close-combat weapon of the Marine Corps. I caressed the .45. It was an original and a collector's item. Worth a thousand dollars or more to the right buyer.

The last pistol was a Phoenix Arms HP25A, a .25 caliber semiautomatic pistol. A concealed-carry self-defense weapon. It wasn't anything I would use.

A shotgun and two rifles stood upright with socks over the ends of the barrels to keep dust from getting in. A Mossberg twelve-gauge pump shotgun. He'd probably bought it in a department store on sale. I'd had a Mossberg twenty-gauge growing up. They were sturdy, reliable shooters.

A Marlin .22. Inexpensive and common. A semiautomatic. It was easy to shoot five hundred rounds in a day. Made for fun while trooping around the woods.

Little more than a toy, but it helped teach shooting fundamentals at a low cost.

The last rifle was a gem, like the Browning. A Springfield 03A3, a former military weapon reconfigured as a hunting rifle. Fired a 30-06 round. Deadly accurate and rugged. A warfighter's weapon without the semi-automatic proclivity to descend to volume of ammunition fired versus the quality of a single well-aimed round.

"You look like a kid in a candy store." Jenny leaned against the dresser with her arms crossed.

"The .45 and 30-06 are both collector's items because they are nice pieces of gear." I smiled. I locked the slide to the rear, sending a round into my hand. I dropped the magazine. "Did you know this was loaded?"

Jenny shrugged while she shook her head. I unloaded them all. Boxes of ammunition sat under the rack bolted to the side wall of the closet. The old clothes within smelled musty. I put the weapons back, giving them one last appreciative look. I would have liked Jenny's dad.

"You haven't cleaned out your parents' stuff."

Jenny hung her head and started to sob. I took her into my arms and gave her as much time as she needed. I pulled a tissue from the box on the dresser and gave it to her.

"I'm sorry…" She started to cry again.

"What are you sorry for? That you care and had no one to share your grief?"

She wiped her nose and looked up at me, eyes red and puffy.

"We're naked," she mumbled.

I had to chuckle. "This is the American dream. I'm naked with a beautiful woman, a cup of coffee, and a bunch of guns. My life is now complete."

She play-slapped me, then chuckled and hugged me intensely, digging her nails into my back. She bit my chest and pushed me against the dresser. I cupped my hands around her butt cheeks and lifted her to carry her the short distance to her parent's bed.

Jenny didn't resist, embroiled in the emotions of leaving a lifetime of history behind. She pulled me so hard against her, I could feel the skin on my back give way. The pain was sharp but distant. The intensity of this moment sealed our bond.

I winced and gasped as she pulled her nails from the wounds. She looked in horror at her hands, covered in blood. She tried to push me off, but I held steady. "I'm not ready to get up yet."

She relaxed. "Are you trying to be tough for me?"

"I will always be tough for you. Don't be ridiculous. I'm perfectly fine. Better than fine. On a completely unrelated topic, do you have Bacitracin and Band-Aids?"

"Unrelated?" Our noses were touching again.

"We better clean up. I want to shoot some big guns. And so do you."

"Of course."

"I want you to carry the little pistol with you this next week, just in case." I finally rolled to the side. My back stuck to the comforter on the bed. I hunched my shoulders to free myself and swung my legs to the floor. Jenny slipped past me and pulled me to my feet.

"Come on. Into the shower with you." She took me by the hand and dragged me to the one bathroom in the house, located off the hall. Old-style, a shower over the tub.

The water felt good. Afterward, Jenny tamped my back dry with a paper towel. I finally got a look at the damage. Four claw marks on each side of my back. Even the most puritan observer would know what they were from.

"Those are some serious badges of honor."

"You shush," Jenny said. The mirror showed her smiling, but she dabbed at my shrapnel scars as well. Love and war in all its glory.

Leaving similar scars. "I prefer the marks you made over mine."

"You were hurt." She ran a warm finger over my ragged flesh.

"It blasted from the side. Got under my flak jacket because I didn't have it fastened all the way. It was hot in the desert. Other guys were hurt worse."

"Is that why it scarred like that? You took care of the others before anyone had a chance to look at you?" She finished covering my new cuts.

"Something like that. Why are we still naked?"

"That's your fault." She slapped my butt hard. I faced her. She threw her shoulders back and lifted her chin. Pride. Confidence.

"I think you're tough enough to enter my world. I expect you're a better shot than you give yourself credit for, too." I kissed her forehead. "I'll get breakfast. Join me when you're ready." I headed into the hallway to find my clothes. I thought I'd left them in the living room.

The range had two sections, an enclosed pistol area and a much longer but covered range for rifles. They had security cameras in key locations, so I kept my ball cap pulled down over my face. Jenny wore a visor that covered some of her face. It would have to be good enough.

We had to sign up for a time slot on the rifle range since most of the lanes were already full. I opted to maximize our time on the pistol range, where we could shoot paper targets that reeled back and forth. We didn't have to wait for the range to clear to put out a target or see where the bullets were striking.

We didn't need to rent weapons and we had our own ammunition, but we needed to get two ports because they only allowed one person per firing port. We sat through a fifteen-minute safety lecture before they handed us targets and eye and ear protection. Once turned loose, we took our assigned lanes.

Miss Jenny knew how to load and unload both pistols. We went through the stance she would use and the grip, keeping the pistol pointed downrange. Couldn't have an accident. "Never point it at something you don't want to shoot."

She took aim and popped off five rounds. I tapped her on the shoulder. She cleared the chamber and put the pistol on the bench in front of her. We reeled the target back to us. She was all over the paper.

"What are you looking at when you aim?"

"Down the barrel, focusing on the target."

"Focus on the front sight post. Let the target be fuzzy. Put that front sight right into the middle of the fuzzball in the center of the target. Breathe out and hold it as you squeeze the trigger. Let the round going off be a surprise. Those are the keys to a good shot."

"Are you a good shot?" Jenny pointed to the .45 on the bench in my lane.

"Throwing the gauntlet down, Miss Jenny? I accept." I picked up the pistol, chambered a round, and assumed my modified Weaver stance, firing across my body as I pulled the pistol into the palms of my hands.

When the round erupted from the barrel, I started to laugh.

"Oh, yeah! Bring it, baby. Rock me!" I focused on the target to see where the round had impacted. Six o'clock low. I raised my aiming point and sent four more rounds into the center of the black. I rolled the target back to me.

"I hit what I aim at." It wasn't bragging. In my world, it was a cold reality.

"I expected." Jenny nodded, tight-lipped and determined. "I need to shoot better."

"This is a nice pistol. Your old man did well with it, and you need to fire both of these, be comfortable with both."

We continued through two boxes of ammunition. Jenny fired the .45 last. She held a tighter group with it than the .25, but it was a big piece of hardware. She shook out her wrists after draining a single magazine. We never fired the long rifle, canceling our lane after the pistol time. We'd taken nearly two hours.

I was satisfied and gratified.

We packed up the pistols and headed out, thanking the kind folks for the use of their range. It had only cost a hundred dollars, but I was far more comfortable. Peace of mind. Jenny would be able to defend herself.

Cancel the contract, I wished. *Cancel it!*

Once we were in the car, I said, "I need to do a little more research. Can we go back home for a bit?"

"Home," she repeated. "Can we go home? Yes. I would love to go home with you."

"I have a little research to do. I thought of a couple things while shooting."

"What are you digging into, if you don't mind my asking?"

I looked at her while she concentrated on driving. "I never realized how important it was for me not to be alone. I'd grown harder than I was comfortable with. I was losing me." I watched the scenery as Jenny drove the speed limit. I approved. "Tricia Tripplethorn. I want to show you a private email she maintains. The cryptic messages within and her answers that she deleted but never removed from the deleted folder."

"People do that?"

"People with something to hide. I don't care about other people's secrets except for how they impact me and this contract."

"Don't I know about getting into other people's secrets," Jenny said, squeezing my hand. "I'm kidding. It's for the best, Ian. All the way around. If you hadn't met me, would you have killed Jimmy Tripplethorn?"

"No. I probably would have offed his wife so there was no one to complain about not fulfilling the hit."

"What if it's not her?"

"That's why I need to keep digging. She's going somewhere on Monday. I want to know where and who she's meeting." I stroked the back of Jenny's hand. "I'm probably going to have to follow her the hard way."

"How good do you think she is?"

"An insightful question, my dear. I think she made me when I was in the hobo outfit."

"Is that what that smell was?"

"I had to pay first to order Chinese. It was a little embarrassing."

"My God. I'm getting a firsthand account of a hitman, and it's not anything like what we see in the movies. Those guys are high-tech, always one step ahead of their marks. James Bond-classy."

"I'm classy."

"You came home smelling of fish."

"Is this our first fight, my love?"

She laughed and shook her head. "Not quite. What you describe makes sense to me—loners who aren't connected and leave no footprints. You can't do that if you are constantly online, connected by radio with a team, always tracking and all-knowing. It is a stretch for believability."

"I have to know just enough to make the hit and leave. No more. I don't need to know every aspect of their lives. The simpler, the better. Nothing about Jimmy's life is simple. Nothing about the Wonderbeast's life is simple. Where is she going on Monday? What does the rest of the week hold? The clock is ticking. To answer your question, never underestimate the enemy. She's the daughter with a billion-dollar inheritance. She's nobody's fool. I will treat her as if she's that good."

CHAPTER TWELVE

"To contemplate is to look at shadows." Victor Hugo

Monday morning came early. Jenny was willing but had a hard time waking up. We didn't have far to go to get back to the hotel, but we'd be in the middle of the rush-hour commute. I wore her father's rain jacket, something she wanted me to have.

Jenny preferred that I drove. I kicked the seat back in her car and connected my music to her radio. It's what I listened to while I drove.

"Rush? I might have to rethink our relationship, Mr. Bragg."

"I have found solace in the words of Neil Peart my entire life. I need Rush more than coffee, I think."

"Damn!" Jenny seemed put out but turned the volume up. "The lead singer's voice gets to me."

"He gets to me, too. Have I told you today how beautiful you are?" Deflecting and distracting.

I could see her out of the corner of my eye, smiling and

staring. "I don't think he gets to us in the same way. I shall concede this one point for the moment, but you can owe me."

"I'll treat you to breakfast."

"Am I that cheap a date?"

"No, but I am." I declared victory. She leaned back and closed her eyes, drifting off in the early morning drive.

We'd stop by the hotel's restaurant, and then I'd work out while Miss Jenny went back home. I wanted to be in place outside the Tripplethorn neighborhood a couple hours early to make sure I caught the Wonderbeast when she left. We had reviewed the emails again and again. I could come to no other conclusion. I doubted anyone would come to their house for a meeting. Too many nosy neighbors.

The neighborhood *watch*.

I carried a bag with my freshly cleaned and folded laundry to my room. Jenny threw her purse inside. I locked the computer and thumb drive in the safe for the time we'd be out of the room.

The nice lady who had hooked me up the first morning was in the restaurant, still setting up even though the restaurant was already open. She smiled at Jenny and me. We were the only ones there.

"No conferences this week. Very few staying at the hotel," she explained.

"We'll do our best to keep anything from going to waste." She had not put out very much, and nothing was under the heat lamp. I stared at the empty space.

"Sausage biscuits coming right up." She wiped her hands on her apron and returned to the kitchen.

"Not eating cereal today?" Jenny wondered as she browsed the sparse cold offerings, settling for a pre-packaged muffin.

I added cream to a coffee for myself, but Jenny only wanted water.

"Not when I can get a sausage muffin fresh out of the microwave." I wiggled my eyebrows at her.

"If you don't mind, I am going to avail myself of your bed for a nap before driving back home."

Her keys were in my pocket. I handed them over before I forgot. She took them with a nod.

"Do I mind if you are in my bed? Let me think about that." I rubbed my chin.

Jenny slowly licked her lips before taking a small bite of her muffin.

The attendant returned. "It's good that your wife is able to join you today. I'm sorry, honey, but you don't look like a morning person, while your man is ridiculously perky."

"*Ridiculously* so." Jenny smiled, and her eyes twinkled with the titles the woman had bestowed on us.

"I'm not sorry, honey," I said, holding Jenny's gaze. The sausage biscuits and hash browns were steaming. I couldn't wait to dig in, but the attendant hovered.

"Ian and Jenny," I told her.

"I'm Rose. Nice to have you in the hotel. Are you here for a while?"

"A little bit. Another week or so, then it's off to the next adventure." I looked at my sausage biscuits. I could smell them, but they had stopped steaming. They were congealing before my eyes. "Thank you for these, they smell great. Righteous, even."

"You enjoy them. Are you newlyweds?"

Jenny smiled. I answered, "Nah. We've been together nearly our whole lives. We just act like newlyweds. Life is too short to give it anything less, don't you think?"

I didn't wait. I slid half the sausage biscuit out of the package and took a big bite.

She gave us the matronly look of approval before heading back to arranging the buffet.

"You still get up too early."

"I know," I mumbled. A few crumbs escaped my mouth. "I also talk with my mouth full."

Jenny shook her head while daintily chewing her muffin. I inhaled my breakfast, eating it while it was at least lukewarm. I stuffed a twenty under my plate, and we left while I was still chewing.

By the time I got my shorts and t-shirt on for the workout room, Jenny's clothes were on the floor, and she was bundled under the covers. I hung the do not disturb sign on the door.

I headed out for a quick hour in the fitness center to tune my body. The hard part of the job was coming. I could feel it.

When I returned, I cleaned up, removed my computer from the safe in the closet, and put it on the desk before folding Jenny's clothes and setting them on the overstuffed chair wedged into the corner next to the window. I peeked behind the curtains. It was overcast. No mountain view. I watched the gray world for a few moments before turning on my computer.

VPN. Browsing. Searching. Tricia Tripplethorn. DN74XTW1. Emails. I pulled up the satellite view of the Tripplethorn neighborhood. There were two exits from the community, but only one led to a main road. From there, she could go anywhere. I'd have to wait for her on that route. What time would she leave for a noon soirée?

It all depended on how far she was going. I had no answers.

Jimmy had scheduled a three-hour meeting in the district campaign office for tonight. I wondered if those were every Monday and every Thursday. It made sense, but I couldn't make assumptions. I needed the next week's schedule.

I accessed the city council's agenda for the next week. Jimmy was scheduled to be at the meetings all week, as usual. On Jimmy's campaign page, he had everything laid bare before the world.

No wonder the schedules had been lying about haphazardly. All one had to do was pull up JimmyTripplethorn4Mayor.com and his complete itinerary was right there. Today and next Monday, meetings in the district campaign office, but on Thursday, the meeting was in the downtown office. Various campaign stops, and then next Tuesday, he was taking a trip to Washington, DC.

That cut my timeline short by two days. I had eight days to make a decision and finalize the contract.

But I'd already made the decision. Jimmy was not going to die by my hand. The jury was out on the Wonderbeast.

More searching. Logged into Facebook with my fake profile and looked for Seattle's future First Lady. Her profile and posts were as fake as mine. They told me nothing, but there was a picture of the backs of the kids looking over the rail toward the grandeur of Seattle as seen from the mouth of Puget Sound.

Nothing to show *Euripedes' Ion*. No picture of Clive Barrows or her stepmother. I ran a quick search to find Clive's second wife. Trinity Johnson was the same age as his daughter. Her father was Senator Abel Johnson.

Who said the practice of kings bartering their daughters to expand influence was dead?

Political royalty. Clive's money, Trinity's influence, and Jimmy's up-and-coming career. The Barrows family was positioned for a major power move.

It left the question of who wanted Jimmy dead? The

Wonderbeast still had the best motive, but she would benefit from her husband's aspirations and her father's influence. A political rival? A slighted former contender?

The aggrieved party had to have money. Big money.

Tricia Tripplethorn, who are you going to meet?

I watched more videos of campaign rallies, looking for the Wonderbeast and anyone who seemed friendly. Her position had always been perfectly choreographed. Never anything out of place.

Well-timed laughs and smiles. Appropriately supportive.

Before I closed my laptop, I set up my two GPS transmitters. I used a fake address for registration. It would be the only time I used the New York City address or the one-time email address. I created a password consisting of the New York address, linking the two to keep them straight in my mind.

I closed my laptop and put it back in the safe and hid the thumb drive behind the light switch. I opted for another business casual look, with Mr. Lawless' old rain jacket topping me off. Jenny had been happy to give it to me.

She was sound asleep. I didn't want to wake her. I leaned against the wall and watched her sleep. I finally gave in and kissed her goodbye, softly so as not to wake her.

Rose let me back in for a second round in the restaurant since I only wanted coffee. I was her best customer. The competition was not fierce. I think Jenny and I were the only ones she had seen that morning.

In my car, I set up my music player and brought up *Power Windows*, yet another exceptional album. *Grand Designs* seemed appropriate for the day's events.

I drove straight to the neighborhood and parked out of

the way, but where I could see. I turned off the engine. Half a tank of gas. I couldn't refill anywhere near here. It would have to do until I was done following the Wonderbeast.

I enjoyed my coffee to go, sipping slowly. It was nine-thirty. Two and a half hours before the meeting. There was a slim chance she was already gone, but the meeting could be less than five minutes away, and she might not leave for a while. I settled in and relaxed. I didn't bother with my phone. I watched the cars drive by. The late commuter rush.

People wearing stoic expressions, driving as a burden. Few looked like they enjoyed being behind the wheel.

Traffic thinned as I entered my second hour of waiting. I selected *Permanent Waves* and turned the volume up. The last song on the album, *Natural Science,* started playing when Barchetta appeared. The Wonderbeast looking angry as she raced down the road in her Porsche Panamera.

I pulled out and followed, leaving one car between us. She took a hard right and headed down the main drag, a four-lane road. I followed from the right lane as well as I could, but she wasn't bothered by speed limits. I couldn't lose her.

A stoplight saved me. I maneuvered into the fast lane, taking a position behind an impatient man in a Ram HD with oversized tires. The Porsche bolted at the green light, slipping past a car turning in front of her on the red. I could hear the engine rev as she launched the land rocket in front of the truck before me.

He took it as a personal challenge. The big beast growled and lunged forward. Once past the slow-lane traffic, I moved back to the right so I could see. She darted between two cars to her side and jammed on the brakes in an erratic move to get into a gas station.

I tapped my brakes, signaled, and took the second

entrance into the station. I parked and put my phone to my head, being responsible by not talking and driving.

The Wonderbeast finished filling her tank and strutted toward the convenience store.

I hopped out and walked behind my car. "But honey, I love your chili!"

Tricia Tripplethorn hesitated and looked at me. I had my head down and my hand and phone over my face to avoid the cameras.

"Let me get some privacy!" I said into the phone and stormed away from the Wonderbeast. She harrumphed and headed inside. I continued talking and walked straight to her car. Once beyond it, I walked back and forth while carrying on a robust conversation with myself. I stumbled and ducked. I tucked the GPS tracker inside the front wheel well and stood back up, brushing myself off. I continued talking while strolling casually to the side.

Wonderbeast ignored me on her way back to Barchetta. "I love you too, honey," I finished when she was within earshot. I hurried back to my car. Once inside, I accessed the app and brought up the device.

Barchetta bolted into traffic. Half a block up, she accelerated like a gunshot onto the on-ramp.

I set my phone where I could see it and followed at a more leisurely pace. Took the access and merged easily into traffic. It was lighter than at rush hour but still moved briskly. I had to concentrate on the Indy 500 maneuvers too many Seattle drivers felt they needed to implement on their daily drive.

A glance at the tracker showed Barchetta hitting ninety miles per hour as she increased the distance between us. I moved into the middle lane and sped up with the flow.

After five minutes, Barchetta was no longer moving. The dot blinked on the highway. I continued and looked for it as I approached, thinking she had gotten into an accident. Flashing lights up ahead did not allay my fears, until the truth was revealed.

The highway patrol had bagged themselves a red Porsche. I drove past, moved into the right lane, and slowed down. I pulled to the side a mile down the road and put on my blinkers. I counted on only one police vehicle patrolling this stretch of road. Once Barchetta started moving again, so would I.

And maybe she'd learn her lesson and take it easy on me. She needed to have more consideration for the one who was contemplating killing her. I chuckled at my morbid humor.

Eight minutes later, Barchetta dodged into traffic. I saw a gap and jumped off the shoulder and back onto the highway. I watched Barchetta take the off-ramp behind me.

"Crap." I hit the next off-ramp a mile away and doubled back. Ten minutes later, I was looking through the area from where the tracker had last broadcast.

No signal.

The app had a feature of last broadcast location, but it only sent a signal every thirty seconds. At the Wonderbeast's pace, that drew a circle a quarter to a half-mile wide. I drove around the streets, using an expanding square pattern to look for where the car might have gone.

We were in an upscale suburban city with mid-rise corporate buildings, high-end shopping, and immaculately maintained greenery and flowers on the island between the separated road lanes. I parked where I could see the road Barchetta would have to take to leave the area if the Wonderbeast was going back to the highway.

More waiting. I turned off the car. I was fine on gas. We

had not gone that far. Noon was ten minutes away. Even getting stopped by the police, she was early.

Who or what commanded her attention like that?

Had the tracker slipped off the car?

I had no other course of action.

So I waited. One in the afternoon. Then two. The clock was crawling toward three when a blip appeared on the screen. "Thank you," I told my phone.

She was headed this way. Her reappearance was not far from where she'd disappeared, but I waited for Barchetta to pass before driving back to the area. A parking garage between three corporate buildings. Each of the big buildings had their own garages, too. Which one had she gone into? I took pictures of the four buildings before accessing my tracker app.

Ninety miles per hour. The Wonderbeast didn't care. I expected that she had not gotten a ticket earlier, waving the Jimmy Tripplethorn get out of jail free card in the officer's face.

I considered her a menace when it came to road etiquette. I thought I'd be comfortable ending her for that alone. Maybe not.

She was stretching my boundaries, though. How could someone be so eminently unlikeable?

But was she bad?

I killed bad people for money. I had to remind myself. She had two children. A husband who liked her in some odd way.

A father who doted on his grandchildren, his daughter's progeny.

I checked the app. Wonderbeast was headed home. She'd get there before the kids returned from school.

"What did you do for three hours?" I asked no one. I wondered about a follow-up email to finalize any details of what that secret meeting was all about. I looked at the map on my phone, deciding to take back roads to get to the campaign's district headquarters. I could get gas and something to eat on the way.

And call Jenny to check in.

She had an in-service day, but she'd have to go back to work tomorrow.

I didn't know what tomorrow would bring for me, but I knew what I had to do that night.

CHAPTER THIRTEEN

"At the moment of truth, there are either reasons or results."
Chuck Yeager

Lunch consisted of a power bar and a cup of coffee from the gas station where I filled up my car. I drove to the campaign headquarters, parking two blocks away.

I forced myself to stroll, not looking obvious. Just another guy going from one place to another. In the strip mall with the campaign headquarters, the businesses were open with their usual customers keeping them engaged. A small group of volunteers and staff busied themselves with setting up for the meeting.

Chairs in place, tables cleared for the inevitable pizza delivery.

Jimmy. Taking care of his people.

I waited at a café table at the end of the strip, where I bought a better meal—a chicken Caesar wrap. I kept my phone on the table and glanced at it while eating. I brought up the app to confirm Barchetta remained at home.

I kept my eyes peeled for Antoinette Bickness' car. It was how Jimmy had arrived last time. Anything could go. It would be best if I intercepted him before he entered the offices. I finished my wrap, cleaned up my trash, including wiping the table to remove any fingerprints, and walked toward the campaign office, stopping near the dry cleaners to lean against the wall and play with my phone.

I glanced up each time a car pulled in. It was taking too long. All the volunteers and staff were in place, but still no Jimmy Tripplethorn.

At a quarter past six, the campaign managers arrived. I put my phone away. Antoinette dropped off Jimmy and Ken, just like last time. I intercepted them.

"Jimmy, I know you're late, but you need to hear the information I have." It was the best I could do without sounding like a nut or conspiracy theorist.

"Mr. Tripplethorn has a campaign meeting. Please contact the campaign office to schedule an appointment."

"This can't wait, Ken," I replied, using his name to show I wasn't a casual interloper.

Jimmy, always accommodating, waved to the staff inside the campaign office. "Randy, right?" he said, demonstrating a politician's mind for remembering names, making each person feel special. "Randy Bagger."

"Yes, Mr. Tripplethorn. A few moments of your time, please."

He put his hand on his campaign manager's arm and nodded. "I'll be right in, Ken. Start the meeting with what we already discussed."

Jimmy looked at me, leaning slightly forward with his hands in his pockets, the body language of someone willing to listen.

"I work for an organization that removes problems from society. For some reason, they have designated you as one of them. I was hired to kill Jimmy Tripplethorn, candidate for mayor."

Jimmy took a long breath, his face contorted with a variety of emotions.

"Who would do such a thing?"

"Once I realized the contract was an abomination, I started looking. Can you tell me where your wife was from noon to three today?"

"At home," he said slowly, making it sound more like a question than an answer. He winced with the realization that he didn't know. I shook my head. Jimmy changed his position. "Not at home, but I don't know where. She's a professional in her own right."

"She is, sitting on a couple different boards of directors as well as her ancillary engagement with Barrows Holdings. Today, she went to Kirkland and disappeared into a parking garage for three hours. I lost her, but the car was there. I have no idea what she did.

"I am not going to kill you, Jimmy, but if I walk away from this job, leaving it unresolved, they *will* send someone else. I'm trying to get the contract canceled, but that means I need to know who hired me. Has your wife transferred a large sum of money recently?"

Jimmy shrugged and made a face. He gestured for Antoinette to go inside instead of joining him on the sidewalk. The staff and volunteers cast furtive glances our way. I put my back to them.

"How large?"

"At least a million dollars."

"She has that kind of money squirreled away, but we don't need it. We have everything we want." Jimmy looked down, momentarily lost in his thoughts. I waited for him to internalize the curveball I'd thrown into his life.

"Do you know anyone else who has that kind of money to spend who wants you out of the way?"

Jimmy shrugged anew. "I'm a politician. I can't please everyone, but don't think I've angered anyone that badly. The current mayor doesn't even want the job. He's going through the motions. There are no other challengers. There is no value in killing me."

"Money is not the problem. There is something else driving this. I don't know what because I'm not on the inside. I don't need to know how the clock works, only how to tell the time."

Jimmy shuffled his feet and remained quiet. He made no move to go inside.

"The challenge is that you can't tell anyone about me. That won't help you. The only thing that will is to find who paid for the contract. After that, I'll take care of it."

"What will you do?"

"Leverage them to pull the contract. I can't just kill them because I doubt the organization I work for will care if they're dead. The organization has already been paid, and they have a one hundred percent success rate, as far as I know. Getting me killed or thrown in jail won't protect you."

Jimmy straightened his back and held his head high. "You're telling me the only person who can help me is the one hired to kill me?" He jammed his fists on his hips in defiance.

"Sounds hokey, but yes. And no, this isn't extortion. I don't need money or any favors. I only want to get myself out of this, and doing that means I need your help. Does the name DN74XTW1 mean anything to you? Does your wife have a piece of paper or a book she won't let you look at? It would contain a list of words with a second list of other words. It's a codebook. She's communicating with someone in code."

"This is the twenty-first century. I can't believe we have codebooks and hitmen. I'm sorry, but this sounds like something out of a movie. There are cameras watching us. You can't go anywhere that someone doesn't know it, let alone kill people."

"And law enforcement using facial recognition software has been made illegal. No one is watching anything because the video surveillance archives are vast. There isn't enough time for humanity to watch it all. I'm not the one with a codebook. That would be your wife."

"Carrying a weapon is illegal, too," Jimmy countered weakly.

I held my jacket open. "No weapon."

"Then how were you going to kill me?"

"What do you say we don't talk about that? Your understanding of how I do my job will make you want to hide in your basement for the rest of your life. Jimmy, help me find the person who paid to have you killed. We need to fix this so both of us can get our lives back."

"I don't know where to start."

"Go to your meeting. Think about it. Give me your personal number, and I'll call you in two days' time."

Jimmy uttered a series of numbers. I typed them into my phone and pressed send. Jimmy's pocket started to vibrate. I tapped end.

"I'll be in touch. I believe you might be the last honest politician, and that gives me hope."

I spun on my heel and headed in the opposite direction from where I parked. I had started our chess match by moving my knight into the center of the board, hoping that Jimmy took it seriously without melting down. If anyone could handle this without showing their next move, it would be a professional politician.

I didn't call Jenny on the way back to the hotel, and I didn't pick up dinner, either. I replayed my conversation with Jimmy over and over. He had listened, which was all I could ask. He gave me the time I needed.

Had I convinced him?

I opened my door and walked in to find the TV on and Jenny propped up on pillows. The menu was gone off the top of the screen and sitting on the low dresser. I picked it up and put it back over the camera.

"That blocks the view," Jenny said.

"It also blocks the camera," I replied. "I'm sorry, I didn't get any dinner. I didn't realize you'd be here waiting. I didn't call."

"You seem put out. I can go." Jenny got off the bed. I took her into my arms and held her close.

"I need to talk, but not here. We'll go for a short drive."

"Whatever you need, Ian." Jenny took my face in her hands while leaning her forehead against mine. "Anything you want."

It was hard not to smile. I pulled her against me. "I have everything I could ever want right now, in this brief moment of time. I want more because I want it to last. But I need to count on others for this one. *They* need to come through for *us* to win."

"I look forward to learning what that means." I let go of her hips. She dropped her hands from my face, yet we stayed nose to nose. Neither wanted to be the first to move.

"Maybe we can just go to your place? I'm going to avoid all things work tomorrow."

"Let the honeymoon continue," she whispered before kissing me and grabbing her purse. I had to get the computer and thumb drive.

Jenny watched me remove the switch plate in the bathroom. I held my finger to my lips and showed her the thumb drive before carefully putting the plate back on.

She raised an eyebrow at me with the revelation.

Naïve.

As everyone should be who's not in the game. But now, she was a player. She needed to learn the rules and get up to speed. Her life depended on it.

I packed my stuff into a bag and motioned for Jenny to lead the way. She headed for the elevator. I paused.

She stopped when she realized I wasn't following. I pointed at the stairs. Jenny turned around without hesitation. I held the door for her. She kissed me before heading down. "I could get used to a gentleman holding the door for me."

We continued to the parking lot, opting for her car over mine. She jumped into the driver's seat. I threw my stuff in the back before climbing into the passenger seat.

"Bad day?" she asked while starting the engine.

"I don't think so, but it was hard." I recounted trailing the Wonderbeast and ended with my conversation with Jimmy.

She listened quietly. "That's a lot to process."

"If I were you, I wouldn't believe me. *True Lies* and Bill Paxton ruined it for us honest guys."

"I love that movie." The corners of Jenny's mouth twitched upward. "You have nothing to gain by playing me. You had already closed the deal and then some."

"I like your logic." Darkness settled over the area with

the coming night. "The last thing I told Jimmy was I wanted both of us to get our lives back. Ten minutes prior, he hadn't known his life was in jeopardy. He took it surprisingly well."

"What do you think he's going to do?"

"I think he's going to ask his wife where she was today. That will be followed by a massive throwdown. Then Jimmy will call me back, angry that I put such an idea in his head. After that, I'll have to confront the Wonderbeast myself."

"Let's hope it doesn't come to that."

"She is a royal bitch." I wanted to think in other terms but couldn't. "Tricia Tripplethorn has a knack for bringing out the worst in people. The worst in everyone except Jimmy, and he thrives in spite of her."

"Why do you think that is?"

"From a woman's perspective, why do *you* think that is?"

"Nice turnabout. I could see him as a possible narcissist, tormenting her every minute they're alone. He turns it off when he leaves the house. She can't and takes out her pain on everyone else."

"I saw him at home with his wife. She was the one shaking her finger and yelling. He looked like a whipped puppy." I looked at the radio. "Mind if I put on some music?"

"Driver's choice. I'll take the classical station." She punched a number on the panel, and the sound of a string quartet materialized. "Maybe she's the narcissist, and he is free when he's outside the house."

"Which leads us back to the Wonderbeast. None of this is Jimmy Tripplethorn's fault."

"I agree. What are you going to do, Ian?" We held hands. I stroked her fingers while I tried to think.

"Talking to you was at the top of my list, so my number one priority is checked off. Next is wait two days before giving Jimmy a call. In between, I'll watch the Wonderbeast's emails. I think she'll head out for another illicit meeting, but since I told Jimmy where she'd gone, she won't go there again. I'll have to play the Race after Red Barchetta game."

"You and your Rush."

"I promise it won't turn me into a devil worshipper."

"That would put a damper on things. Are you hungry?"

"Getting there. What did you have in mind?" I was close to the point of eating anything put in front of me, even shoe leather. I had only managed half of my chicken Caesar wrap before tossing it.

"Grocery store. I want to see how you shop for groceries."

"This is your devil worshipper test? I always put the cart back in the rack. Always. And I take grocery shopping seriously because I love to eat, but I usually don't have a kitchen."

"Now you do. And you've been through my cupboards. You know what's in the house, or more importantly, what's not there."

I took a deep breath. Reflection. I'd been chasing that question the entire time on this operation. Everything that made for a good hit was missing.

Jenny pulled into her local supermarket, a chain store. "Do you mind if I drive?" I asked after selecting an upright cart. I didn't see buying a whole lot. "Steaks, sweet potatoes, steamable green beans, rock salt, and Italian dressing. A leafy salad mix. Muffins and sausage patties and eggs. A little lunch meat or sausage. How about tater tots? Then we could get a fresh pie from the bakery. And ice cream."

"You had eight seconds to think about this, and you already have a full list? I'll drive. You pick and load."

Staying true to my proffered menu, we quickly filled our cart. Jenny glanced at the freezers as we walked by without taking any ice cream. Her face dropped, and she frowned.

I pointed at the cart. "That's a big pie, and there are only two of us."

"We don't have to eat it all, but we are obligated to eat it right." I swallowed hard before turning around and heading back to do battle with the brands. We selected a pint of Tillamook, made nearby in Oregon. "A girl's gotta have her ice cream."

I knew it would be nearby. I'd spotted it at the end of the aisle. I left the cart to grab it: a can of whipped cream.

"What's that for?"

"The good dessert that comes after dessert," I replied casually. It was impossible to miss the sparkle in her eyes. "I'll start the two steaks marinating, and we'll grill them tomorrow. For tonight, salads, eggs, and sausage. We better get cheese, too."

Jenny wasn't sure. She didn't move the cart. "You want to wait for steaks?"

"Not wait, prepare for optimal flavor and enjoyment. Open your eyes and behold your new world."

"I like the way you wait."

"Waiting doesn't mean we have to do nothing."

CHAPTER FOURTEEN

"We can easily forgive a child who is afraid of the dark; the real tragedy of life is when men are afraid of the light." Plato

I sat at the dining room table, reading the Wonderbeast's emails. I'd already looked at her secret account. She had not sent a message. I wondered if Jimmy had broached her absence from the family home. Maybe she didn't need to flail and send a message. As a narcissist, she would make it her sole mission to get Jimmy back under her control, not questioning anything she did.

I wanted to think Jimmy would stand up for himself better than that.

We had not yet cleaned the pistols. The gun oil and cleaning kit were stored with the ammunition at the bottom of the closet. Even the rag to use on the weapons was clean and neatly folded. I brought it all to the living room to set on a magazine on the table.

I could take the M1911A1 apart with my eyes closed, but I had never seen a weapon like the HP25A. A quick search on YouTube showed me what I needed to know. I had to leave the magazine in and hammer back to break the weapon down, not anything I would have considered intuitive. I verified they were both unloaded before taking them apart, wiping them down, and scrubbing the carbon out of the recesses and off the movable parts. After they were clean, I applied a thin layer of oil to each, dry-fired them, and put them back on the table.

The ammunition was limited, but I didn't expect to get into a protracted firefight. In a home defense firefight, the most ammunition people use is a single magazine. It's not like the movies.

I loaded two magazines for the .25 and two for the .45. I liked the feel of the M1911A1. It was a weapon made for war, and it delivered like no other.

Jenny walked up behind me.

"What are you doing?"

"Cleaning the pistols. Drinking some coffee."

"It looked like you were lost in a dream. What were you thinking, Ian?"

I put the pistol down and pulled Jenny onto my lap. "I was thinking about war and the power of this pistol. I never carried a pistol back when I was in the Corps. My weapon was an M4, but when they put me on sniper duty, I got to carry an M14. One is good for clearing buildings. The other is good for reaching out and touching someone."

"How much of your life does war consume?"

I ran a hand through my hair and blew out a breath. "That is a tough question. I guess my answer is more than it should, but it's kept me alive. And then it made me a rich man, only until it tore me down again when I rejected it. I respect the weapon and the peace it can bring when used as intended."

Jenny laughed. "You're starting to sound like a politician."

Her smile and the music of her voice made for the start of a good day, no matter what else happened.

Breakfast was followed by intimate time, but then Jenny had to go. She needed to wrap things up at the school since it was the end of the semester. She had reconciled herself to her last few days of working in the district.

She struggled to pull herself from my arms as the clock raced onward. Our foreheads and noses touched.

"I don't know what to tell you," I said, "besides take care of today's business today. We'll handle tomorrow when it comes. In between, we'll live life to the fullest."

Jenny closed her eyes and nodded slightly before kissing me one last time, desperately and passionately. She was acting like she understood the game. Every moment could be her last.

"Wait," I said when she reached the door. I retrieved the cleaned .25 from the table, chambered a round, and held it in front of her.

"Those aren't allowed in the school. And if the police came for me, I wouldn't shoot them."

I had to agree. "You're right, but it wouldn't be the police. Be at peace and come home to me when you can."

I held the small pistol in my hand. It was little more than a deadly toy, but it would kill at close range, fired at the most vulnerable areas. I watched Jenny get into her car and go. She glanced at me in the doorway. I waved like a dutiful house-husband. She laughed and mouthed the words, "I love you," before backing into the road and driving off.

I returned to my computer. *Better together,* I thought. It applied to how I felt about Jenny and me. More fulfilled.

But it didn't make me better at my job. Being a loner was best, except when the plans and ideas weren't gelling. Like The Peace Archive being a government organization.

Was I a government killer? When I cut ties with that same government, would it be problematic as long as I remained in the United States? As long as *we* remained.

Better together.

I had too many questions about my target. Jimmy seemed like a good man. What was he doing with the Wonderbeast? Even her old man had someone to complement him. The more I thought about it, the more I felt there was a boyfriend. The Wonderbeast had to be involved.

The political rival angle made little sense unless a major player, like a corporation, had tried to buy him, and he wouldn't have it. That had happened often enough throughout American history that candidates were leveraged in a different way. Most corporations expected political leaders to wax and wane, fall in and out of favor, but business rolled on.

Most had limited exposure to the fallacies of political expediency.

A rival with lots of money? People didn't get into politics if they didn't already have a lot of money. Even Jimmy. It wasn't his, but it was there. But there were no rivals.

I stared at my computer, but nothing jumped out at me.

Keep my eyes on the prize.

I had a goal, a much different goal than I had last week.

A world cruise.

I checked the sites and found one leaving out of Italy at the end of the month. Tickets for a luxury suite were fifty grand each. A hundred grand for six months of seeing the world? Hell, yeah.

I closed the site and dug back into the Wonderbeast's emails. On Google, I could access her personal calendar and drive, but she didn't keep anything there. Wherever she managed her schedule, it wasn't in the usual places. I headed back to the dark web to search for everything that hinted at Tricia Tripplethorn.

Two hours later, I felt like I had wasted my time, but I had learned a great deal about where she was *not* active. I was confident that I had done my best. I'd sleep on it, and maybe a new way to approach it would come to me.

I headed outside to get some fresh air. I had not been around the yard to see what the Lawless family had done with their landscaping. The grass needed to be cut. Weeds needed to be pulled. Bushes to be trimmed.

I found a lock on the shed, but the keys hung on a hook by the back door. I opened it to find moss and mold, and a rusty lawnmower. Aged lawn implements. Sandpaper and oil had been Mr. Lawless' friend. I would put his supply to good use.

The mower came to life quickly once the oil and gas were topped off. I made quick work of the lawn, cleaned the rust off the pruning shears, and attacked the hedge between the yard and road. A small bowsaw needed oil and a gentle sanding to make sure the blade wasn't pocked and weakened. I removed some lower limbs that looked out of place and dragged them behind the house, cutting them up into smaller sections before dumping them on an ancient brush pile, a remnant from a time long past.

An afternoon snack and plenty of water before I turned back to the yard. A manual edger helped me clean up the sidewalk and the driveway. Then the hard work of pulling the weeds from the expansion joints of the concrete. I used a life vest from the shed to kneel on.

There was no boat. The vest was another relic from the

time before. The material within crumbled under my knees, but it kept my body from abuse. Helping me with the weeds would be the final act of its long and storied existence.

I finished late in the afternoon. It had been a good day, time away from the war to contemplate what needed to be contemplated. Despite the manual labor, I felt refreshed. I removed the steaks from the refrigerator and put them on the counter.

The charcoal grill was long dead. I would have to cook them on the stove, but Jenny's mom had a well-aged cast iron skillet. As an alternative, it would suffice. I checked my phone but hadn't missed any calls.

As I looked it, it rang, but it wasn't Jenny's number.

Jimmy Tripplethorn.

"Jimmy," I answered.

"I need to see you at a place outside of prying eyes. There's a private meeting area in an equestrian center next to the Redmond Watershed. Tomorrow, lunchtime. I'll text the address."

"This sounds like something your father-in-law would set up. Have you involved him?" The words came out of my mouth, but I didn't want to be that contentious. I was forcing myself into a corner. I tried to relax.

A car pulled into the driveway. Jenny.

"This is something beyond my ability to handle. I needed a person I could trust."

"I hope you're right. If this is a setup, you're going to lose. Come alone. Just the two of you, I guess. I'm already not liking the setup, but I'll make do. I hope you can live with the outcome."

I ended the call as Jenny walked through the door.

"The yard looks..." The smile froze on her face when she saw me. "What's wrong?"

"Jimmy. I have to meet him tomorrow, some horse ranch beside the Watershed. He's bringing Old Man Barrows."

"He's bringing his father-in-law to discuss the wife, his daughter?" She shook her head. "Don't go, Ian. I'm afraid."

"Would you be less afraid if you came with me?"

"Well, I-I don't know."

I waited.

"I guess seeing it in person would convince me you're not Bill Paxton."

I laughed. Then I let go of her and laughed harder. "Here I was thinking you were worried about me getting killed, when it was really that you don't want me to be a liar." I chuckled some more.

She slapped my arm. "You stop."

"It's dangerous because Barrows has the kind of money where he could make people disappear in a way that no one would ever know they existed. But Jimmy will be there. The squeaky-clean politician. Will Jimmy get his hands dirty? I can't believe that. I have to go. You do not."

"I think I need to go, too. I don't want to be without you. If that means we both die tomorrow, so be it. At least we'll be together."

"Putting it that way makes it sound dramatic. I was thinking that if it was a hit, they wouldn't pull the trigger with an unknown third party there."

Her mouth dropped open. "You want to use me as a human shield?"

"I'm pretty sure that's not what I said. How do you like your ribeye, medium rare?"

"You are not going to change the subject as if life and death are an oh-by-the-way." She put her hands on her hips, her purse and strap tangled on her arm. She yanked it off her shoulder and slammed it on the table.

I didn't say anything. I wasn't sure where I had gone astray.

"We need to talk about whether we are going to survive tomorrow or if Wednesday is our last day on this planet."

"I told you everything there is to know. I don't have anything else. Anxiety or worry is a construct within our minds. In the Marines, I learned not to worry about tomorrow. Sure, plan for it. Be ready for it. Stay fit to help get through it, but worrying ruins today *and* hurts your chances at having a good day tomorrow. Please, Miss Jenny, there is nothing we can do about tomorrow right now. Tomorrow, we will go early and scout the area, then we'll get into position to watch. If they set up an ambush, we'll see it, and then I'll simply execute the original contract. If this is a setup, all bets are off, and Jimmy can kiss my ass."

Jenny started to sway, grabbed the table, and dropped into a chair to keep from falling.

The game's embrace was dark and too often cold. There would be more shocks before Jenny was on the inside.

No one wanted to see anyone else's dark side, but I had opened the doors and shined the light into humanity's worst recesses in only a few sentences. I kneeled beside her, then took her hand and kissed it. Her arm hung limp.

"Come back to me, Miss Jenny. We'll know where we are tomorrow. I err on the side of caution, but I sincerely believe Jimmy isn't the double-crossing type. Clive Barrows? You don't get to be a billionaire without making enemies you have to deal with."

"This is a lot to take in. I don't doubt what you're saying, Ian, but I'm a schoolteacher. I live in a quiet community and have a boring life. I'm new to the international-man-of-mystery stuff."

"When I followed you into your room on the first night of the rest of my life, I thought you were in my room. Shows you how sharp I am. When you untied your robe, that was it. I was yours from that moment on. And you have very much done the international man of mystery. My back still hurts, by the way."

"You are so bad." She pushed me away, but a smile touched her lips. "You don't worry about tomorrow?"

"Worry is a waste of time. I give things the appropriate amount of attention and then I move on. We'll go early tomorrow to scout the approaches to the meeting site. We'll find the bottleneck, and that is where we will see anyone who enters or leaves. We'll scout an egress in case of an ambush, and we'll go armed. If anyone comes after us, I'll take them down."

"I think you're trying to put my mind at ease. I'm not sure it's working."

"I got this. It sounds worse than it needs to be. Which reminds me, we need to buy a remote camera that we can hook through a Wi-Fi. I saw an electronics shop in the strip mall with the grocery store. They'll have something. But first, let's take a stroll through the yard. I love the smell of fresh-cut grass."

Jenny studied me. I stood back and relaxed as her eyes ranged across my body. "I expect you'll help me navigate the shark-infested waters of your world, Mister Bragg."

"As much as I can. I've grown fond of having you around."

"And you want to show me your freshly mowed yard?" A question.

"Of course, so you can appreciate my contribution to our partnership as I appreciate yours."

She leaned back, and a quizzical expression flashed across her face. She settled into blinking slowly and shot me a warm smile. "I never thought about it that way. I saw it as more defensive. Kind of like, 'Look at me. I cut the grass. I cooked. I did the dishes.' But it's not that at all, is it?"

"We'll figure that out together." I pointed at the front door and motioned with my head. "Come on now. Freshly mowed yard. Then steaks."

"You got the grill going?"

"The grill has seen its last steak. Your mom's cast iron will do them up nicely."

"That's Grandma's," Jenny corrected. She stood and held out her hand. I took it, and we headed outside. A quick tour of the yard, then a trip to the store to pick up a four-pack of wireless security cameras.

After that, we made sure the rest of the evening was about only today. We would take care of tomorrow when it came.

CHAPTER FIFTEEN

"But he did not grow too proud, and he kept that garden as a mongoose should keep it, with tooth and jump and spring and bite, till never a cobra dared show its head inside the walls."
Rudyard Kipling

I tested the cameras and made sure I could see them through Jenny's phone. I would have to leave my phone near the cameras to act as the Wi-Fi for them. I had a double ziplock to protect it from the rain.

I used Google Maps to do an in-depth study of the area, map mode, satellite view, and the best granularity through the street view. Multiple paths through nearby neighborhoods offered a wide variety of escape routes, but the least likely would be going through the watershed. We'd arrive on foot from the neighboring wilderness.

I had to get my cameras in place before the advance teams arrived, if there were going to be any. That meant an early morning.

I think Jenny was getting used to my embrace of the

best part of the day. As long as I had the coffee ready, she was willing to give morning a chance. She also walked around naked at that time of day. I had not gotten used to that yet and didn't know if I ever would, but I liked it a lot.

We headed out early to beat most of the traffic. I had to play Rush. Jenny tolerated it. I jammed *Signals* for the trip to the hotel.

Our first stop was the hotel to pick up my car. I didn't want Jenny's associated with this meeting, even if we were going to hide the vehicle.

We stopped in to take advantage of the breakfast. Rose was there, along with a handful of guests. "I missed you yesterday."

"We got trapped away from the hotel, so we honeymooned over there for a while. We just made it back but need to head out again. No rest for the weary."

The heat lamps were cranking and trays loaded.

"A conference?"

"They arrived last night." Rose waved me away from the heat lamp meals. "Get your coffee and find a seat."

I wiggled my eyebrows at Jenny. She smiled back. The conspiracy to one-up the other guests was well underway. We did as advised, taking a table closest to the swinging door leading to the kitchen. I kept my rain jacket on since I had the M1911A1 tucked into the back of my waistband. Jenny kept her purse on her shoulder because the .25 was inside, despite her protests. Rose reappeared and dropped off two plates with a breakfast that did not look microwaved.

"A little something special for our special couple."

"So much better than we deserve!" I jumped to my feet and gave the older woman a one-armed hug. "I am already enjoying them way too much."

"Go on, you two. Eat and keep up your strength. I remember what it's like to be a newlywed."

"We just act like newlyweds," I corrected. Jenny giggled, but she was already eating. I joined her, trying to eat slowly to enjoy the fresh sausage and crumbly biscuits. A minute later, they were gone.

I sipped my coffee and waited for Jenny to finish.

Rose stopped by to take our plates. "Magnificent, Rose. I can't thank you enough. We hate to eat and run, but we have to go do great things. Maybe they are small things, but we'll do them in a great way."

"Keep that attitude." Rose turned to go back to her duties. I tucked a twenty into her apron before she could object.

Jenny and I strolled out. "That was an unexpected pleasure."

"Everybody loves some Ian Bragg." Likeable. Loyal.

"What's not to love?" She wrapped her arm around my waist, and I wrapped mine around hers. We walked out of the hotel, hip to hip.

In my car, my hobo clothes in the trunk did not do the interior any favors. I opened the door for Jenny, and she started gagging when she was only halfway in. I hurried around to the driver's side to get in and start it, open the windows, and turn on the fan.

"That is the worst man-smell that has ever polluted my body." She held her hand over her mouth while pinching her nostrils closed.

"I don't think I'll need them again. They might have a date with a dumpster."

"And make the dumpster smell bad."

I put Rush on and dialed up *Roll the Bones. Dreamline* started jamming. "This could be our song. Listen to the words, Miss Jenny."

After it finished, she tapped the screen to replay it. After the second pass, she turned down the volume. "The resolution for *our* song has been forwarded for consideration. I second the motion. All in favor, say aye."

"Aye," we agreed.

"What a strange way to pick a couple's song," Jenny started. "But my life stopped being normal the second you walked into it. I don't get picked up in bars."

"Good, because I don't pick up women in bars."

"Yet you did."

"Guilty as charged, and I throw myself on the mercy of the court. Today we focus on today. Let me talk through what we're going to do..."

When we reached the entry to the equestrian center, Jenny hopped out while I turned around. She positioned one camera in a tree that faced down the entry road. She put a second looking toward the equestrian center and hid the phone behind it. Jenny's total time outside the vehicle— fifteen seconds.

We drove away from the entrance, stopping a second time to tuck another camera in a second tree. We continued three blocks farther before turning into a powerline trail access. We parked where people parked before they hiked into the watershed.

Jenny pulled out her phone and brought up the cameras. Three screens showed a full-color view of the road leading to the center. The smart camera recorded a frame a second unless the motion detector activated, then it recorded at full speed. It maintained a record of each activation, and we could browse those separately.

We left our parking spot and cruised three different

egress routes out of the area. Once past the entrance, a car could easily disappear in the neighborhoods with their various winding streets, most of which were secondary routes into adjacent neighborhoods. A veritable spiderweb of roads. We picked the route closest to the powerline trail, winding along a road that was little more than an alley.

After making sure we had it down, we returned to the parking area and got out. Time to hike our route to the center.

Jenny wore a big black overcoat, nicer than a usual hiking jacket. It was cold, and she needed a jacket. Everything else in the closet consisted of bright colors. I wanted something that stood out a little less, especially if we were running for our lives through the woods and brush.

My overcoat was dark gray, still muddy from my foray to the campaign office.

We strolled away from the car, holding hands and walking without urgency. A casual hike for a nice couple.

Who happened to be heavily armed and ready to do battle. At least I was ready. I doubted Jenny could pull the trigger unless she saw her death as imminent, or she thought she needed to protect me. I kept my concerns to myself. It was nothing to worry about. One never knew until the fight started. At that point, all souls were bared before the world.

"You're a good soul," I blurted, building on my thoughts.

"Thank you, but where did that come from?"

I told her about my philosophy.

"Let's hope we don't have to find out," Jenny stated matter-of-factly. We continued talking softly about the trail and the scenery. An eagle flew overhead.

"That's good luck," I claimed. "I'll take it and any other

omens that are casting positive vibes in our direction. Cross your fingers."

"And my toes, I suppose."

"If you can, make it happen." We took a hard left on the first hiking trail leading into the watershed. We had to go single file, so I took the lead while Jenny checked the cameras. We had not seen any other vehicles with people inside. Nothing like a surveillance van. Nothing like what the movies showed.

We ran into a problem when we were even with the equestrian center. There was no trail leading that way. I headed into the brush first, trying to stay on high ground to avoid tramping across marshy areas. When I saw the fence up ahead. I started breaking branches so we could find our way back to the trail. It was a board fence to keep horses in. Easy to duck under and climb through.

I turned back. Time to wait in the car until closer to our appointment. Jenny blocked my way, wearing a lopsided smile. "And here I thought we were going to meet a billionaire and the future mayor of Seattle." She pointed at her shoes, covered in mud and grime.

"I'll bring a rag when we come back. Anything from the cameras?"

She checked the live feed before digging into the activated images. A couple of workers at the center and that was it. I looked back at the center. Both cars in the employee parking lot accounted for.

"No bad guys," she told me.

I worked my way back to the trail, clipping branches to finish marking the way.

"If we did all this prep work for nothing, what would that tell you?"

"Better safe than sorry?" She patted her purse.

"Player," I declared. "That is exactly right. Then we review how we can do it better next time."

"How did you do all this alone? I'm surprised it didn't drive you insane."

"Who's to say I didn't reach the precipice, ready to fall in? It's much better with a partner."

"I really don't want to be doing any of this," Jenny declared.

"I don't either. Not anymore, but as long as I'm still in the game, I'm going to do it the best way I know how. The only way out is to win."

We didn't talk about anything else. We walked single file back to the powerline trail and then held hands for the return trip to the car. I took solace in the simple act. The world would spin faster soon enough.

When 11:30 AM rolled around and no one lined the roads waiting for us, I suspected my feelings about Jimmy were right, although one never knew about the inestimable Clive Barrows.

At 11:45, we left the car and started hiking back down the trail into the watershed. We turned off at the broken branch exit and headed into the backside of the equestrian center. When we reached the fence, we used my hobo t-shirt to wipe off our shoes. Jenny wrinkled her nose at the smell and gave me the hard side-eye. I stuffed the rag into a bush, wiping my hands on its leaves before climbing through the fence. We waited at the back of the property until Jimmy appeared in his vehicle with his father-in-law in the passenger seat. They parked next to the horse barn and got out, standing around uncomfortably until Jimmy spotted me.

He waited. We walked toward him while watching the entrance. Jenny was mesmerized.

"Watch your phone. Look for anyone coming in," I

whispered harshly. She fumbled with her phone, almost dropping it. She brought up the video feeds.

"Road's clear," she said softly.

I picked up the pace. Jenny strode by my side, checking the phone every couple of seconds. The two men moved into the open.

"Jimmy, Mr. Barrows."

"Randy," Jimmy replied. "That's not your real name, is it?"

"It is not. My name is Ian Bragg, and this is my wife, Jenny."

Clive scowled. Jimmy's trademark smile was missing. We stood uncomfortably for a few moments. "Is there a room inside?"

"This is all the privacy we need," Clive replied.

Jimmy pulled a notebook from an inside jacket pocket and handed it to me. I thumbed through the neatly written pages.

"The last message he sent was a chair, the deck, a cloud, and Margarita." I showed Jimmy the entries. It was an address in Kirkland.

Clive looked at it before turning his steely glare on me. "Do you know who Daniel Nader is? Manager of the Xterra Worldwide hedge fund?"

"Daniel Nader. XTW. Was he born in 1974?" I asked the question but already knew the answer.

"Sounds about right. How did you know that?" Clive wondered.

"How did you know it was him?" I pressed.

"A father knows these kinds of things."

Jimmy looked away. The conversation was between Clive Barrows and me. Jimmy was hanging onto the out-of-control roller coaster. I expected most political lives had backroom deals where a person like Jimmy was uncomfortable with but had to let slide. "I need to talk to this man about canceling the contract on Jimmy."

"Already done. Daniel Nader put out a contract on Jimmy so he could have my daughter to himself," Clive stated, leaving no doubt about the finality of the statement. "But I have one other thing that needs to happen. Despite what my business challengers might say, I have no idea how to hire a hitman, but Mr. Nader has intruded on my daughter's life one too many times. I will pay you one million dollars to remove Daniel Nader of Xterra Worldwide from this existence."

Jenny coughed. I looked hard at Jimmy. "Is that what you want?"

"I want my wife back," Jimmy pleaded, looking at the ground, his hands in his pockets.

"And I want my daughter to know her place. This is a message that has been a long time coming. It has to be sent. She will hear it, loud and clear."

"Accident, or mugging gone bad?"

Clive Barrows didn't hesitate. "An ugly accident. He cannot suffer enough for what he's done."

"Does Nader deserve to die for something more than pissing you off?"

Clive Barrows studied me, the corner of his mouth twitching up as I met his gaze.

"His hedge fund is built on a Ponzi scheme. He's defrauding his investors. My daughter isn't his only conquest. One of many. I have no idea what she gets from her interactions with him."

Jimmy had his back turned to us. He couldn't watch and tried not to listen, but his father-in-law made sure he heard every word.

"I'll check into Nader's business. I need to confirm the contract is canceled, and then Mrs. Tripplethorn will arrange a meeting with him. I'll take care of it as long as the money is in my account by Saturday. Do you have a pen and paper?"

Clive removed a notebook from his sports jacket and handed it over, along with a gold Waterman.

I wrote down my transfer account and the routing number for my bank in the Caymans. I would move any money from the transfer account into my final and secret account as soon as it arrived.

"It'll be done later today."

I handed the notebook and pen back. I shoved Tricia's codebook into my pocket.

"I'm sorry, Jimmy. I'm sorry you had to find out about all this, and that you had to see the kinds of things people do when they aren't under the spotlight of notoriety."

Jimmy nodded and kicked at a rock. This was not something he wanted to be a party to, but Clive was teaching *him* a hard lesson, too.

"I hope Tricia returns to you, not because she doesn't *have* a choice, but because you are the *best* choice."

Jimmy turned around to face me, creases making him look much older than he had two days prior. "You are a strange man, Mr. Bragg. You seem to understand a great deal about how the world works. In a different situation, I would have liked you."

"In a different world, yes. For now? You won't see us again. I'll conduct my due diligence to ensure Nader's a viable target. Once confirmed, I'll meet the contract terms. Then I'll be gone."

Clive Barrows held out his hand. We shook on it. A million-dollar deal. Jenny was still reeling from the day's revelations. She had turned pale.

Clive gestured for Jimmy to get into the vehicle. I guided

Jenny away from the meeting. "Just breathe, sweetheart." I rubbed her back as we walked. "We're a helluva lot closer to being free than when we got up this morning."

Jenny turned to me, forcing herself to relax. "I'm okay, honey." She clicked her phone and looked at the time. "That took four minutes."

"When there is one hundred percent focus on problems, they tend to get taken care of quickly."

Jimmy backed out and drove away. Neither he nor Clive looked at us.

"We might as well leave by the front door." Jenny looked at me, confusion gripping her. I explained. "Take the road. Grab my phone and the cameras on the way out. I'm okay not walking through the mud again."

She took a deep breath. "Practical." She closed her eyes and tipped her head back to drink in the smell of the horse farm amid the cool, moist air. I stayed close, resting my arm across her shoulders. When she opened her eyes, she smiled, close-lipped. "Clear-minded. Focus. No judgment, just action. This is a rough game, and men like Clive Barrows are not afraid to play it."

"To teach his daughter a lesson regarding consequences. Jimmy was having a hard time. I don't think he expected what Clive had planned." We walked down the road that led out of the center. "Hang on. Let me grab my t-shirt."

I jogged to the fence and crawled through to grab the rag before returning to Jenny.

She looked at the stinking t-shirt in my hand.

"What?" I asked her. "I'm not going to litter."

"The future mayor of Seattle is right. You are a strange man. So loveably, wonderfully strange." I held her hand as we walked, jaunty. I felt good. Jenny was improving quickly. "You called me your wife. How am I supposed to take that?"

"I feel like there's no answer I can give that would be satisfactory. How did you take it?"

"I'm still figuring that out."

We stopped by the tree to grab the cameras and my phone, then hit the second tree closer to the main road. We strolled the neighborhood street. I kept my head on a swivel as we walked, watching everywhere at once.

"I thought you said we were free?"

"It could have been a setup, but Jimmy was there, arranging a hit on his wife's lover. Even as a setup, that would be a lot to ask the public to accept as a made-up story. It sounds true, but one never knows. Maybe we should have walked through the watershed."

"Is paranoia a key trait of the players of your game, Mr. Bragg?"

"For those who survive, yes, Mrs. Bragg."

Jenny squeezed my hand as we walked. I picked up the pace since I didn't want to be out there anymore. I preferred being a long way away and out from under the spotlight. Jenny started to breathe hard in the final block to the car. We jumped in, and I drove away without even spinning up my music. Through the neighborhood on the twisty, narrow lane. Two side streets before going the long way around to get on the highway that took us toward Jenny's place.

Jenny put the music on for me, clicking through to replay *Dreamline*. Our song.

I dodged off the highway and made a loop to make sure no one was following, not once but twice. The second time I refilled the gas tank so I could watch the traffic.

Nothing seemed out of order. When we left the

highway, we drove a roundabout way to get to Jenny's house.

Once inside, I brought up my computer and accessed my transfer account. The money was already there. I showed it to Jenny and finally relaxed.

I moved it to my secret account and breathed a sigh of relief.

"I thought you were more a nerves-of-steel guy," Jenny quipped, pushing her way closer to sit in my lap and pressing her forehead to mine.

"Everything has changed, Miss Jenny. I realized that you were now at risk and will be until we're out of here. I'll check on Nader, but I suspect he's a scumbag. If so, I'll take care of business, and then we'll disappear. Jimmy and Clive can continue their manipulations, mixing politics, family, and business."

"I understand." Jenny's arms felt warm around my neck. I stroked her sides. "Are you petting a dog?"

"What?" I realized what I was doing and stopped. "I'm thinking. The money is a nice bonus to take the edge off disappearing."

"If I may be so bold, how much do you have?"

"*We* now have four and a half million in cash."

"More than most people make over their lifetime."

"It is. And it will last us the rest of ours if we don't get wrapped up in buying stuff."

"Does it look like I'm a big fan of material wealth?"

I chuckled. "I noticed you have at least three purses and, like, ten pairs of shoes."

"Your experience with women appears to be extremely limited. My international man of mystery has never had a serious girlfriend before. Clearly."

"I resemble that remark." I squeezed her tightly, inhaling deeply of her scent. "I need to start digging into our Daniel Nader. I have to focus for a while and find what I need to find. I have to build a profile and then start working on a place to take him down. One last job and then retirement. Why don't you give your sister and brother a call? You said you talk to them a lot."

"I do, but I'm not sure how much I have in common with them. I can see the conversation now. 'I met a man, but I can't tell you about him. I'm going to leave everything for him and he for me.' Makes us sound like hippies."

"When you say it like that, it does. It's better than, 'My boyfriend and I are running from the mob, but we're loving life.'"

Jenny kissed me warmly and fully before standing up and leaving me be. I watched her retreat into her bedroom. I pulled the .45 from the back of my waistband and put it on the table next to Jenny's purse. Then I opened my computer and launched into the dark web to find everything there was to find on my new target.

CHAPTER SIXTEEN

"Chess holds its master in its own bonds, shackling the mind and brain so that the inner freedom of the very strongest must suffer."
Albert Einstein

The rest of Wednesday came and went. I would have thought I'd have gotten an order calling me off the hit, but there was nothing.

Then, Thursday morning disappeared. Digging through the financial machinations of Xterra Worldwide threatened to melt my brain, but I kept at it and then bounced those procedures off comparable hedge funds.

What could have been considered a competitive advantage in setup and execution looked questionable. A man like Clive Barrows would know if it was legitimate. He'd said it wasn't. Clive had reasons to lie, but I didn't think he had.

The more I read about Dan Nader, the more he came across as shady. He and Tricia Tripplethorn would have

made a great power couple. Invited to all the best parties, even though no one wanted them to show up.

Being unlikeable wasn't a death sentence. Not even in my book. But cooking the books and destroying the futures of how many investors? I didn't find anything specific, but there was enough smoke swirling around Xterra Worldwide to tell me there was a fire.

Nader had a good legal team. They had a number of challengers tied up in court, where they would remain quagmired for the next decade. Nader thought he was bulletproof. He'd find out how wrong he was and soon.

I couldn't give Tricia any additional time to warn him. On Thursday, I drove Jenny to the hotel to pick up her car. She had to go to work, and I needed to scope out the places in the Wonderbeast's codebook that I could use for illicit meetings.

I checked out a parking garage, a mall, a sports stadium, and a ferry terminal. The mall had the fewest cameras, but I had no idea where he would park. It was such a huge area with a wide variety of options. I suspected the plan was to drive around until he saw Barchetta. I went with a parking garage instead. I entered at 1:07 PM and circled downward. I reached the lowest level and selected a spot on my way toward the ramp up. Few vehicles parked down here. It smelled of sewer runoff.

The lone camera to cover the lowest level had a broken lens. I walked up the ramp to the next level, and the next after that.

Ground level was three floors up. Four other cameras were in place, but they had seen their best days. I had my floppy hat on my head and my coat pulled up. Despite the time of year, the air contained a bite from the mist and lack of sun. No one would question a coat and hat.

The only camera that looked to be marginally

operational was the one at the entrance, where drivers entered and left the garage. Out the back, a temporary entrance for construction workers had been opened. Judging by the footprints, half of those using the garage walked in and out using the alternate entrance where there was no video coverage.

It seemed too easy.

That made me question it. I left by the construction entrance. No one cared. I could not see any observation of the area. Around the corner, through the shadows into a building, out the side entrance to a small parking area. Street parking, too. Places to eat. And most importantly, busy enough not to be seen. Business casual was the dress of the day. No suits in this part of town, but no t-shirts either.

I had my plan. Tonight. I needed to send an email. In between, *Working Man* played in my mind. I drove out of the parking garage at 1:53 PM.

I returned to the hotel, cleaned out my room, and checked out, agreeing to pay for one last night. They wanted a forwarding address to send the refund since I had paid in cash. I told them they could check the room now while I waited since I was going to be on the road for another month and would have no access to my mail. I sat in the lobby and browsed my phone.

A television above a fake fire played the news. Jimmy Tripplethorn stood larger than life in the middle of the big screen. I cocked my head to hear what he was saying. The city council had had a disagreement regarding homeless strategies. Three of the members had walked out in protest. That was when Jimmy'd had his epiphany. He'd committed to living on the street with them for a week. They'd called it a stunt and would have nothing to do with it.

Jimmy told the reporter that the cameras needed to stay away so as not to pollute the process. He'd take nothing with him, nothing that could be stolen, nothing to call his own. He'd figure it out like they had to.

People in the crowd were screaming at his lunacy. He'd get killed. He'd get kidnapped. He'd be injured in ways from which he would never recover.

"If I'm going to lead these people to a better place, I need to know where they are now. What their problems are, why they're on the street. I must leave my family behind to experience what the homeless experience every day. If we're to make this better, that's what I must do. I've invited other councilmembers to join me, but they have declined. They will defer to my judgment. You can trust that I will give this my best effort, and it's going to start today. Right now."

I found myself standing close to the television, taking it all in. I had met Jimmy and knew this was no stunt. He was punishing himself for what was going to happen. He was willing to die because of what his wife had done and what his father-in-law was doing.

"That is a new level of crazy," the lady from the registration said. "Leave it to Seattle to bring out the nuts. Your review is complete, sir. I have your refund."

I clenched my teeth while watching Jimmy hand his suit jacket to an aide, along with everything in his pockets. With one last wave, he walked away from the crowd.

I signed for my refund and thanked the hotel for a great stay.

"Did you get what you wanted from your stay?"

"That and much, much more. I will stay here next time I'm in the area."

I hurried to my car and raced out of the parking lot. I needed to pick up my gun and get downtown. I drove with the traffic to get to Jenny's house, sometimes fast, sometimes not.

When I got there, I changed into my freshly washed hobo clothes, checked the M1911A1, and pocketed a second magazine. I had no idea what I would run up against. I assumed I was going into a war zone. The movie *Escape From New York* came to mind. *Call me Snake.*

"Why do you have to go? There has to be someone who is protecting him."

"He doesn't have security. I learned that when I was casing him. He's on his own. Even if he wasn't, I think he would have sent them away. He's trying to kill himself." I clenched my fists. "Dammit, Jimmy!"

"You're going to protect him?" Jenny looked sad even through her smile and sparkling eyes. "I could not be more proud of you. Do what you have to do and then come home to me, Ian."

"Two birds with one stone," I said, popping open my laptop. I looked up the words in the codebook and logged into the Wonderbeast's email.

Chair. Basement. Wind. Chocolate.

I clicked send and then deleted it from the sent folder. I bundled my business casual clothes into a paper bag and threw them into the car. Jenny held the door as I got in.

"Come home to me," she reiterated.

"I will. I don't know when, but I will. Be ready to go when I get back. We won't have much time."

She nodded and closed the door behind me.

Even driving opposite traffic, the trip downtown seemed to take forever. I parked in a long-term meter lot and paid for a full day. I shuffled away to find out where Jimmy had gone.

Trooping the city streets looking for homeless people wasn't easy. They hid in the shadows of both nice buildings and dives. It was getting dark, and then it would get real hard. I backtracked to where he started near City Hall and retraced his steps as he had walked away. I shuffled and limped, my overcoat hiding the .45 and my other gear.

How far would Jimmy have wandered?

A couple of boozers were drinking from a bottle.

"You see the future mayor walk through here?" I asked, trying not to sound too coherent. "I have a bone to pick with him."

"Nah. Got any mickey?"

"Nah. I got rolled last night. Got nothing left." I muttered and shuffled away. I kept my head down but darted my eyes left and right, looking for those who didn't want to be seen. The invisible people of the undercity.

An hour passed, then another. Darkness fell. A light rain started. Another hour. Hundreds of dirty faces peered out from under ad hoc shelters. None of them were Jimmy. All of them were miserable.

I walked into cubbyholes and through alleys to see who hid there.

Up ahead, another alley on the edge of downtown. A white shirt. A commotion. I hurried to it. The councilman on the ground. Three homeless men kicking him.

I surged in like a freight train.

A right cross downed the first. A knee kick dropped the second. The third faced me, and I stepped into an uppercut that lifted him off his feet. The man with the injured knee tried to crawl away, but I caught him and hammered a fist into his temple. He crumpled to the ground.

Blood dripped from Jimmy's nose, his mouth a mess

from a split lip. His hands quivered from the pain wracking his body. He curled into himself, seeking solace in the fetal position.

"Come on, Jimmy, stand up. We need to get out of here." I thought of different leverage. "What about your kids?"

"I've failed my kids. I've failed my marriage. Nothing else matters. Leave me alone," he mumbled and covered his face with his hands, one finger sticking up at an odd angle. I took his hand and straightened the finger. He gasped at the pain and feebly pulled his hand away.

"Only dislocated."

Jimmy whimpered.

I put my back to a dumpster to keep the three vagrants in front of me and any newcomers from sneaking up behind me. "You are better than the rest of us, Jimmy. As much as you might hate it, people like me exist. People like me will keep you safe so you can take care of everyone else. We'll do what we do in the background, but you need to stay in the light, make the rest of the world a place where people can live better lives. I am going to stay with you out here until you learn what you need to if you want to get the right kind of help for these people. Now come on, we have to go."

"Won't the police be coming?" he asked.

"No, Jimmy. There's your first lesson. Police don't see homeless-on-homeless crime. No one does. Decent people avoid these wretched souls. Most of them have mental health issues; they are broken and forgotten by society. They keep living the only way they can."

I pulled Jimmy to his feet. "Are you hurt?"

He looked at me through sad eyes. "My dignity. My pride. My sense of right and wrong. And my nose."

"It's going to need some work unless you like the

washed-up boxer look." Jimmy put his arm over my shoulder.

We made it to the corner and then moved slowly down the street until we found a basement entrance that was dark and unoccupied. Jimmy sat on the stoop and wedged into the corner of the door and the frame.

"Weren't you supposed to kill me? Let me go, and you'll fulfill your contract."

"I said I wouldn't, and that means that I won't let you kill yourself either. You have a lot to live for, Jimmy. Don't squander it on a rash decision. Your kids need you. This won't bring your wife back to you. What she needs is someone to spank her."

"I don't abuse my wife."

"I'm not talking abuse, Jimmy. No wife-beating. Those aren't real men. I'm talking the right amount to send a tingle through her body. Ignite that passion. She fires on all eight cylinders."

"You're now an expert on what my wife likes in bed?"

"I'm now an expert on what Daniel Nader likes to do to the women in his bed." Jimmy lunged at me. I caught his weak effort at a punch and pushed him back into the doorway. "Sit your ass down. This isn't to make you feel bad. It's for you to retake control of your life. You wouldn't have pulled this if you hadn't already surrendered. Cut the crap and get back to winning the mayor's office. To raising your children to be decent citizens like you."

"You don't think this will do it?" He gestured toward the blood on his shirt, barely visible in the dim light that penetrated into the depths of our nook.

"Win hearts and minds? Maybe if you do it right, which you aren't. If you get beaten and carried out of here, you won't win the sympathy vote. You'll convince everyone that you're not as smart as you want them to think. And what if you get your brains splashed across the pavement? How will that help these people? What kind of crackdown would that lead to?"

Jimmy didn't answer. I checked my watch. It was late, going on eleven. "Why don't you get some sleep? I'll stand watch."

The future mayor wrapped his arms around himself and tried to get comfortable, but he was cold and wet.

I sat on the ground and leaned back across Jimmy's chest. He shivered against me for twenty minutes before drifting off. This was not how I had intended to spend my evening. I had expected to get some serious naked time with Miss Jenny, but that would have to wait. I sat on the ground in the mist in a basement stairwell in the butt-crack of the high-rent district.

You want me on that wall! Prophetic words. No one wants to know how sausage is made, only that it tastes good. No one wants to know the lengths hard souls will go to keep the rest safe.

I kill bad men for money. I was going to have to change what I told myself. *I keep good men safe.* I could live with that.

CHAPTER SEVENTEEN

"Tactics flow from a superior position." Bobby Fischer

Jimmy woke around four in the morning, stiff and stuffed up. I moved away, then stood and stretched. Jimmy looked around.

"Gotta take a leak?" I asked. "You know, there are no bathrooms for the homeless."

He hung his head in shame. I pointed to a small gap between the buildings. He favored the leg that had been injured as he limped over to take care of business, his head twisting back and forth as he watched for people who might see him.

"Can you stand guard for a while? I need to get some sleep."

Jimmy looked at his wrist, but he had taken off his watch. He tried to guess the time from looking at the sky.

"It's four in the morning."

"You stayed up the whole time?"

"Night is the most dangerous. It's why you see a lot of

them sleeping during the day, or slugging the last from their bottle in the evening to take the edge off what the darkness brings."

Jimmy held himself and shivered before tenderly touching his lip. He winced at the pain. He blew his nose onto the ground, ejecting a bloody snot ball. He took a deep breath through his nose.

"Stand guard. You were former military. Which branch? Army SF?"

"Marines. Army operators were good. I liked working with them. The D-boys were a strange bunch, but they accomplished the mission."

"D-boys?"

"Delta Force. Elite, but under the radar. Like Seal Team Six. Still, I'm happy to have been in the Corps."

I took the spot in the doorway, pulling my collar tightly to my ears as Jimmy sat with his back against me. I unbuttoned my coat so he could pull a small part of it over his arms.

"Why are you here, Ian? Even my own people didn't come."

I closed my eyes. "Your people respect you and your wishes. I guarantee they're worried about you. I think you'll see them this morning, bringing breakfast for you and any other homeless in the area."

"I had you to protect me, so I didn't get the full experience. If they bring food and water, I won't experience what the others are going through." Jimmy's hair remained plastered to his head as he shook the rain and mist from it.

"You just slept in a doorway after getting the shit kicked out of you. I don't need to jump into the abyss to see that it's a terrible fall. Have you seen the horrors within?"

Jimmy nodded but didn't speak.

"To learn the best lessons, one must be uncomfortable and open. You've been both. You have seen exactly what goes on down here. A week of this might break you, and then you won't be able to help them. What is your goal, Jimmy? I know the answer. You thought you wanted to die, but you couched it in understanding the homeless. You were playing politics, giving yourself an out. When the angry bums were beating you, you curled up. That tells me you were trying to protect yourself. If you wanted to die, you would have taken it all, wide open. Kick me in the Jimmy, you pricks!"

I chuckled at my joke. Jimmy's chin sagged to his chest.

"You've learned hard lessons. It bothers you because you're a good man. How many times are you going to make me say it? It hurts me, especially telling it to a politician. I have no respect for your chosen profession, no disrespect intended."

Jimmy perked up. "None taken. My profession created this." He spread his arms wide to take in the entirety of our basement entrance.

"That's crap. Politicians might have created conditions that people did not react well to, but you didn't create this. Every society in the world has homeless. How do you keep people moving forward without leaving an entire class behind? Social programs without being a socialist. Necessary but evil, but they aren't. It's not Robin Hood, taking from those who can afford it and giving to those who don't. It's about serving the needs. There are homeless down here who aren't homeless. You'll see them show up in the daylight, set up, and look miserable in order to beg. Some make their living that way, probably more than working fast food. But they ruin it for the real homeless."

"You're telling me to go home?"

"I'm asking you if you learned what you need to know to help these people."

"I'm not sure."

"You think about it while I catch some sleep. You're harshing my homeless buzz, Jimmy. Let me sleep in this doorway while smelling your piss. Next time, try to shoot it farther away."

"You are a hard man, Ian Bragg. As much as I know I shouldn't, I like you, and I never properly thanked you."

"I don't know why you're still talking while I'm trying to get some shut-eye," I grumbled. Jimmy snorted.

"Have it your way."

"Does that make me the king, the burger king?" Jimmy snorted a loud kind of laugh, the type you give when you're free to be yourself.

I relaxed into the wedge. It wasn't that uncomfortable. Being up for twenty-four hours straight was the best submission to sleep's mystic rhythms.

"Go on, get out of there!" a gruff voice shouted. "Move along, now."

Jimmy had fallen back asleep, but no one had caused us any problems. Pre-dawn was the time for waking and moving, finding a new spot. Jimmy stood, cracked his back, and offered me a hand up. I checked the time. Two and a half hours. It was nearly seven in the morning.

It would have to be enough sleep.

"Is it time to take your newfound knowledge into the council chambers?" I asked, hopeful that Jimmy had seen the light.

He studied me while I yawned. I didn't bother covering my mouth. I closed my jacket.

"You have a wife." Jimmy talked as if he were thinking.

"I should be next to her right damn now, Jimmy."

He held up his hands. "Yes, Ian. I've learned what I need to know. Let's head to my campaign office. They open at seven. We can get cleaned up. I need to start crafting a proposal."

"Good choice. I want to get out of here. I have an appointment with my wife for some private time, and I don't want to miss that."

"Take it from me. Don't make her the second choice too often. You won't like the result."

Jimmy hobbled up the short stairs and ended by hopping on one foot.

"Hang on." I bumped his hip and grabbed him to shoulder some of his weight. "It'll loosen up after you use it a bit."

"I should probably stay off it," Jimmy countered.

"Welcome to Marine Corps rules. You need to walk, you walk. There is no other choice. I'm not going to call a cab."

"You have your phone with you?"

I looked at him. "I'm not here to make a statement. I also have money and a gun."

"You can't have a gun down here." Jimmy looked shocked.

I found his surprise amusing. "I can take on three men when they don't see me coming, but next time, it might be five, or it could be druggies with guns. This is a dangerous place, and I'm not going to risk my safety without giving myself a fighting chance. The homeless have to live with it every day, so you need to do your politician thing and try to make it less horrible."

"Fine. Can I use your phone to call my wife?"

"No. You are not using my phone to call your wife. I'm

not happy that *this* number is on *your* phone." We headed uphill, walking slowly while Jimmy powered through the pain in his knee. He needed to get it looked at, but later. His homeless lesson was not yet complete. The pain would drive it home better and make him appreciate it, especially after he crossed the finish line.

"Sorry. I didn't think that through."

"Call her from your office. We'll be there shortly." I wanted to get something to eat. It had been too long since my last meal.

And coffee.

We rounded the corner and I stopped. I pulled Jimmy back. "The press is waiting for you, so this is the end of the line for me. Can you make it the rest of the way?"

He took one step and almost fell. "I don't think so."

"You know I can't be seen with you. I'll find someone to help you. Get around the corner and lean against the wall." I turned Jimmy loose and made myself scarce, heading downhill. I walked quickly up the parallel road, catching the side street to emerge above the campaign office. I staggered and stumbled my way toward the crowd. I stopped when I got close and shielded my eyes. The reporters casually eased away from me. "It's Jimmy Tripplethorn!" I pointed down the road.

The press glanced at me only to see where I was pointing, and I kept my arm in front of my face to block any pictures. Cameramen and reporters took off down the street. I stumbled onto the side road. Once out of sight, I picked up my pace.

I needed to beat the rush to the coffee shop. I buttoned my jacket to look more presentable. I walked with a purpose. People would pick up on that without knowing what made me different. I removed a twenty from my wallet to wave at the barista. I was willing to pay anything for a cup of coffee at that moment in time.

My kingdom for a horse, or something like that. I had a full day ahead and didn't have time to go home. I would only get one shot at completing the contract on Daniel Nader.

His appointment with destiny raced toward me at the speed of cold molasses.

There were two others in line at the open-air shop. The mud and dirt on my jacket convinced the next person in line to keep their distance. When I reached the counter, I put the twenty down and slid it over before ordering. Two cups of coffee, one with plenty of room for cream, and a blueberry muffin. They handed them over and waved at the next customer.

I plied my coffee with as much half and half as would fit before retreating to a table, where I enjoyed sitting down on a seat that wasn't a concrete step. I slugged down the creamed coffee as if it were milk, then ate the muffin slowly, savoring it. When I was finished, I wiped my table down and dumped my trash. I walked away with my second coffee still steaming.

No one had messed with my car despite its remaining in the day lot overnight. It started right up, and I put on my music because I needed that as much as coffee. I dialed to *Middletown Dreams* and pointed the car's nose out of the lot. I checked the map app to find a YMCA not far away. I drove straight there.

I was happy to pay for a shower and use of the bathroom, cleaning up and dressing in my slacks, dress shoes, and a button-down shirt. I was as refreshed as I needed to be for what I had to do. My old clothes went into the dumpster on the way out of the building. I called Jenny from the parking lot.

"I missed you," she said when she answered.

"I let Jimmy know he was harshing my newlywed buzz. Our first night apart, and I am completely destroyed."

"Are you on your way home?" Her sultry summons made me wish it were true.

"Only one more thing to do, and then I'm coming home for good."

"I'll be ready for you." We listened to each other breathe for a few moments before Jenny continued, "I saw Jimmy's return on the news. He made a profound statement, before one of his staff took him to the hospital. The talking heads at the news stations seemed concerned about his physical health, but when he talked, he was bright and engaging. Does he owe a good night's sleep to you?"

"We should discuss what the finer points of a good night's sleep looks like. But yes. I watched so he could sleep after getting himself beat up by a few angry bums. I convinced them of the error of their ways *before* Jimmy was battered into a coma."

"Of course you did. You're an educator, just like me."

"I like how you think. I need to go, but I'll be home this afternoon. I love you, Jenny."

"Please stay safe, Ian. I love you, too." She ended the call. I looked at the blank screen before I powered the phone down and tucked it into my shirt pocket.

I headed to Kirkland, turning up the music and sipping my coffee as I ran through scenarios in the variety of ways they might play out. I was like a pilot practicing emergency action drills to be ready in case something happens and there's no time to think, hoping the whole time he never has to implement them.

CHAPTER EIGHTEEN

"Be ready to pay the price of your dreams. Free cheese can only be found in a mousetrap." Paulo Coelho

The parking area I had picked was full, as was the secondary spot. It bugged me, but not enough to get angry. I drove two blocks farther away and parked at a short-term metered spot on the street. I sat in the car and waited with the window rolled down, leaning back to take in the nice weather. Parking patrol did me the courtesy of not coming by.

As the time counted down, I left my spot and drove around the block to check on the parking area. Two spots had opened. I drove in and shut the car down. I acted like I was on my phone while I casually wiped down the inside of the car, the steering wheel, the seat belt clip, the gear shift, the radio, and more.

In most of my DN74 scenarios, I would abandon the car where it was.

Once outside, I locked it with the key instead of the fob

to surreptitiously wipe down the door handle. I took care of the back door on the way around the trunk and to the other side. I had already wiped Jenny's prints from the passenger side. She had touched everything, it seemed, so I wiped everything, twice.

I carefully tossed my sports coat over my shoulder to keep the pistol from flying out and held it with one finger while I walked into a nearby building, through the lobby, and with my jacket on, left through a side door. Around another building, into a crowd, and then by myself once outside a store camera's view. I entered the parking garage by the construction entrance and walked down the rear stairs to the basement.

I waited at the bottom of the stairs, ready to climb up if someone was coming down and stepping into the garage if someone arrived by car and came toward the stairs.

Pictures on the open net showed Daniel Nader with his 2007 Porsche 911 Turbo Coupe. It looked like a flattened VW Bug to me, but it didn't act like one. It was a street-legal race car. It embodied the persona of Xterra Worldwide's chairman.

The clock slowly wound down. A car made its way to the basement level, but it didn't sound like a sports car. I stepped into the roadway as the wheels squeaked on the turns to the final level. I walked down the middle, my hand inside my jacket, gripping the M1911A1. A Prius appeared. I waved with my free hand and stepped aside for the car to pass, but the driver maneuvered it into an empty spot.

I kept walking. The driver took her time getting out. I heard the throaty growl of the Porsche. Two levels above.

She was out and walking. The car beeped when she locked it as she kept going. The growl was slow and deliberate. Searching. Not in a hurry. He was in complete control. Make her wait. Make her beg for him. Walking speed. Around a corner and down. I hurried toward the stairway to give myself the length of the parking area in which to work.

I checked the pistol. A round in the chamber. Thumb on the safety and pistol in my hand. A robbery gone awry. Blow his head off and keep walking. I'd be long gone by the time anyone came to check.

The silver Porsche turned the far corner. The driver, with his arm hanging casually out the window, approached me agonizingly slowly. I walked down the middle of the lane, raised my pistol, and aimed at him.

The challenge was on, and his fight or flight fear response activated. He snarled through the windshield. He jammed the gas pedal to the firewall and redlined the engine as he charged.

I stopped and danced back. A new plan instantly flashed into my mind. I gave him the finger with my left hand while continuing to aim with my right. Like a matador, I balanced on the balls of my feet, dodging at the last instant. The brakes squealed for a millisecond before the Porsche slammed into the back of a Nissan Maxima. The airbag popped into Nader's face.

I stuffed the pistol into my waistband while running to the car. I reached through the open window to wrap an arm around his head. I pulled and twisted. He was strong and starting to fight. With a desperate surge, I pushed away from the car, using the door and my body weight for leverage, falling back, bending and twisting. His neck snapped. I shoved him back into the driver's seat, looked around quickly, and brushed myself off. I strode toward the stairway, expecting the Prius driver to appear, but she was long gone.

Upstairs to the ground level. No one. I moved the pistol to my jacket pocket, then took the coat off since it was covered in talcum powder from the airbag. I carried it over my shoulder as I walked across the short open area, into a different building, and out the far side, where I made a beeline straight for my car. I jumped in, carefully backed out, and drove away.

As I cleared the downtown area, I still had not heard a siren. I continued driving the speed limit until I was thirty miles to the east, then pulled into a Denny's. I headed inside to order breakfast for lunch. I ate casually, leaving my phone off.

After I finished, I asked the cashier if she could call me a cab. It arrived in under five minutes. I jumped inside, carrying nothing except my bundled-up suit jacket. I gave the driver Jenny's address. He headed out, and thankfully, he wasn't a talker. We listened to the oldies station as we churned through the miles.

Once in the driveway, I gave him a generous tip and wished him well. The fresh air smelled like home.

Jenny waved from the living room window. I smiled, but I didn't feel the internal peace I'd thought I would.

CHAPTER NINETEEN

"You cannot run away from the truth because truth will find you." ColoZeus Benz

The weekend rolled around before the news of Daniel Nader's accident and untimely demise hit the airwaves, but then it exploded. An SEC investigation had been ongoing. The implication? He'd committed suicide rather than face the impending charges.

It became a big story that was serving to gut Xterra Worldwide. A day ago, people's investments were safe. Today, they were gone. The fallacy was that the money hadn't been there yesterday either. They'd only thought it was. With spotlights shining into the void of Daniel Nader's hedge fund, the ugliness was clear for all to see. The investigators, both media and government, were far better at rooting out irregularities than I could have ever been.

I remained validated. I had only killed bad people. It was time to leave the game.

In other news, Jimmy roared back into the public eye. His ratings jumped. He looked more confident. Instead of being in the background, he kept Tricia by his side, touching her, holding her.

She masked her sadness well, but her eyes told the truth. Her dad had delivered a lesson on brute force and the use of power to shape the world. Jimmy had been given a new life. It didn't look like he was going to squander it. Tricia had a new life, too: dutiful wife and supporter of Jimmy Tripplethorn.

On the sale boards, a red Porsche Panamera showed up, discounted nicely for anyone with fifty grand to spend.

As I did, I checked my accounts each day. In my deposit account, two amounts showed up—a four-figure deposit and a six-figure deposit. Adding the two together delivered a phone number. No new gigs were shown on a hidden bulletin board.

My phone was two days beyond its useful service life. I should have destroyed it immediately following Nader's hit.

Jenny wasn't up yet. I wrote a note that I had gone out to the store to get something special for lunch. I needed to do that, but I also needed to be a long way away when I powered my phone up. Even though the GPS was off, a phone could still be tracked.

I'd make the call to The Peace Archive and then destroy the phone. I borrowed a hammer from the shed.

I took Jenny's car and drove two towns to the south on a main artery leading back to the big city. In a mall parking lot, I dialed the number.

The line connected as if someone answered, but no one spoke. I waited. They had sent the note to contact me. The ball was in their court.

"We know what you did."

A simple sentence made by a computer modulated voice. Ambiguous. A threat. They had made the first move in a verbal chess match. They were searching to see where I was. They'd figure it out, but they didn't have any assets close enough. I'd give them two minutes of my time, and then I would disappear.

"So what?"

"It's bad for the group's reputation. Pressuring clients to keep their money while not satisfying the contract is very bad for business."

"I doubt that. Don't drop contracts on good people, and you won't have these kinds of problems. You should be thanking me for cleaning up your mess. Next time, make sure you get it right."

I hung up and turned off the power. I started the car and hurried onto the main road, accelerating on a vector away from Jenny. Five miles distant, I stopped at a hiking trail's parking lot. On one of their decorative boulders, I hammered the phone into non-existence before depositing pieces and shards into each of the lot's four garbage cans.

I casually drove toward home, stopping at the first grocery store and meandering through the aisles, looking for something I wanted to cook for lunch. I settled on burgers with freshly baked rolls for buns. I knew Jenny failed miserably when it came to selecting the proper mustard for each occasion, so I picked some up, along with pickles and barbeque sauce in lieu of ketchup.

The self-checkout was efficient. I was done in under a minute. The drive back to Jenny's house was uneventful, as all drives should be.

My thoughts were heavy since I knew we needed to go. This afternoon, we needed to be winging our way to Italy, probably never to return to this town. It was the life I had promised Jenny, and she had accepted.

When I pulled up, a car was parked on the street across from Jenny's house. I'd been there on and off for a week and had not seen anyone park in that place before. I pulled in behind the car and jumped out, ducking behind my open car door.

The engine revved and the car spun out, sending rocks and dirt my way. I backed up and raced into the driveway, sliding to a stop. I bolted into the house and sprinted down the hall to find Jenny still asleep.

I leaned over the bed to kiss her face, fighting to slow my breathing. She moaned softly in the delight of being woken in such a way. She tried to pull me into bed.

"We have to go. Right now. They've found me, and they aren't happy."

"The police?"

"The Peace Archive. We're on the wrong side of a group of hired killers. We need to regain the high ground."

Jenny blinked the sleep from her eyes and helped herself out of bed. "What's that mean?"

"It means our plans for a world cruise are temporarily on hold. I need to deal with this, but I have to make sure you're safe first."

"We can fight this together." She wrapped her arms around my neck and pulled her naked body tightly against me.

"If we want the freedom to do this, we need to run. Right now. Clothes on your back. We'll take your phone, but power it down. We'll buy what we need on the way."

"What about our home?"

"Our home has become wherever we are. It cannot be here because they know about this place, which means they know about you. You have a target on your back, Miss Jenny. Don't be afraid, be alert. We will select the battlefield, and then we will win this fight. Nothing matters right now besides surviving the day."

Jenny backed away from me until she leaned against the wall. Her eyes glistened. My reality had been fine when people didn't want us dead.

I ran back to the front room. The car had not returned. I went outside to check for an improvised device, but if there had been one, it would already have detonated. We didn't have a propane tank outside or an easy way to build a weapon.

I grabbed the remaining ammunition for the two pistols. Into the kitchen to take a few non-perishables in case we couldn't stop. Jenny appeared wearing jeans and a loose top, hair still messy.

"You look beautiful," I told her.

"Can't they wait for a decent hour to deliver their vendetta?" She stared out the living room window.

"We plan for tomorrow while living for today. Every day from now until we're done." We took two coats on our way outside. She wore her workout shoes and carried her purse. Good choice.

I had my computer. I had planned on donating it to Goodwill, but I hadn't scrubbed it clean yet.

I locked the front door because it needed to appear normal. We drove out earlier than we wanted, but on our way to somewhere else.

"How did they find us?"

"I don't know. They could have dug through my VPN to find me. Or they got my name from the hotel, and then got your name because I fell in love."

Jenny took my hand and held it as we drove away from all things urban. Fifty miles away, I spotted a car sitting in a yard with a price on the windshield.

I held a finger to my lips. "Let's get something to eat before we keep driving to Boise. No one will find us there." I parked at a local diner. We stood outside the door, where I kissed Jenny passionately and whispered into her ear, "I'll return with the car, and then we'll set a trap for whoever is following us."

She nodded. Jenny had turned pale from the stress of the day's ordeal. She went inside, and I jogged away. Across the highway to a frontage road and back to where I'd seen the car for sale. A Toyota Corolla in decent shape. Forty-five hundred dollars. That would take most of my remaining cash, but I could Western Union some more.

I knocked on the house door. An elderly gentleman answered.

"I'd like to look at your car."

"My granddaughter's car. She used it for college."

"How great is that? A grandfather making sure his family gets their education. Looks like a decent daily driver." He grabbed a key off the hook by the door and followed me back to the car. He started it and let it run. It sounded good, was mostly clean. "Let's take it for a ride."

I hopped in the passenger seat and we took off, driving a mile down the frontage road before pulling into a turnaround. We changed places. It drove fine, but it wouldn't win any races. It had a few thousand miles left on it. That was all we needed.

I thrust my hand toward him. "I'll pay your price in cash right now."

"Damn, sonny. I just put the sign on it this morning."

"Then serendipity smiled on both of us." I started counting out the bills.

"I'll get the title. She signed it before flying to Japan for an internship." He disappeared into the house. I finished at forty-five one-hundred-dollar bills. I reversed them and counted again.

"Congratulations," I called after him. He shuffled back into view, waving the paper. We traded money for title.

"You can fill it out when you take it to registration."

"Easy day, my good man. I thank you again." We shook a second time, and I hopped in and drove off. It was that simple. Across the road and into the Walmart parking lot next to the restaurant. I parked close to the entrance, slipping between other cars. I strolled into the store, along the wide walkway just past the registers, and out the garden entrance.

Jenny was picking at her food when I joined her. I initially sat across from her, but that wasn't what she needed. I moved and slid in next to her. I kissed her ear and nuzzled her neck. She shivered and leaned against the wall.

"What are you doing?"

"Making time with my gal?" Judging from the look on her face, that wasn't the right answer. I leaned close. "We're going to go to the hotel on the other side of Wally World. We're going to get a room and park your car right in front of the door. We're going to wait for whoever shows up, and I'm going to kill them."

Jenny closed her eyes. "Do you have to?"

"Yes. They'll keep coming until they find it's too dangerous, which means too expensive. We make the hit and we disappear. After this hotel and abandoning your car, there will be no way for them to find us."

"Just like that?"

"Just like that. Being an international man of mystery comes at a steep price. I'm sorry, Miss Jenny. I truly am. I'm sorry for being so selfish as to drag you into my world."

She smirked. "Does love have to have a trade-off?"

"To me, the answer must be yes since this is the only time I've been in love."

"Me, too. It takes the edge off the bad stuff." She tipped her head up enough to smile at me.

"The bad stuff. We'll see what we can do about that. Get our room, and then we need to go shopping."

CHAPTER TWENTY

"We may be likened to two scorpions in a bottle, each capable of killing the other, but only at the risk of his own life." J. Robert Oppenheimer

We were too early for check-in, so we paid for two nights to get the room today and through the night. I checked in under a phony name, one The Peace Archive knew, paid with one of my pre-paid cards, and registered Jenny's car.

In the room, I pulled out my computer to access the hotel's internet. I used the VPN to get to Western Union and sent five thousand dollars to the Walmart customer service counter for my pickup.

I needed a burner phone. Jenny remained distraught, unsure of what to do with herself. I made sure the wireless security cameras were ready to go, then closed my laptop and pocketed my thumb drive. Jenny stood at the window, peeking out. I leaned past her to close the curtains.

"I expect if they're out there, they can see us much better than we can see them."

She hung her head, but I pulled her away from the window, just in case. I doubted The Peace Archive would spare her. No need to make it easy for them if they planned a drive-by hit.

I slid my arms around her waist. "Are you Bonny, or am I?"

She stared at me. "We're better than Bonny and Clyde, aren't we? They killed people and stole money."

"I don't steal money," I conceded. "And you don't break any laws because you are my angel."

She snorted. "That's quite a stretch."

"Just trying to take your mind off today's minor issues. I'm willing to profess my love for you if that would help."

She cracked a smile for only an instant, but I saw it.

"We are well into the game, but checkmate is not imminent. We have our main pieces in the middle of the board, vying for a superior position and pressing the other through constant attacks until victory." Jenny's beautiful green eyes sparkled in the sketchy light of the motel room. "They will only have one, maybe two assets assigned. That's it. The Peace Archive has worldwide reach but is still a small operation. Plus, I had a few days left to satisfy my contract. They had to put the counter operation into play in a day, no more."

"Then what?"

"Then we go on our world cruise. Give them time to calm the hell down. Then we'll find a nice country we want to live in."

"I've heard Cabo San Lucas is nice," Jenny offered.

"Or the southern coast of Spain. How about Tuscany?"

"Can we get visas without letting anyone know where we are?"

"With money, all things are possible. Think about a new name for yourself. Your days of being the unrepentant Jenny Lawless could be quickly drawing to a close.

"Jenny Bragg?" she offered.

"I can go with that. Eldon and Jeannette Bragg. I go by Ian and you, Jenny, but in any documentation, it won't be obvious."

"Is it that easy?"

"Much easier doing a variation on an existing name. Getting that through the system is almost effortless, but The Peace Archive knows that, too. Still, they don't have unlimited reach."

"Is this our life now? Cheap motels and running from shadows?"

"We're not staying here. You deserve far better than this. So, nice hotels." I smiled while stroking her hair. "We're not running from anyone. Never take your foot off the gas. As soon as we get defensive, they'll have us. Are you ready to go to Wally World?"

"Do you have your pistol?"

I tapped the back of my pants. "I do. Why?"

"I have mine, too." She pointed to her purse.

"We *will* win this game."

"Win or die trying?" Jenny started to sink back into the doldrums.

"There is no try, according to Master Yoda. We shall do unto others as they would do unto us."

"Quoting movies and clichés?" Jenny rotated her shoulders, forcing herself to relax.

I hugged her for a long, long time. She had to go through all the emotions and settle into her new normal. I went out to the car and set up three security cameras, looking left, right, and out the back. I wiped down the inside of the car. When I returned to the room, Jenny was ready to go.

The customer service clerk was exceedingly patient and thorough with the Western Union forms, forking over the money after fifteen minutes of documentation exchanges. We grinned like two college kids getting their allowance.

Walmart had the disposable phone I wanted. We picked up one with a data and voice plan. We left by the garden entrance, walking beside a family into the parking lot and staying behind taller vehicles until we were in our new ride.

I explained my plan to Jenny, keeping it simple. We had to draw out whoever they'd sent after us. I assumed they were already here. We'd been in this location for more than four hours.

We backed out and casually drove through the parking lot, Jenny keeping a keen eye out for someone sitting in their vehicle. We found a couple of candidates to watch. We finished our tour and parked where we could see them.

"If they saw us leave, they'll be waiting for us to return," Jenny said. "How do you think they're going to do it? A sniper rifle from a mile away?"

"Operators travel light. That was one of the critical factors in getting hired—the ability to improvise. If they rushed to get here, they don't have a rifle, not one that is sighted in, anyway. I think they'll go with something like a fire-bomb through our window."

"But we won't be there."

"We have to go back now, but we'll be out of there when they come for us."

"What makes you so sure?" Jenny squinted at one of the potential vehicles as a woman and two kids climbed in. The man who had been waiting fired up the engine and quickly drove away.

"This isn't something they'll do in the daylight. They'll

wait for darkness, especially if they think we're not going anywhere. We'll be going to bed early tonight, honey."

"I can't wait," Jenny deadpanned.

"I can't wait until we're in a comfortable hotel with each other for company. Plan for tomorrow but live for today."

Jenny turned toward me. "I look forward to it. You owe me a back rub."

"I'll enjoy paying my debt, even if it doesn't end in sex."

"Even if..." Jenny chuckled lightly. "It'll end in sex. That's part of the deal, and you better pay up, mister."

"I shall do my very best, but unfortunately, not tonight. I think tonight will be car city, just until we have our target locked."

We looked at each other before steeling ourselves for the return walk to the motel. We headed back into Walmart to buy two sandwiches to complete our cover by carrying a bag and getting a throwaway dinner at the same time.

I couldn't spot our pursuer, who I felt was nearby. I couldn't scan the area without looking obvious. We hurried along the walk in front of the rooms before diving into ours. I moved a chair to the window and pulled the blinds and curtain up in one corner. I looked out while bringing up my new phone, getting it online, and downloading the security app. I accessed the three cameras and brought up the feed through the hotel's Wi-Fi.

"What do we do now?" Jenny asked.

"Wait, but be ready to go. We'll only have a few seconds when the opportunity arrives. That's when we'll make our break."

"I still don't see how we'll draw them to us."

"Hubris," I explained while watching out the window.

The inside lights were off, and Jenny was antsy. I reduced the screen brightness on my phone so it didn't highlight my face like a bad ghost show. "They need to suffer the pain of coming after me when the contract was canceled. I cleaned up their mess. That made someone angry, probably whoever brokered the contract."

Jenny was still trying to get her head wrapped around it.

She laid down and forced herself to relax. We talked about anything and everything. What we wanted to see from the world. Archaeology. Mountains. Rivers. Wildlife. Art. Opera. Most importantly, we were destined to conduct a food tour of the world. Wherever we stopped, we agreed to try the local specialty. We both loved a good meal. I also loved a bad meal when I was hungry enough, but we would avoid those as much as possible.

I opened my sandwich and ate it slowly.

Jenny fell asleep while I watched. I couldn't keep myself from glancing at her. I considered myself lucky at having been graced with her presence. She was easy to fight for and willing to fight with me once she knew what she had to do.

By six in the evening, I saw what I had been waiting for. A big orange self-moving truck parked at check-in.

"Jenny, get up. We're ready to go."

She popped her eyes open and jumped to her feet. I had to keep her from running out the door.

"Hang on. We have to wait for the van to block the view. Then into the breezeway to the back of the hotel, across the parking lot, and into the field beyond. Don't run, just a fast walk, and don't look around. People remember folks who act like they have something to hide.

Check-in complete, a young couple with a small baby

climbed back into the van. Short haircut. My guess was military on orders. He pulled out, maneuvering slowly through the parking lot. I took a quick look around and wiped the table where I'd been sitting. I turned the doorknob with my shirtsleeve. The truck started to pass. I threw the door open and Jenny popped out, hurried to the left, and dove into the breezeway beside our room.

I pulled the door shut behind me and followed, clearing the opening before I could be seen. Through the breezeway and into the parking lot at the rear of the motel and into the field beyond where people walked their dogs. We slowed and walked casually, hand in hand on our way around the far side of Walmart. It made for a longer walk than I'd intended.

We ran into Walmart to buy a pair of binoculars and toiletries. We hurried out, a sense of urgency hanging over our heads. I could feel it, like my combat sense in the Marines.

I drove across the highway to a small hill that overlooked the area. We settled in to watch. As the sun breached the horizon, we found that the entire area was lit up like daylight. I checked the camera feeds on my phone, plugging it into the charger sticking out of the car's twelve-volt power outlet.

"Why are we up here?" Jenny asked.

I took her hand and watched the motel parking lot through the binoculars. "Getting into a gun battle in the motel parking lot wouldn't be the best. All we need is to find our mark, then we'll pick the time and place of his demise. Never let the enemy select the battlefield."

"What about innocent bystanders?"

"There won't be any. We'll make sure of that before we take care of them."

"What about the motel?"

"That's on them if they hurt anyone."

Jenny turned on the radio and searched until she found a rock station. Modern rock. It was different from what I liked, but it was what she wanted to listen to.

"Not going to fight me?" She pointed at the radio.

"I don't want to fight with you, and I won't let your poor taste in music be the catalyst to start one."

Jenny turned to me, rubbing her chin as she contemplated my countermove. "I think those are fighting words. Are you always playing chess, Mister Bragg?"

"Why, Mrs. Bragg, I'm sure I don't know what you're talking about."

"Since you brought it up, are you going to give me a proper wedding?"

"Proper...hang on." A car moved from a spot close to the highway, circled the lot, and then drove slowly around for a second pass. I pointed at the screen. Two people in the car. They slowed to a stop behind Jenny's car. A woman got out, carrying a brick attached to a bottle.

She took two steps before winding up and launching it through the window of the room. It caught on the curtain but had gone in far enough to burst into flames inside, igniting the bedding and the carpet. The woman hopped back into the car, and it drove slowly away.

Emergency lights started flashing on the side of the building. A few more seconds and the first people emerged from their rooms. The smoke pouring out of the first-floor window expedited the departures.

The nondescript four-door parked at the edge of the Walmart lot, facing the motel.

"You drive," I said, jumping out and climbing into the back seat.

"Where?" Jenny wondered.

"Walmart. You're going to make one pass around the back of the lot before pulling past, keeping that car on the passenger's side. Put something in your ears. Earplugs if you have them."

Jenny moved both front seats up to give me more room. I rolled the rear passenger window down and wedged myself in, crouching low.

Jenny stuffed torn tissue into her ears. With trembling hands, she drove away from the overlook. I held the M1911A1, relaxing my grip as the blood started to race through my veins. Jenny's knuckles turned white from the death grip she had on the steering wheel.

Def Leppard popped up on the radio station. Not a bad way to head into battle.

"Those two just tried to kill us. I am not cool with that," I told Jenny.

"I'm not either," Jenny agreed, her voice less confident than mine. I let my anger drive me. I only kill bad people.

"Whatever you do, don't look into the other car. Focus on what's in front of our bumper."

These two were just like me, operators working for The Peace Archive. When did they start churning out contracts on just anyone? I was no threat to them. Whoever was in charge had his ego bruised when an operator wanted out of the game. I had no idea who that person was or where the business was located, if anywhere. The contracts were arranged online through a maze of secret locations and memorized passcodes.

No one knew anyone except for the recruiters.

Dumbasses.

They were going to forfeit two of their people in a senseless vendetta. Or was it only one with his partner? It was hard to recruit operators two at once.

Like Jenny and me.

Into the game. All the way in. And these two were on their way out.

What a waste of life.

Across the highway and into the parking lot. In front of the store to head up the aisle next to where they were parked. Around the end, turning toward the store. Approaching at a regular speed. The car jerked as Jenny's arms tightened from the tension seeking to seize her. She muscled the power steering, the resistance hers. She brought the car next to the one with my targets.

Time slowed as it always did during the moments right before the hit.

I raised the pistol over the window ledge, let the driver come into sight, and fired, taking the man in the face, blowing the back of his head over the passenger, the woman. She started to yell, facing me in terror or anger. I couldn't tell in the last instant of her life. I raised up and fired, hitting her in the chest. She flopped against her door.

The thunder of the .45 firing from within the car. Like a silencer, little sound escaped. I dropped into the space between the front and back seats, making myself as small as possible.

"Keep driving."

"Where?" Jenny's voice shook.

"Back to your house, Miss Jenny. I'll put you in your shower and then your bed. We're safe until we leave the country."

I touched her on the arm, making her jump. I reached over my head and rolled up the window. Jenny turned left past the store as firetrucks' lights and sirens stopped traffic on the road between Walmart and the motel.

"Drive carefully. Watch for people walking and

gawking. They're watching the firetrucks, not us. Slow and steady."

Back past the storefront and to the road next to the diner where we had been earlier. Onto the highway on our way to a place of comfort and refuge.

CHAPTER TWENTY-ONE

"A great storm is like a sunny day to a person of great faith. A gentle wind is like a great storm to a person of great fear."
Matshona Dhliwayo

Jenny made it thirty miles before she started to cry. "Pull over," I said, resting my hand on her arm. She bolted from the car as soon as it stopped. I jumped out and ran after her. She pulled up after fifty feet, knees shaking and threatening to buckle.

I caught her and held her tightly.

She had been roused from her bed way too early and chased through the country by ghosts, who then tried to kill her. It was a lot for a person to internalize.

I held her as late-night traffic drove by, tired drivers minding their own business.

"We need to keep going," I told her. I was unhappy with my pragmatism, but the farther we could get from the fire and the killings, the better off we'd be. She nodded but didn't speak. She continued to cry. I put her in the passenger seat, fastened her seatbelt for her, kissed her on the cheek, and closed the door.

I drove the rest of the way to her home, parking on the street two houses down. No lights lined the windows of the houses. Early morning. Working-class, taking Sunday off. I carried our stuff while holding onto Jenny and getting her into the house. I closed the curtains before turning on a light.

She flopped onto the couch, face red and puffy.

I sat next to her and pulled her to me. She buried her head in my chest and started to mumble. "What did we just do?"

"We taught people that they shouldn't try to kill us." It was the complete truth. Unrepentant. I would do it again if The Peace Archive made me.

"I am not good with killing people. I thought I might be, but I didn't know. How could I?"

"You couldn't. The first one changes a person forever. You're upset because you care. I'm upset because those two people tried to kill you."

"They were trying to kill *you*," Jenny corrected.

"A firebomb isn't a precision weapon. I wonder who else they injured in that hotel? People like that don't belong on the same planet with you and me."

"My ears are still ringing." She hadn't blocked the worst of the noise. "Is this our life now?" She'd asked the same question before.

"No. Our life is out there, exploring the world. If we tried to stay here, this house would become a fortress. There's no need for that. We can preserve the memory of your parents and keep the house intact. Do you have any friends who can stop by and check on it every now and then?"

"I do." She sniffled. I got up to find a tissue, bringing back the box. "I'm not going to need that many."

She took one and used it. I ran a single finger along her neck. Skin as soft as satin. She shivered. "I want you, Ian," she said softly.

"You've got me," I replied, not understanding.

She stood and pulled me after her on the way to the bedroom. She was caught in the tidal wave of emotions that came from the culmination of our day.

At that moment in time, I wanted her to the exclusion of everything else going on in our lives. We wanted to celebrate that we were still alive.

"Is it common?" Jenny asked.

"It what common?" I was confused, half-dazed from expending my remaining energy. The day had been a test of wills, taking all my focus.

"Making love after a hit?"

"I don't know. I've never done it before. The rush is from surviving something dangerous. We all love a good rush."

Jenny smiled up at me. A nightlight on the bedroom wall sparkled within her beautiful eyes. "Is that a pun?"

"It might be. I want you to know the lengths I will go to protect you. I will never hurt you. As odd as it may sound, I'm not a violent man. I don't need anger in my life. I get no jollies from it. My job was my job. I believed in what I was doing. Still do. There's no place for bad people here, the really bad ones. I've made the world a safer place. That's what I tell myself."

"What if those two were on their way to make a hit? Take out a drug kingpin who goes after something big?

They're not able to finish him before he executes his plan, and a lot of people die because those two are no longer with us."

I shook my head. "That's a pretty extreme hypothetical. It begs the question, though. Is there a backup for the primary operator? I haven't thought about it. There probably should be. They sent me a note to call them when they already had people on us. Suggests there's a backup operator on standby. Damn, you're smart. I should spend more time with you."

"What's our next move?"

"You have a passport, don't you?"

She nodded. "I needed one a couple of years ago for a retreat in Canada."

"I can't believe I never asked before. Good. We're not stymied. Next move? We fly to wherever we're catching our world cruise, assuming that's what you want to do."

"I do, as long as there won't be people trying to blow us up."

"There are no guarantees, but we'll live for today, every day. We'll fly to London, take a train to the continent, then fly to Italy, catch our cruise, and relax on deck between luxurious and glorious stops."

"Simple as that?"

"The world will leave us alone if we don't involve ourselves in its affairs. When we get on the plane out of here, we'll officially be retired."

"*Officially.*" Jenny sounded skeptical.

"As much as we can be. Are you ready to sleep now?" I could hope.

"You're going to roll over, and in fifteen seconds, you'll be out cold."

"You say that like it's a bad thing. I think you should try

it. You might find that you like it." I snuggled closer to her perpetually warm and soft body.

"That is a good way to get yourself hurt," Jenny replied, lightly scratching my back with her fingernails. "I'll lie here for a while, start tossing and turning, and finally fall asleep right before you get up."

"I don't know what to tell you." I was fading and fought a losing battle against it. The past week had been hard on my sleep cycle.

"Empathize. Feel for me. Whisper sweet nothings into my ear."

"You are the most magnificent woman I have ever met," I told her. With my arm draped across her waist and a breast as my pillow, I disappeared into a dreamless sleep.

It was light when I awoke. I froze, trying to remember where I was. Jenny had rolled to her side, but I still had one arm around her. I kissed her back lightly before freeing myself.

I peeked out the window. No cars on the street. I couldn't see where we had parked our new ride. It was probably still out there. I started a pot of coffee, turning on my computer while it brewed. I didn't use Jenny's internet but rather used the data plan from the burner phone in addition to the VPN.

I then accessed the cameras from the car. They were still taking pictures. I went back to the active shots from the motion sensors, starting from the moment the woman jumped out of the car carrying the firebomb. They'd driven away after tossing the bomb and starting the fire.

Others rushed to the room and yelled in the window,

looking to help. The fire department arrived. I ran it back. They drove up moments after I had terminated the targets. No one acted strangely during the time when someone might have heard the gunshots. The sirens, the alarms, the fire, and the muffling from firing inside the car had made it a clean hit.

The firetruck took care of business, cleaned up, and drove off. Most of the residents packed up and left. With the parking lot mostly empty, I could see the four-door in the distance, facing the camera at the edge of the screen. The two had not yet been discovered.

That's a bit of good luck, I thought. I gave them the finger. *No one even noticed you died.*

I checked on cruises. The ship leaving from Italy appeared to be second best. A Viking cruise was leaving out of Miami in a couple of weeks. Nearly six months underway. I changed my search criteria to high-end cruising and realized the options were limited and ridiculously expensive, with Viking getting high praise.

Two weeks? We could drive to Miami, traveling with luggage like real humans instead of flying with the clothes on our back and taking the train. Jenny could take her own clothes and ease into life on the road. Or on the run. However it turned out.

I looked at the cost of the best suites on the ship. Only fourteen of those available, with nine hundred other cabins. A quarter of a million dollars for the two of us. I expected that bought a certain amount of privacy. A smaller ship, focused on delivering passengers to exotic ports around the world. No cabarets. No entertainment. The ship was a vehicle to move people from one place to another, not a destination in and of itself.

A few things to do before anyone realized we were still

in the area. Maybe today. No later than tomorrow. We had plenty of food. The burgers I'd bought were in the refrigerator. I'd put them there barely twenty-four hours prior.

It felt like a week.

CHAPTER TWENTY-TWO

"O love, be moderate, allay thy ecstasy,

   In measure rain thy joy, scant this excess!" William Shakespeare

Jenny joined me when it was nearly lunchtime.

"Did you sleep well?" I hugged her, ending with my hand on her butt as I always did. She shook her head and gave me a half-smile.

"I shouldn't have, but I did. I feel better, as if yesterday was a bad dream."

"And that's how you do it. Live for today, plan for tomorrow. Yesterday is gone." I pointed at the computer screen. "What do you think of this?"

She walked through the itinerary from Miami and around the world, ending in London. I had put together a rough schedule for a drive from here to Miami. "I like it, but why five days in Vegas?"

I kneeled next to her. "Jenny, will you marry me?"

She pursed her lips and looked at herself and then

down at me. "It has been your presumption since we met that we would marry, even that we already were. *Now* you want to make an honest woman of me?"

"You've always been an honest woman." I wasn't sure what plays were being made. I had just proposed to a naked woman. I'd failed on the romantic side.

"You want a real piece of paper?"

"I want some things to be normal." My knee started to hurt. I stood. "Maybe I do want the white picket fence and apple pie."

"We don't need a piece of paper, Ian. I'm perfectly happy, loving as we do."

"Even if it's Elvis who marries us?"

"Why didn't you start with that? I'll marry you just to get a little time with Elvis."

"Burgers?"

"What burgers?"

I pointed at the kitchen. "For lunch, since it's lunchtime. I'm famished."

"You want me to get dressed, then?"

"I'm good with a come-as-you-are lunch, but what do you say we pack and leave today? I'd like to get out of here, just in case someone checks."

Jenny lost her smile. "I understand."

"The good news is that no one has discovered the bodies, not yet." I brought up the latest images from the cameras in her car. I pointed in the distance.

"How can you tell?"

"No yellow tape around it. I watched the feed from the brick-throwing until the firemen left. No one stopped by the car. I'll call and have your car towed back here. Lunch, we'll pack, and then it's off to Vegas sooner or later."

Jenny kissed me. "I'm going to take a shower. You can

start lunch in about fifteen minutes. I look forward to making time with Elvis."

She had taken it surprisingly well. I was proud of her. I watched her walk down the hallway. She glanced over her shoulder and caught me staring unashamedly. I waved. Jenny crooked her finger at me.

Two days after that, with Jenny's car safely in the driveway and the cameras removed, I dug into the dark web and pulled up the board where The Peace Archive put their targets. Bids were made on a different page.

They had established me as a target in the formal bid process. There were no bids on my picture. I wouldn't see who bid or how much, only the number.

Employee needs to be found. Last seen in Washington. Extremely dangerous.

They weren't wrong. No one in their right mind would bid on that job. Looking for someone who didn't want to be found would have been bad enough, but going after an operator? If anything, The Peace Archive would tag the two men who'd recruited me and make them do it.

I almost felt sorry for the skipper and the platoon sergeant.

Almost.

We hit the road in the car that I'd bought for cash and never registered. We took our time, driving casually, staying off the radar. Stopping at nice boutique hotels to enjoy the luxury that I wanted to wrap Jenny in.

When I could.

Las Vegas was a town where anything could be had for a price. Anything. We needed new identification to stay off the radar.

When I'd hired on with The Peace Archive, I had the impression that it was a United States-only organization. I had nothing concrete. It could have been solely based on my bias or the fact that none of the jobs that popped up over the past six months had been anywhere else.

All we had to do was leave the country.

There aren't Yellow Pages for fake ID, so I thought we'd try a different route. A legitimate one.

"There's no backing out," I told her. "One and done. I'm not a good-time guy where you marry me, clean out my bank account, and move on."

"Do I have access to your bank account?"

"There is the inevitable question. The answer for now is no. Money destroys too many relationships. If it takes me handing over all my money for you to trust me, then you don't. If you trust me to begin with, you won't pressure me. I will share the numbers with you as I've already done, and you will have all you need. I will spend nothing without telling you. Fair enough, for now, at least?" I didn't want to be destroyed if I was wrong about Jenny.

I didn't think I was, but stranger things have happened. I had seen it in the Corps. A newlywed had returned home to find his wife living with another man. I looked into Jenny's eyes and got lost in them, as I usually did. She matched my gaze before finally replying.

"Are you saying you'll be my sugar daddy?"

"I'm sorry, what?" Not the answer I was expecting.

She leaned close. "How about we go see Elvis?"

"Deal, future Mrs. Lawless."

"Now it's my turn to ask. What?"

"They know me and my name, but who will be looking for Jeannette and Eldon Lawless? I'll change my name on the marriage license. We're a modern society, aren't we? Who's to say which party has to change their name?"

"Mrs. Lawless sounds like my mom. Maybe Ms. Lawless since I heard it a billion times as a teacher, even though it doesn't make me feel special."

"I think you'll get used to it, especially if it means people aren't waiting to kill us."

"It's my wedding day, and you have to bring up the target part. We enjoy two days of travel bliss, honeymooning like teenagers, laughing and taking in the sights. How about I call you Mr. Rain on My Parade?"

My mouth worked, but no words came out. I was ill-equipped to respond to emotional arguments. "Yes, dear?"

She cocked her head to look at me. "What?"

"I've heard from men I respect that sometimes the right answer is simply 'Yes, dear,' and then do what she asked."

Jenny smiled. I think she used emotional arguments to throw me off my game. She struck me as every bit as logical as I was. I decided she was playing three-dimensional chess. I needed to up my game.

"Your friends are wise in the ways of the world."

"I also know beyond a shadow of a doubt that I could not have been blessed by a better partner in life. Whether or not we go see Elvis, I love you, Jenny."

"Me, too, Ian. I'm sorry I waffle, but I'm still trying to get my head wrapped around this life. I'm coming around, already getting used to it. I don't want to go on a world cruise right now. I'd rather just settle someplace and relax. Watch TV, see what Vegas has to offer."

"We can disappear in Vegas. Many people do."

She chuckled and shook her head. "Disappear above ground, to be clear." We kissed tenderly. "Elvis is waiting."

We held hands as we walked to the small chapel. My mind raced. I wanted to get out of the States for a while and throw The Peace Archive off the scent. That wasn't to be. Sometimes the best answer was "Yes, dear." Now I had to figure out what that meant. Ian Bragg's name couldn't show up anywhere in Las Vegas.

I didn't have a birth certificate with me, but Jenny had hers. I had my passport and the wedding chapel considered that good enough, based on the logic that one had to produce a birth certificate to get a passport. It was not necessarily the same for a driver's license. Still, they did the paperwork and didn't blink at our name request. We hadn't been the first. I don't know why I was disappointed.

Jenny kept the man talking while he filled out the form, and he put Jeannette as her first name, despite what was on her birth certificate. Our legitimate approach to changing our names worked far better than digging out a forger. Fake ID was nothing to take lightly with law enforcement stings plaguing the net.

I wanted zero interaction with law enforcement.

Who was going to give newlyweds a hard time? Surely not Elvis. Unfortunately, it was the old and heavy Elvis who performed our ceremony, but he had a respectable voice and put on a great show.

We sealed our marriage with a kiss between lovers, slow and tender. Elvis cleared his throat. The next couple was waiting. We paid our fee and tipped him with a hundred-dollar bill.

I would become Ian Lawless for the time being. I had a mission because offense made the best defense, and I refused to live my life on the run. I'd go underground to find The Peace Archive. If I had to terminate every one of their operators, that's what I would do. They shouldn't have come after me, and they shouldn't have tried to kill Jenny. They would pay dearly for that, far more than the price of a single contract.

We went with a long-term rental of a furnished house. The man was military, following a divorce, shipped overseas and stuck with all his stuff. I spoke his language and gave him the sympathy of a veteran who had seen it before. He felt like we were doing him a favor. I agreed. We paid six months' rent and the deposit in advance.

I put my computer on the table and accessed the Wi-Fi, using the VPN to get onto the net. I wondered how much longer the sergeant would pay for it. I had his email and a new account I created just for correspondence with him. He even kept the utilities in his name, which limited our exposure from whatever compromised system appeared on the dark web. I'd send him money to cover the internet and cable bill and more, like pictures of his stuff if we moved it.

He deserved to know his place was being taken care of. His life had raced into the dumper right quick and in a hurry. Peace of mind was my gift to him.

We moved in with what we carried in the car. Two roller duffels and a few disposable grocery bags filled with stuff. It was more than I liked.

I put everything in the living room. The house was a little bigger than Jenny's, with a similar layout.

I hooked my music player into the flatscreen's soundbar and dialed up *Dreamline*. I started jamming while Jenny put things away.

"Dance with me." I boogied over and dirty-danced around her, trying to guilt her into dancing.

"This isn't dance music." Jenny dug her fists into her hips.

"Charlatan!" I cried in mock disdain. She hesitated to

make her point before relenting. The song ended, and I pulled her close to whisper into her ear, "Live for today."

"I know," she replied. "Mr. Lawless." She shook her head. "That is too weird."

"We'll get married again somewhere else, and you can be Mrs. Bragg next time."

"Is it real? Are we married? It was hard to take it seriously with Elvis singing *Love Me Tender* and shaking his belly at us."

I took the certificate off the counter. "It is one hundred percent valid. I've known you for a grand total of two weeks, and here we are. I look forward to a lifetime of learning about you."

"Two weeks? Is that it? Seems longer."

"A spear right to the heart! You're making me old before my time."

"Two weeks," Jenny reiterated. "I met the future mayor and the Baron of Ball Street. I walked away from my career and my house. And three people have died."

"You never said a word when you met Jimmy and Clive."

"No. Their business was with you. I had nothing to add."

"Which reminds me, let's see what's up with Xterra Worldwide."

Jenny slid a chair next to mine and leaned her head against my shoulder to watch. I dove into the dark web first to scan the backdoor articles. There was a lot of speculation in most, but two were substantial. Shareholders had filed a class-action suit to recover their investment when fund prices tanked following Nader's untimely death. I searched throughout to finally end up on the regular internet, where an article reported his death as an accident.

I stroked my chin.

"What's wrong? Isn't that what you wanted it to be?"

"It is, but there should have been some kind of investigation. The ruling came quickly."

"But he was dirty."

"In a big way. Maybe that's all it is. They didn't rule it suicide by car. Accident. The easy way out."

"Search for those two we left in the Walmart parking lot."

Jenny was insulating herself against what we had done by making it impersonal but removing the killing-them part. I searched by the town name, and it came right up. A double murder in a sleepy town. The victims had not been identified. The police suspected it was a gang hit related to a drug deal gone bad. The article mentioned the motel fire. Nothing was said about Jenny's car. She had destroyed her phone, leaving her on the outside looking in when it came to being connected to the greater world.

"You need a phone."

"Why?" she asked, having embraced the freedom of not being connected.

"In case I need to get hold of you, or you need to make a call."

"Where are you going that I won't be with you?" she shot back.

"Well, nowhere, but in case we have different errands to run."

"Uh-huh. Already kicking me to the curb. I see how you are. You can apologize by taking me out for a nice dinner."

"Vegas, baby!" I searched for the finest dining in Vegas and was buried under pages and pages of five-star restaurants, two of them dedicated solely to steakhouses. "Anything you want."

"All of it, dinner every night at a different place if we

want." As I had suspected, we would live the world gastronomical tour. I was good with it. We needed to get a gym membership, too.

"And we will never run out of great places to go. I have to warn you, despite my usual approach of carrying nothing and moving around a lot, I am a creature of habit. When we find a place we like, I suspect we'll go there often." I checked the prices of the steakhouses and picked the third most expensive. "How about this one?"

"If we like it, what's wrong with going back?" She reached past me and clicked on pictures of the patrons. "Looks like we need to buy you something to wear. You can't go like that."

"Do you have something to wear?"

She looked sideways at me. "Despite your orders that I should only bring practical clothes, yes, I have two outfits that go with one pair of dress heels. I even brought lingerie."

My man instinct kicked in. "Can you model it for me? It *is* our wedding day."

"Maybe." She let it hang. "I'm not sure you deserve it yet. We'll see how well you treat me at dinner."

"Only the best. We're going to need a car. We can't drive this one for too much longer, and we can't ditch it here."

"A quandary, but you'll think of something. Let's get unpacked and make believe we live here, even if only for a short while."

CHAPTER TWENTY-THREE

"It was a time for warm embraces, for smiles, for toasts and reconciliations, for renewing old friendships and making new ones, for laughter and kisses. It was a good time, a golden autumn, a time of peace and plenty. But winter was coming."
George R.R. Martin

Life in Vegas was pleasant. We grew comfortable, and that was when I started to worry. I wanted to go into town less and less, but Jenny liked getting out, so we compromised and went somewhere every day, often simply hiking in the hills. There were numerous trails in and around the greater Vegas area. We'd joined a gym early and went nearly every day.

When I was in the Marines, we were warned against falling into a routine. Terrorists exploited habit.

I checked The Peace Archive board daily. Jobs came and went, all in the US, and the hit on me still had zero bids. They updated it once a month with a new minimum. It was up to one and a quarter million when it finally received two bids.

And then it disappeared. Someone had been hired and was on my trail.

"It's time for us to go," I told Jenny after we returned home from the gym.

"You have something planned?" Jenny smiled and sauntered toward me.

"I'm sorry." The look on my face explained it to her. It was as if I had stabbed her in the heart with an icicle. I gave her time to herself while I sulked, looking through the stuff we'd bought, ready to leave it all behind.

As we had to.

I walked outside and scanned the neighborhood, looking for someone who didn't belong. Everything was in its place. Normalcy. People at work who worked during the day. People at home who worked at night. Nothing untoward.

Yet someone was out there. They wouldn't have taken the job if they didn't know where I was. We still had the Toyota. I should have gotten rid of it already. Three months and I'd lost my edge.

Complacency was an ugly word in my business. It benefitted the operator. With one last look, I went back inside.

I had thought about what it would take to live normally while maintaining a low profile. I wanted to do that for Jenny. I looked in the refrigerator—leftovers like we always brought home, but we didn't have a dog. We couldn't get one because we knew this day would come. There was nothing I wanted to eat.

My stomach was twisted in knots. I sat on the couch with my head in my hands.

The last few months had been magical. The higher we

soared, the farther we had to fall. Here we sat, in different rooms, lamenting our lives.

The best defense... I jumped online and started searching the boards where my type might hang out on the dark web. Just because I never interacted with others, it didn't mean they didn't.

Jenny emerged from the bedroom, eyes clear, walking with a purpose, straight to the counter with my stuff. She took my music, plugged it into the soundbar, and dialed up *Dreamline*. When it started to play, she jacked up the volume.

"Dance with me," she mouthed. She might have said it out loud, but I couldn't hear anything except our song. I was up like a shot, slipping past her so I could run my hand over her magnificent body.

And we danced, making it mean something. When the song finished, I paused it.

"Thank you."

"I'm sorry for being selfish," she started. I tried to stop her, but she waved me off, hugging me to her and resting her forehead on mine before she continued. "I knew this day was coming. I will do what I have to. This life is about us, not a place or things. Tell me what we need to do and how I can help you help us."

"I was just looking at that. How about a staycation? Right here in Vegas. We need to draw the operator out."

"What do you mean? What operator?"

"Someone bid on the contract and The Peace Archive removed it from the board. That means they know where we are and have sent someone after us."

"Why do you still have access to the board?"

"It's not something that anyone controls. I expect I wouldn't be able to bid, but seeing it? That's open before God and the world."

"As long as you're on the dark web and in the right place behind a maze of gateways."

"There is that. Maybe God is a hacker." I looked at the screen and dug into the site. There was no way to leave them a message. Nine jobs were open at present, an increase in the usual targets. The Peace Archive was growing.

I accessed every potential target. Bad men and bad women. "Why did they accept the job on Jimmy?"

"Soft spot for the Wonderbeast, wanting her to find love in the arms of her bad-boy billionaire?"

"I can't believe that. Bad-boy billionaire!" The look told me I was getting close to crossing the line, but I pushed it. "Don't tell me you read that stuff."

"You're my bad-boy millionaire. Everyone deserves to find love."

My mouth hung slack as I tried to generate a witty reply. Nothing came to me.

"Maybe The Peace Archive is run by a woman."

"Then why are they trying to take me from you?"

"Maybe they don't know about me."

"You're blowing my mind with insight that makes more sense than anything I've been able to come up with. Way to go, partner. Even though they found me at your house. It still doesn't add up."

"What do we need to do?" Jenny rubbed her nose on mine, but she was focused on the business at hand.

"If Ian Bragg pops up all of a sudden, they'll suspect it's a trap. But if Ian Bragg appears on a third-party site, a net crawler will pick it up. I'm thinking the gym. Public but private enough. We need to ditch the car and pick up a rental. Where do you want to stay, my dear?"

"Ooh! A staycation." Jenny was as warm and loving as ever. We had grown close enough to marry and even closer afterward. The rest of the world disappeared into a foggy haze while we stayed in focus. "I'll pack my trash, and let's get on it."

"You're starting to sound like me. The Marines have landed. Oorah, hot mama."

"You are such a bad influence. A bad-boy millionaire sweeping small-town girls off their feet. So bad."

She leaned in for a kiss, and we almost went over backward. She pulled me to my feet. "A quick goodbye to the house?" She nodded toward the bedroom.

Sometimes, it was important to make time for that which mattered.

"And then we'll hit the road. How about Bally's?"

"I can't wait."

We drove down the Strip past Caesar's and Bally's on our way out of town. Jenny tapped me on the shoulder. I winked at her.

"Are you sure about this?"

"Wipe down anything you've touched. And yes, I'm sure. Gotta find us a respectable-looking hitchhiker."

On the second loop, a young man appeared on the side of the road, looking very much like a surfer. Out of place at the south end of the Strip. We pulled over.

"How far are you going?"

"All the way to the City of Angels!" He tried to climb in the back.

"Wait." We both climbed out of the car, dragging our overnight bags with us. I left it running and handed him the title. "Do us a favor and take the car to LA for us? We'll be along in a couple months."

"Are you sure, man?"

"We are. And here's a hundred-dollar gift card for you to buy gas. You got a phone number?"

"Yeah, man!" He was overjoyed and grabbed and hugged me. He spouted a series of numbers. Jenny made like she was typing them into her phone.

"Peace, man! And take it easy on our baby. Drive carefully."

The young man bounced with joy or drugs. I didn't care which as long as he made it to California before self-destructing.

He jumped into the driver's seat and raced off, nearly hitting a car since he didn't look before merging. He threw his arm out the window and waved at us.

"He's probably not even going to make it out of town," Jenny said. We watched him drive under the highway and onto the ramp, accelerating south.

"Maybe he'll make it. Traffic is light. There's probably a reason he doesn't have his own car."

"Do you think he'll realize he has the title and can register it in his name?"

"I wouldn't count on it." We walked to the next light and crossed the street to a small restaurant, where I called a cab to take us to Bally's.

The ride was short but long. Too many lights missed. The zone pricing guaranteed a set fee no matter how long the ride took or distance traveled, as long as one stayed within the zone. I paid in cash with a generous tip. We strolled in like we owned the place, straight to the concierge since we were too early to check in. We asked them to store our small bags, and they promised to call us when our suite was ready. I gave them my number and my name.

Ian Bragg.

From there, we walked through the inside air

conditioning to Paris, where Hertz maintained a counter. Renting the car was easy. Again, in the name of Ian Bragg. We listed Bally's as our hotel. We picked up the car and parked it not far from the rental area.

I scanned the dark recesses of the garage before we got out. There wasn't anyone else around. We needed to get back to where there were people.

No collateral damage.

I was counting on that rule from The Peace Archive. They needed to isolate me, which meant they had to follow me and determine a pattern. Identify a weakness and make the hit.

We walked through the shops, stopping at a French restaurant for lunch. It was Paris, after all.

We sat as far inside the restaurant as we could. I had my back to the kitchen. It was the best tactical position I could find. Jenny shifted to the side to let me see the entrance and watch as people passed.

I received the call that the room was ready.

A French dip sandwich was as adventurous as I was going to get. Jenny ordered a salad. We needed to eat lightly and avoid drinking. We had to be sharper than the person hunting us.

I made sure no one was nearby. "Tell me the plan again."

Jenny repeated it to me. If we assumed her suggestion was correct, that they didn't know about her, that gave us an advantage. Any little bit mattered in the game of life and death.

I'd been training Jenny in my business the entire time we'd lived in Vegas, but we hadn't hit the range like we should have. She could repeat the finer points of being an operator, but would they be habit? Could she employ them to save her life?

We ate quietly, each in our own thoughts. I war-gamed the scenarios. I couldn't see every step. That was dangerous. I couldn't afford blind spots.

If anything happened to me…

"I need to give you my account information."

Jenny knew what I was thinking. "Don't say that." She hung her head.

"I said I'd take care of you for the rest of your life, and you promised me the same. Mine might be shorter, and you've made me whole. If I'm not here, you deserve all the good things money can buy."

"I don't want it."

"You might need to run, and that takes money. In that case, buy yourself a nice place in Tuscany and live on a wine orchard."

"Don't say those kinds of things."

"Then we need to win this fight. It's coming and soon."

"I have the .25 caliber, and I'm not afraid to use it."

I had to smile at her. Defending her mate. The lioness unchained. Fierce, determined. "Are you making fun?" Defiant.

"I am not. Maybe we'll go to Tuscany, although I don't like wine. I can tolerate Peroni whilst you imbibe the nectar of the gods."

"Promise me, Ian. Both of us will go."

"Pinky swear." I held up my little finger. Jenny hooked hers around mine, locking it in a death grip.

The server stopped by with the check. "That's so cute. What was the promise?"

"My wife will let me drink beer while she enjoys her wine. Only the best from Boone's Farm and Bud," I replied.

"Boone's Farm isn't that good," the young woman replied. "But I've had worse."

Jenny coughed to hide her laugh. I paid in cash and we

left, heads on swivels, looking for a person who was trying not to be seen.

We continued to our room, where they'd already placed our luggage. The fifteen-hundred-square-foot suite offered plenty of space and entertainment, meant more for group parties than a couple who tended to stay close to one another. A full-body shower topped off the amenities. I was happy it had a coffee maker. Vegas skimped on those to drive people out of their rooms and into the casinos.

"The plan starts this afternoon with another workout and a picture."

"I'll be here and worried until you walk through that door." Jenny hugged me. Before I left, I showed her my bank site and how to access my accounts. I wrote down the account number, everything except the last four digits. I made her memorize those. We checked the account together. We'd only spent fifty grand in our three months in Vegas.

"That's a lot." Jenny pursed her lips and stared at the screen.

"Keep it in perspective. Two hundred grand a year. Four and a half mil means twenty-two and a half years before we need to get a job, but the majority of these funds are in market bonds drawing a little better interest than your average, so we're up to about thirty years before we might run out, but probably not. We could invest a mil or two in some good blue-chip stocks and see where that takes us."

"Make sure you're here to implement that plan. I have to admit I've grown accustomed to not working. I rather enjoy your company and would be greatly put out should that stop."

Jenny was speaking my language. I would be put out, too.

"I shall endeavor. Today isn't the challenge. That starts tomorrow after the gym slips a picture of me into their social media page with a daily workout routine."

Jenny clenched her teeth before walking to the window and looking down the Strip. I hugged her from behind. "I have to go. I'll make it look good, and I'll come home to you super-buff. You won't be able to keep your hands off me."

"I'll hold you to that. Be careful, Ian."

"You know me, the master of paranoia."

I left the room and took the elevator to the ground floor. I meandered along the walkways to the garage entrance, where I waited for a crowd of people. Twenty minutes later, I had my company and followed them into the parking area. They split off quickly, having parked closer than where the rental car was. I stayed close to the cars, circling my level once, checking for occupants before continuing to my car—an all-white Nissan Sentra in a sea of white four-doors.

I pulled out of my space. Within seconds, a car was behind me. I drove out of the garage faster than I wanted to give myself distance, watching in front and behind. Can't hit a pedestrian. The car followed. A driver. No passenger.

The light turned red as I approached, forcing me to wait. I was the first car in line. It turned green and I raced across the intersection, swerving to miss a taxi that ran the red to turn in front of me. I fled away from the Strip on my way to the gym. My heart hammered a staccato against my breastbone.

Why was this so intense? I used to be better.

I still was. Thanks to consistent workouts, I was as fit as I'd ever been. So much training for Jenny to make sure she was ready, even though she'd said she wouldn't be.

Nerves. A mentor who was unsure.

It wasn't about me. I grunted with the recognition. My pulse slowed. I was concerned about Jenny. Keep my wits. That was the best way to keep her safe. Just like the couple who fire-bombed us.

I fought for a cause, and that realization mattered.

The chess match had been underway, but the pawns had finally been cleared away for the major moves.

Once away from the Strip, traffic lightened. The mirrors showed me the car from the garage, still following. I took a right turn at the next major intersection, then another right turn, and then another, back onto the main road. It would confirm if the car was following.

But if they knew which rental was mine, they could have put a tracker on it, like I had done to Mrs. Tripplethorn. I had been betting that they had not been close enough.

This was Vegas, and I was betting with my life. What other assumptions could we have gotten wrong? My heart started to race once again.

I continued to the gym and parked as close to the front as I could get, jumping out as soon as the engine shut down and hurrying inside. I waited around the corner and watched the lot.

The car from the garage.

Got you, you bastard.

But he didn't park on the other side of the lot and wait. He picked a spot in the middle, hopped out, and walked toward the gym entrance. He lifted his keys over his shoulder to lock his car.

It wasn't my intention to engage on this day. The plan had been to take care of it when Jenny was in place to surprise the tail. A distraction. No plan survived first contact.

I needed a new plan. A side entrance. I could hurry out and run around, but the rental was compromised. I was left with one choice. I stretched my fingers and cracked my knuckles, bounced on the balls of my feet, and focused my attention on the man coming in the door.

He entered and stopped before me. "Ian," he said casually. "Is there somewhere we can talk?" I'd never seen this man before. A little older than me. Fit. Hard eyes.

"I'm pretty sure I don't want to do that. What will it take to remain retired?"

"There's no hard feelings, Ian." The man shrugged. He held his hands in front, then turned in a circle to show me that he carried nothing. I didn't know if I could take him in a straight-up fight. I was confident, but there were deadly people out there. This man had to have been in the game for a while. One didn't get old in this line of business by not having an edge.

The smoothie bar had two customers, a power couple on display drinking their wheatgrass nasties. I led the way to the counter and ordered two small berry blends. He said he didn't want anything. I ignored him. We took a table as far away from the others as we could get.

"You tried to kill me. I don't take that lightly."

"It wasn't me. And you made them pay for that miscalculation, costing us our only operator couple unless you and your Jenny Lawless come back into the fold."

I stared at the man. Denying what he knew would have been a waste of time. He'd made the boldest of moves, placing his queen in the middle of the board. Attacking that piece would accomplish nothing. A diversion was required.

"Back into the game? I was looking at retirement. Only if you don't hook me with a clean target like Jimmy

Tripplethorn. That was a garbage contract. We're better than that."

"You shouldn't have accepted the work. We have to manage the contracts we get."

I shook my head slowly. "You know how it works. Without the full background on the target, we're shooting in the dark. Trust is hard-earned and easily lost. I trust good work will come with the contracts. I shouldn't have to double-check my employer. That was a bad move by the company."

Our smoothies arrived. I thanked the chef. My counterpart never took his eyes off me.

"Drink up. The desert environment can take a lot out of you." I took a sip, smacking my lips when I finished.

"Why did you contact us?"

Using my real name had triggered alarms, but they'd arrived in no time. This guy must have already been in Vegas. It made sense to have someone here. One could get anywhere in the world from this city. "What should I call you?"

"How about Dave?"

"Dave it is, then. I let you know where I was so I could kill whoever came after me. My apologies to those you leave behind."

"You won't do that. My colleague is entertaining your Jenny right now. You don't want to see her die because you were hasty."

"Yes, let's not."

Had I trained her well? Would she get angry enough to defend herself? We had bet on an assumption and gotten it wrong. We had bet with our lives. I tried to sit still, but my blood was raging.

Jenny stood at the window, staring mindlessly down the Strip. She heard a card tap against the reader on the door twice before there was a gentle knock. She hurried to the door and opened it. Before she could close it on the stranger, he forced his way inside.

He carried no weapon, but Jenny felt the icy tingle of fear spike through her body.

"Sit down, please." A soft baritone. Dark brown eyes. Light brown hair. Taller than Ian. Wider, too.

"What do you want?"

He pointed at the couch. Jenny's mind raced. She jumped when the door clicked closed, leaving her alone with the stranger.

She took one of the throw pillows and sat wedged against the armrest. She clutched the pillow to herself. Her head throbbed with the force of blood rushing through her veins. What had Ian taught her?

Kill the man.

Maybe. Disarm him. But he's not carrying a weapon.

Find out what motivates him. She studied the stranger as he adjusted an overstuffed chair to face her and sat down. He wore slacks and dress shoes with a designer polo shirt. He looked like a television stereotype. Jenny found herself relaxing. He was there to intimidate Ian.

It also showed that her husband had been right. No plan survives first contact with the enemy. Their plan was out the window.

She assumed they were waiting for Ian to get back, but he had the .45 with him, and he'd shoot first. She secretly wished for that.

Her small pistol remained in the purse on the counter in the suite's small kitchen area, far out of reach. It might as well have not been there.

Improvise. What could she use as a weapon? She

scanned the room. A lamp. A remote on the coffee table. A magazine. Her pillow. Nothing in her pockets. Two hands and two feet.

She put her pillow to the side and stood up. He gestured for her to sit down. "I was on my way to the bathroom when you interrupted. That doesn't just go away."

"No. Sit down."

"Screw yourself." She remained standing. The man launched to his feet in a flash of speed, his face contorting with anger. He came over the top of the coffee table and grabbed Jenny, dragging her back into the bedroom, where the bathroom was situated. He propelled her toward the toilet, keeping his foot against the door to prop it open.

"You're going to watch?"

"If you have to go, then go. If you can't, then sit on the couch."

Defiantly, Jenny bent at the waist to pull her pants down to sit on the toilet without giving the man a look. She covered herself while he focused on her eyes. It took a while to start, but thanks to a couple of glasses of water at lunch, she managed enough to establish credibility with the man. He looked away when she stood.

"I *told* you I had to go. Ian said you people were decent. I think he might have been misled."

"The couch."

Jenny passed him, uncomfortably close. He walked behind her to resume his seat on the chair.

A professional. Why were they keeping her alive and unharmed? She couldn't help smiling. Because they knew that harming her would send Ian against them. They didn't want that. They were going to use her as leverage.

Her phone rang. She started to move, but the man pointed at her. Jenny remained where she was while he got up and walked to the counter. The phone was in front of her open purse. She couldn't tell if he saw the pistol. She'd find out soon enough. He kept his eyes on her until the last moment. He scooped up the phone and returned to his seat. He scowled at the name on the screen. "Honey badger?" he asked.

"Ian."

He tapped accept but didn't say anything.

"Jenny?" a voice from the other end.

"No," he answered.

"Good. We're having a little conversation here. I just wanted to make sure everything was in place. I'm going to give Ian the phone. He wishes to talk to his wife."

The man handed the phone to Jenny. She took it gingerly and looked at the screen before holding it up to her ear. "Ian?"

"Hi, beautiful. Everything okay there?"

"As good as can be expected. Will you be home for dinner? I was thinking Italian."

"Probably fairly soon. I was hoping for Wahlburger's."

"You and your burgers. Soon, then."

The man motioned for the phone. She handed it over, and he put it on the side of the table nearest him. He sat back down.

"We aren't vegetarians or vegan or kosher. There's a lot to be said for a good burger with melted cheese and the right bun. Not too much bread, with a covering of lettuce, tomatoes, and pickles. So good. The trick is barbecue sauce instead of ketchup."

The man stared at her. She shrugged and turned her head to look out the window at the Strip. Her mind raced, looking for a way out.

"Now you know that she's fine, we can continue our conversation," Dave said.

"At some point in time, are you going to tell me what you want, or are you going to play the intimidation game? It's getting rather tiresome."

"*Are* you intimidated?" the man asked.

I didn't dignify that with a reply. It was closing on the time where I was going to kill him right there or die trying. I had consumed my energy smoothie but he hadn't touched his. That wasn't very cordial of him.

"Are you going to drink your smoothie?"

"No. I told you I didn't want it."

"What *do* you want?"

Dave stared back, keeping a blank expression. I matched his look, breathing regularly and slowly. He finally picked up the drink and raised it to his lips. My fist acted almost of its own accord. Coming from under the table behind the cup, punching through it to Dave's nose. The berry blend erupted into his face and over his head.

He threw out a hand to block my follow-up, but he was blind. I slapped his hand out of the way and grabbed the back of his head to drive his face into the table. He fought me, and it didn't hit as hard as I wanted. I squeezed the back of his neck with all the strength in my hand. He held his hands out in surrender.

"A rag, please? We've had a minor accident," I called toward the counter.

I remained behind Dave, quickly checking his pockets for a weapon, removing the switchblade before returning to my seat. I kept the knife in my hand, finger on the button.

The clerk returned with the towel. "Oh, my!" She started wiping, but he took the towel from her. "Do you want another one?"

"No, thank you, ma'am. This was great. When bad boys spill their drink, they don't get new ones." I held out a twenty for her. "Thanks for your help."

She took it without a word, smiling as she walked happily back to the counter.

It was important to be likable in this line of work. Earn their loyalty. She wouldn't call the police. That's what I hoped for, in case she had seen what happened. Maybe she still wouldn't. Twenty bucks was twenty bucks.

"I asked you a question, Dave. What the hell do you want besides a greatly shortened lifespan?"

He slowly wiped his face and neck. He was covered in purple and red smoothie. His nice clothes were ruined. Fire burned behind his eyes. He had lost the initiative and his dominance. He blinked to clear his eyes from the burn of berry juice.

"We want you to meet with the Archive's leadership team."

"Then why are you trying to jack me around? Playing games with an operator will get you killed. If you thought you were having an effect on me, you grossly misjudged me. Did you believe I was going to open wide and devour whatever you were shoveling? You have to know that if you don't say the right things, you are going to die."

He tossed the rag on the table. "The arrogance of confidence. We like that."

"The arrogance of stupidity and overplaying your hand. There's no chance in hell I'm coming to the Archive."

"Neutral ground is fine. The leadership team can be here in a couple of days."

"Then why the games? Did you have to see what would happen if you tried to pin me in a corner?"

"We did."

I didn't understand. I needed more information.

"I need them to be a little more professional. Call your boy and tell him to leave my wife alone. Then you'll make reservations for us at SW Steakhouse, where this so-called leadership team is going to wine and dine us. The Archive charges an astronomical price for its services. It can treat its people a little better than sending dickheads like you on power trips. It's a dangerous world out there. Don't be a victim of it."

I dialed Jenny's number. It took a while before the line went live. I handed the phone to Dave.

"You no longer need to secure the room," Dave said into it.

"Roger," the voice on the other end of the line replied.

"Give the phone to Jenny before you go," I said. Dave relayed my message.

"Hi, beautiful. Is the bad man going away?"

"He was professional about the kidnapping, but he's gone now. I'm in the room, and I'm not scared, Ian."

I didn't know why she added that last part. "Kill the next person who tries to enter the room. Except me. Don't kill me, and I'll call before I try the door."

"Of course, darling."

I hung up.

"You got yourself a wildcat, it seems. Congratulations." Dave glared at me.

I glared back. Dave had lost the power struggle. He no longer held the upper hand. I felt the implied threat. *Shame if something happened to her.* But his queen lay toppled in the middle of the board, my queen looming. Checkmate in five.

"Is there anything else? We like to eat early, around six in the evening. Make it so." I slid my chair back and stood. Stepping past him, I slapped him on the back. "Don't make me hunt you down. Best thing for you and whoever gave

Jenny grief is to disappear. I'm willing to talk to the leadership team, but there's no value in threatening us. That won't turn out well for anyone."

He nodded almost imperceptibly. A lackey. A field manager. I'd suspected The Peace Archive had people like him, but I had never encountered one. Quality control, thought they knew the job better than those doing it. I tossed the knife into a garbage can outside the doors to the gym, continued to the rental car, and eased out of my parking spot.

I needed to see that Jenny was okay. I thought we had at least a two-day reprieve. No one would come after us before the meeting. But I'd been wrong recently about too many things.

I had to think about what a meeting meant while seeing that we both survived to make it.

CHAPTER TWENTY-FOUR

"A man might befriend a wolf, even break a wolf, but no man could truly tame a wolf." George R.R. Martin

I called, and Jenny let me in. Once I was inside, she threw herself at me, hugging me intensely. "I'm so glad you're okay." Her voice was muffled, with her face buried in my neck.

"They should have never come here."

"But they did. I thought it was you, and I opened the door. It was a good lesson. I'm sorry, Ian, but you've been right all along. I'll carry the pistol. I'll be aware. I am not afraid to defend myself."

"We have two days to act like normal people. I don't know why, but I believed my new buddy. We might as well take advantage of it. Let's buy swimsuits and go to the pool."

She let me go, stepped back, and started to laugh. "Now that I commit to packing heat, you tell me I don't need to."

"The next two days, anyway. Packing heat? Do people still say that?"

"I do."

"Fair enough." I reached for her, but she held me off.

She gestured toward herself. "Does this look like a bikini body?"

"Yes. Let's go to the pool so you can show me off to all the hot showgirls."

"How close were you?" Jenny asked, closing with me to touch her nose to mine.

"Not very. My guy was a lackey. He got into a dick-measuring contest, which he lost. I suspect the operator was here."

"What kind of contest?" She kissed me to keep me from answering. "Never mind. I didn't feel like I was in danger. He didn't appear to be armed."

"A good operator doesn't need to be armed, as my guy found out. He walked away covered in berry smoothie." Jenny squinched her eyes as she tried to decipher what I meant. "I punched it into his face. He also got his head slammed on the table. I'm not sure how that happened. He seemed a little clumsy."

"I'll take your word for it." She twisted her mouth as she thought. I watched her, smiling. "Instead of a swimsuit because I really don't want to go out there, let's find a thigh holster and go skirt-shopping."

I liked it. "From this man's perspective, I like how you think. We'll save the skin show for the privacy of our cool suite. Please understand, I'm proud of who you are. I don't want you to feel ashamed of your body."

"I'll still hold it against you," she purred.

"I *like* a good pun. And holster shopping. And skin. Today is going to have it all!" I watched her as she got ready to go, looking for signs that she was trying to hide not being able to cope. But she wasn't. She went about her business as usual. Those months of training hadn't been a waste. The catalyst had come with the intruder. She now understood why I had to eliminate the two who firebombed us. There are rules to the game.

And The Peace Archive had broken them.

"You look magnificent. Utterly stunning, even though I prefer you *au naturel*, as in without the warpaint."

Jenny had gone all out: a full spa treatment, hair, and professional makeup. Her black dress highlighted her figure in the best ways, and it was long enough to hide the holster and pistol. I wore a dark blue pinstriped silk suit without a tie. I carried the Browning at the small of my back in a holster designed to hide the bulge. As long as I kept the jacket on, no one would see my piece.

We sported an expensive look to go to an expensive restaurant to talk over life and death issues. We had already scouted the place to make sure we knew the general layout and available exits.

This one was for real, with only one chance to get it right.

We waited at the entrance, but the host didn't let anyone stand around unattended. "Do you have a reservation, or would you like one?" the middle-aged man asked.

"We'll be joining others. I'm not sure how many are in the party. My name is Ian Bragg."

"Mr. and Mrs. Bragg. Welcome. I'll show you to your table."

It wasn't quite six yet. Very few diners were seated. No one was eating anything more substantial than appetizers.

The Archive leadership had not arrived before us. We had a table for four discreetly distant from nearby diners. We put our backs against the wall. The server showed us a bottle of champagne. When we nodded, he cracked it open and poured two flutes. Our water glasses had not yet started to sweat. They were fresh as well. He retreated to the kitchen, leaving us to ourselves.

Jenny sniffed at the champagne.

I held up my glass to her. We clinked them and took small sips. "If they wanted to kill us, they wouldn't do it in the middle of a pricey choke-and-puke with a tainted five-hundred-dollar bottle of champagne."

"Choke and puke?"

"I'm jonesing for a good burger right now. And some salty fries." I liked what I liked.

"He dresses up, but we can't take him anywhere. You look incredible, by the way."

"It's the haircut, isn't it? Short hair drives 'em crazy."

"Who's 'them?'" She winked at me and took another sip from the champagne flute. "This is good."

"I expected no less. I can't imagine why they want to wine us and dine us, but this might be our ticket out of the limelight."

"You didn't play that today."

"I knew I forgot something. I'll listen to it in my mind." I closed my eyes, but Jenny poked me in the ribs. "Or not."

"I think they're going to offer you something. Another gig." Astute. I had been thinking the same thing.

"We'll find out soon enough." I jerked my chin toward the entrance. Jenny and I stood as the host guided two men toward us. They wore expensive suits and walked like executives, swaggering but with a sense of purpose. They didn't delay crossing the dining area. The server had the glasses filled before they arrived.

The first was older, probably sixty, but in good shape. A vein on his neck stood out, suggesting low body fat. He offered his hand.

I took it. "Ian Bragg and my wife, Jenny."

"My name is Charlie French, you can call me Chaz. My colleague is Vince Trinelli."

I shook Vince's hand, too. Jenny followed suit, hesitantly. I pulled out her chair for her, then took my seat once she was settled.

"I see why you were smitten, Mr. Bragg. I expect you were powerless against such a divine beauty's charms."

Jenny wasn't impressed. We waited for Charlie to get to the substance of the conversation.

He looked around casually before starting. "Vince and I started The Peace Archive nearly twenty-five years ago. We took all the jobs for the first ten years before news of our success filtered to those we were willing to do business with. Then we started hiring. You came to us about a year ago on a sterling recommendation from a couple of our members."

"You prefer military?"

"Yes, and police. We used to interview all the candidates personally, but we saw the value in absolute anonymity, so we stopped those about ten years ago." He turned to Vince, who continued the history lesson.

"We still interview our regional coordinators. These personnel make sure the jobs are clean and that the gigs are for the detritus of society. Some, like Jimmy, get past us. Once we dug into what happened, we realized how masterfully you handled the situation. The regional coordinator overstepped her bounds in multiple ways. She should have transmitted the cancellation to you but didn't. When she realized the dog's breakfast she made of it, she modified the hit to be on you instead to cover her errors, which only served to compound them. If you hadn't dealt with her, we would have."

Her... The bomb-thrower had been the coordinator. Her husband, the driver, had been the bystander.

"They shouldn't have come after us."

"I agree," Chaz replied. "The Pacific Northwest is an active area." Jenny's ears perked up. "I've sent the one you know as Dave there. We would like you to take his position here."

"You put out a contract on me." I wasn't amused.

"We knew you were checking the boards. You couldn't get into it all the way, but it was a contract for location only. Faking the bid served its purpose since you contacted us by using your real name."

"The best defense is a good offense," I countered while trying to look deeper into their words.

"So Dave tells us. He spoke highly of you. It's extremely rare that someone secures an advantage over one of ours, and you've done it twice. If we were to run a selection program for advancement, it would look like what you've done. Afterward, you stayed off our radar for three months, despite our best efforts to find you. You are at the top of your game, and we don't want to lose what all operators should aspire to."

The server returned and provided a verbal menu. Jenny and I had already discussed what we wanted since eating at nice places had become one of our favorite pastimes. I deferred to her. She liked ordering for both of us. "Eight-ounce Kobe tenderloin for my husband, four-ounce for me, both medium-rare. Grilled asparagus and a single serving of the Russian Osetra, please."

I was trying to get my head wrapped around what Chaz had said. They hadn't been trying to kill me?

"Did Nader cancel the contract on Jimmy?" I asked, even though he had already said it was.

"He did, knowing there would be no refund. I don't know how you did it, but that was the right way to go about it."

I didn't clarify the details. Jenny squeezed my hand. I turned to her and she smiled at me, the dimmed lights highlighting her beauty. A stream trickled to the side of the seating area, part of the landscaping for the perfect ambiance for high-end dining.

"A position here. What does that mean?"

"It means half a mil a year as long as you bring in three contracts, and then you get ten percent of the contract price for every completed contract. Dave made one point three million last year, hanging out in an expensive apartment in Vegas. Where have you been staying?"

I chuckled but didn't answer.

Vince slid a gold card across the table. "Did we mention an unlimited expense account?"

Jenny and I looked at the card.

"Is there a way out of the game? We want to take a world cruise that might take a year or two. We can do it now. It would be a lot more fun if we didn't have to keep looking over our shoulder."

"A set time, one-year renewable. Strict non-disclosure. We don't tolerate competitors from within."

"You know who I am. You know all about me, and you know I am a man of my word. I guarantee that if I take this, I will never work against you. I'm either in all the way or out."

"We know that. Despite what you may think, people successfully retire from this business."

"If I take this, I want to be one of those, and sooner rather than later."

"Take the card, Ian, and then we'll explain what your job entails."

"I'm not a salesman."

"No. You're an operator and a damn good one, with a nose for the truth. We have all the contacts we'll ever need. You only have to talk to them to make sure we have the truth on the target. You make the recommendation to us, and we post the job. When we get a bid within the parameters of payment and time, we take it and start the clock running."

"Simple as that?"

"The truth is a vicious taskmaster, Ian."

CHAPTER TWENTY-FIVE

"What a man does for pay is of little significance. What he is, as a sensitive instrument responsive to the world's beauty, is everything!" H.P. Lovecraft

The evening ended with a handshake. I picked up the gold card and slid it into my pocket. I gave the men my current phone number, and they countered with a password to access The Peace Archive's internal web. They said I would find everything I needed there.

"I will send my final answer in the morning after we've had a chance to talk privately."

"Of course. Do what you think is best for you and your family."

The two men strode out as confidently as they had entered, eyes scanning the area for threats as was their habit. The restaurant had filled, leaving only two or three tables empty. Jenny and I sat back down after Chaz and Vince walked away. We ordered one molten lava cake with two spoons and sipped the champagne.

"Is this what you want to do?" Jenny asked.

I thought for a long time before I answered. "I was afraid I had put you at too much risk. That we couldn't just live, like we were able to the last few months. I want more of that and less watching the shadows."

"They said you were fine, they wouldn't come after you. If we quit the game now, we have everything we want."

"I want to be able to bathe you in diamonds."

"I don't need that garbage, Ian. You are such a *man*, doing manly stuff. How about us just being together? That's good enough for me. We can get a cheap apartment in Cabo. Then I'll put on a swimsuit for you."

It was impossible not to smile at Jenny's offer. "The siren's call of pleasure and peace." I squeezed her hand. She narrowed her eyes with a twinkle and a smile, knowing what was coming next. "What if we can make a bigger difference in the world?" Jenny waited for the rest of it. "What if I can fix what's broken with the Archive and make sure what happened to Jimmy doesn't happen to anyone else? Keeping bad guys off the street is worth our time and effort. *In my opinion*. What does the other half of this partnership have to say?"

Jenny sighed and rolled her head. "I loved the past three months. It sounds like you want more of that and a job, too." She air-kissed me. "Can we have normal lives?"

"A different normal." I paid the check with my new gold card. It went through without a hitch. I left a hundred-percent tip. "When I say we can change the world, I mean it." I looked around before leaning close. "What if I take over The Peace Archive?"

"There go our peaceful lives." Jenny kissed me. "Easy come, easy go. We better get back to the gym in the morning. I think we have our work cut out for us because *we* have to be better."

"*We* need to find out what that looks like for us. Can we be who we are while also doing this job?"

"We can't be anyone else," Jenny replied. She held her champagne glass up. I clinked mine against hers. "Like you believed in Jimmy, I believe in you."

"Peace through superior firepower." I quoted the Strategic Air Command motto, the nuclear bomb people.

"Peace through peace. What if we work ourselves out of a job because there are no more bad guys who deserve the Archive treatment?"

"Then we shall turn in our gold card and retire while we're still young enough to enjoy it."

"I'll always be twenty-nine," she deadpanned.

I looked at her. Another masterful play that forced me to change the way I looked at the board. "More of that. On our toes. I don't think this job will be as easy as they made it sound. But..." I took a few moments to shape the rest of the words. "A better society. Clear the worst of the evil away so the rest of humanity can simply live."

"We'll adjust." She drained her flute. The server magically appeared and topped off our glasses, removing the empty bottle. "I will be what you need me to be. The same and different. Like those crazy kids who met a lifetime ago in a bar over a *Shirley Thunderbolt*."

"*Thunderbolt Special*," I corrected. She wiggled her eyebrows at me.

"What do you say we grab a couple from a bar in Bally's and go wild?"

We stood, complimented the server on the meal and service, and hand in hand, we walked out. *Dreamline* was playing in my mind. "A better world awaits, Miss Jenny. To shape it, *we* will be what we have to be."

The End

If you like this book, please leave a review.
Reviews buoy my spirits and stoke the fires of creativity.
Don't stop now! Keep turning the pages as I talk about my
thoughts on this book and the overall project called the Ian
Bragg Thrillers.

AUTHOR NOTES - CRAIG MARTELLE
WRITTEN JULY 26, 2020

I can't thank you enough for reading this story to the very end! I hope you liked it as much as I did.

Can you tell I love all things Rush? This book is an ode to their musical genius. I hope you're able to listen to the music as you read. Even if you don't listen to their songs, understand the power they hold for those of us who do.

I live in the interior of Alaska, about 150 miles from the Arctic Circle. I wrote this entire story after the sun rose and before the sun set a single time. No. I can't write 70,000 words in a single day. It's light for about seventy-three days straight during our summers. And then I published this book at the beginning of our six-month winter. We live the extremes. We only had a couple of days in the 80s (Fahrenheit) this summer. I expect we'll pay for the mild temperatures with a brutally cold winter. The weather has taken it easy on us for the last couple years. The coldest I've ever experienced is -74F. I went outside in that for thirty seconds, and I thought I was going to die. -40F (it's -40C, too) is bad enough. I filmed my wife tossing boiling water out our front door and watching it vaporize instantly. An interesting phenomenon that only those who have seen ambient (not windchill) temperatures at the extreme range will understand. I don't recommend it for the weak of heart.

Which is me, so I spend a lot of time indoors in the winter. I write a lot, but I get caught up on sleep that I missed out on during the summers. I'm lucky to get five hours when it's light all the time.

What about Ian Bragg? He came about as an idea—a man of honor who is also a hitman. How can he reconcile that dichotomy? A vigilante for the just? And then one who falls in love, softens, but still has to do what he has to do? I believe there are people out there like him. Why can't they work for an organization like The Peace Archive? Anything is possible.

People do what they do because something drives them. Ego to be the best. Money. A conscience. Combine all of those, and you have Ian Bragg. Falling in love was easy but dealing with the consequences of that made this story what it was.

As for names, Ian Bragg came to me out of the blue, and at the most basic level of efficiency, Ian is only three letters, very quick to type. Call Ian's name an author's shortcut. For our politician, I wanted something exotic and memorable. I had heart surgery in January which was the perfect way to greet the year that would be 2020. One of the underlying issues they suspected was sleep apnea so my sleep doctor is Dr. Clay Tripplehorn. I like to memorialize the good people who help to keep me alive and kicking.

I'm off to write the next chapter in the Ian Bragg thrillers.

Peace, fellow humans.

If you liked this story, you might like some of my other books. You can join my mailing list by dropping by my website **craigmartelle.com** or if you have any comments, shoot me a note at craig@craigmartelle.com. I am always happy to hear from people who've read my work. I try to answer every email I receive.

If you liked the story, please write a short review for me on Amazon. I greatly appreciate any kind words; even one or two sentences go a long way. The number of reviews an ebook receives greatly improves how well it does on Amazon.

Amazon -
www.amazon.com/author/craigmartelle
Facebook -
www.facebook.com/authorcraigmartelle
BookBub -
https://www.bookbub.com/authors/craig-martelle
My web page -
https://craigmartelle.com

Thank you for joining me on this incredible journey.

OTHER SERIES BY CRAIG MARTELLE
- AVAILABLE IN AUDIO, TOO

Terry Henry Walton Chronicles (#) (co-written with Michael Anderle)—a post-apocalyptic paranormal adventure

Gateway to the Universe (#) (co-written with Justin Sloan & Michael Anderle)—this book transitions the characters from the Terry Henry Walton Chronicles to The Bad Company

The Bad Company (#) (co-written with Michael Anderle) —a military science fiction space opera

Judge, Jury, & Executioner (#)—a space opera adventure legal thriller

Shadow Vanguard—a Tom Dublin space adventure series

Superdreadnought (#)—an AI military space opera

Metal Legion (#)—a military space opera

The Free Trader (#)—a young adult science fiction action-adventure

Cygnus Space Opera (#)—a young adult space opera (set in the Free Trader universe)

Darklanding (#) (co-written with Scott Moon)—a space western

Mystically Engineered (co-written with Valerie Emerson) —mystics, dragons, & spaceships

Metamorphosis Alpha—stories from the world's first science fiction RPG

The Expanding Universe—science fiction anthologies

Krimson Empire (co-written with Julia Huni)—a galactic race for justice

Xenophobia (#)—a space archaeological adventure

End Times Alaska (#)—a Permuted Press publication—a post-apocalyptic survivalist adventure

Nightwalker (a Frank Roderus series)—A post-apocalyptic western adventure

End Days (#) (co-written with E.E. Isherwood)—a post-apocalyptic adventure

Successful Indie Author (#)—a non-fiction series to help self-published authors

Monster Case Files (co-written with Kathryn Hearst)—A Warner twins mystery adventure

Rick Banik (#)—Spy & terrorism action adventure

Ian Bragg Thrillers—a hitman with a conscience

Published exclusively by Craig Martelle, Inc
The Dragon's Call by Angelique Anderson & Craig A. Price, Jr.—an epic fantasy quest

A Couple's Travels—a non-fiction travel series

Made in the USA
Las Vegas, NV
16 January 2021

16055752R00154